# Bolan lo[...] toward the second jeep in [...]

He stood on the accelerator and gunned his vehicle at the open doors, taking scattered hits before he cleared the threshold. The warrior fired the Colt one-handed, uncertain whether he was scoring with the short, sporadic bursts.

The grenade went off beneath the jeep in the barn and blew its fuel tank, shooting plumes of burning gasoline in all directions.

Seconds later the Executioner was out of the compound proper, unopposed, and heading toward the perimeter. His leg hurt like hell, and he was sitting in a pool of blood. But there were other things to consider—like fuel.

He found the headlight switch and twisted until the dashboard came alive. Speedometer. Tachometer. Odometer. The fuel gauge.

He was running for his life on less than half a tank of gas.

Bolan cursed as the headlights illuminated the steep walls of a gully less than ten feet in front of the jeep. When the warrior hit the brakes the tires dug for purchase in the sandy soil. But it was no good. The vehicle lost it, plummeting into empty space.

The Executioner never heard the walkers coming, never felt their strong hands as they lifted him from the wreckage.

# Accolades for America's greatest hero Mack Bolan

DON PENDLETON's

# MACK BOLAN.

# LETHAL IMPACT

## A GOLD EAGLE BOOK FROM

# WORLDWIDE.

TORONTO • NEW YORK • LONDON
AMSTERDAM • PARIS • SYDNEY • HAMBURG
STOCKHOLM • ATHENS • TOKYO • MILAN
MADRID • WARSAW • BUDAPEST • AUCKLAND

First edition December 1992

ISBN 0-373-61429-2

Special thanks and acknowledgment to
Mike Newton for his contribution to this work.

LETHAL IMPACT

Be peaceful, be courteous, obey the law, respect everyone; but if someone puts his hand on you, send him to the cemetery.

—Malcolm X

The savages have put their hands on each of us, in different ways, and now it's payback time. Their tabs are overdue, and the Executioner is coming to collect.

—Mack Bolan

## PROLOGUE

The six-foot tiger snake was coiled to strike, its body twisted in an *S* shape, the flat head aimed directly at its enemy.

A whistling vibration rent the air as something hurtled toward the reptile, a threat beyond the realm of instinct or experience. The tiger snake never felt the sharp point of the wooden spear that clipped its spine and pinned its thrashing body to the ground. Swift death, and then there was nothing left but reflex action—sinews whipping mindlessly against the earth.

Mawulan waited for another moment, finally retrieved his spear, and used its hardened point to flick the reptile's head away. He crouched beside the twitching body, digging in his leather belt pouch for a flat stone knife with which he slit the ventral scales from end to end. His fingers cleared the body cavity in one smooth motion, and he sorted through the entrails, picking out the stomach and intestines, shoving the rest into his mouth.

This was his second day without a taste of water, and the vital fluids of the tiger snake would spare Mawulan from the need of opening a long vein in his arm and using blood to slake his thirst. The desert wouldn't claim his life tonight.

He couldn't risk a fire while he was being hunted, but the coals would only dry his kill, in any case. His need for moisture was as great—or greater—than his need for meat. He used the flat stone blade to skin his kill and strip the pale meat from the serpent's skeleton, consuming it in three- and four-inch strips.

A teenage male of the Arunta tribe, Mawulan wore no clothing to protect him from the desert's broiling heat by day or chill by night. His only garment was a plaited belt of hair, from which the smallish leather pouch was hung. A wooden boomerang was tucked inside the belt, against his hip. His spear and thrower lay beside him on the ground.

He didn't fear the desert vastness, but he missed his people now, the family and tribe that he'd known from birth. His flight had broken with tradition, might have placed them all in danger, but he had no choice. Mawulan couldn't bear to watch what happened to his people any longer, see the crawling things they had become.

It would be better, he decided, for a man to seek his own fate in the desert, live or die with courage and in defiance of his enemies. If he was killed, at least the choice of when and where he died would be his own.

Since fleeing from his village two days earlier, he'd been forced to travel after nightfall, hiding from his enemies by daylight. It demeaned him, digging burrows in the earth or curling up beneath a shelf of stone, afraid to venture out in case he might be seen. His enemies were everywhere in their machines, on land and even in the air.

Just yesterday they had almost had him, circling the rock pile where he occupied a narrow crevice, screened by shadow and a few dry strands of grass. They had sent two scouts with thunder sticks to search the desert fortress, but his enemies were lazy, careless when the sun beat down on their heads. They'd missed him quite

by accident—or by the will of desert spirits, in response to urgent prayers—and had gone back empty-
handed to their vehicles.

Mawulan had another six or seven suns to travel yet
before he reached the mountains in the north, a part of
what the white man knew as Arnhem Land. He'd be
safer in the mountains for a while, and over time his
enemies would cease to look for him, assuming he was
dead and gone.

The thought of finally returning to his village never
crossed Mawulan's mind. He understood that there
would be no better time ahead, no respite for the people who had given him his life. They lacked the strength
or will to rise against their enemies and make a stand.
It was the reason he had finally decided he must run.

He finished off the snake and dug a shallow pit to
hide the entrails, skin and bones. There was no point
in leaving markers for the men who followed him. They
had a great enough advantage as it was, with their machines and thunder sticks and magic eyes that could
identify a target from a mile or more behind.

Mawulan rose, picked up his spear and thrower.
They would do him little good against the trackers,
with their weapons that could kill from far away, but
they were all he had. Like most Arunta, he had never
killed another man, but he wasn't afraid to fight. His
people had been victimized for long enough, and if his
enemies weren't content to let him go, then some of
them would feel Mawulan's wrath before he died.

He understood that they were more concerned about
what he might tell the world than about the loss of one
more slave. To them, Arunta life was cheap and easily
replaced by means of seizing other bodies, sweeping up

whole villages if necessary. But, if once their secret was revealed . . .

Mawulan had considered telling all, if he could reach the outside world, but logic told him that his words would fall on deaf white ears. If anyone took time to listen, they would almost surely laugh the story off, equating it with myths and legends from the Dreamtime, when his race was young. They wouldn't understand—or care—about the suffering his people bore from day to day.

And so he simply ran. Without specific goals in mind, and no intent to meet with white police or journalists. If the pursuers had been able to divine his thoughts, they might have been content to let him go, but they couldn't afford the risk.

And, to be truthful, they enjoyed the hunt.

Near midnight, walking in the wan light of a quarter moon, he heard the sky beast coming, dark wings whipping at the air. Mawulan turned and stared along his path, watching as the monster's glaring eye swept back and forth across the desert floor.

So they were stalking him by night, as well as in the daytime.

Still a mile or more away, the flying devil held a steady course, as if it could detect his scent. Mawulan glanced about and found no ready place to hide himself. He'd be forced to run or stand and fight, and neither option bore much prospect for success.

He set his face due north and ran, an easy loping stride that could sustain him through the night with only two or three brief stops to rest. But there was no resting now that they had found his tracks and sent a demon out to run him down.

The light was drawing closer, sweeping back and forth across the barren desert floor. Mawulan felt it licking at his heels, a living flame, and knew that there were only moments left before the flying monster spotted him and descended for the kill. The shock waves from its thrashing wings beat down upon him, whipping dust across the sterile landscape in its wake.

The sudden glare of light was blinding, brighter than the sun. He tried to dodge away, elude the monster's gaze, but it was faster, veering slightly to correct its course, pursuing him. Through squinted eyes, he saw the first small puffs of dust as something struck the ground in front of him and to his right.

The demon swept past and raced a hundred yards in front of him before it turned and doubled back. Mawulan halted in his tracks, aware that he had nowhere left to run. The spear he carried, taller than himself if planted upright on the ground, was fitted to his thrower in another heartbeat, cocked and ready for the pitch.

He watched the airborne beast bearing down upon him, nearly blinded by its giant, burning eyes. He couldn't gauge a proper distance, but the beast was large enough and closing fast enough that he wasn't concerned about a miss. Inflicting mortal wounds would be another problem, but he had to fight with what he had.

Mawulan hurled the spear with all his strength. He didn't hear it strike the belly of the monster, falling harmlessly to earth. By that time he'd seen the demon's second, smaller eye begin to wink, along one side. Erratic spurts of sand and rock chips marched past him, dragon quills that slapped against the arid soil.

He sidestepped, drew his boomerang and waited for the devil to return. Another pass, and if the boomerang struck home—or if the demon's burning eye incinerated it—there would be nothing left except his small stone knife with which to fight.

So be it.

Thunder beat his ears, and a sudden sandstorm whipped at his naked flesh. Mawulan flung the boomerang and instantly lost sight of it as he recoiled from the impact of a stunning blow against his hip and thigh. He toppled backward in the dust, his leg on fire. The demon swept directly overhead and swung around for one more pass.

Mawulan ran a hand across his wounded hip and leg. The flesh was torn and bleeding freely, and pale bone was visible beneath. He couldn't stand, much less escape his superhuman enemy, but he could still resist.

Returning for its final pass, the monster swung away from him and circled widely, fixing Mawulan with its glaring eye and settling to the ground amid a roiling cloud of dust. He raised one arm to shield his eyes, and saw the belly of the beast disgorging smaller monsters in the shape of men.

At last he understood his enemies. They weren't human, after all.

It helped explain their actions, and the easy way they killed. Disguised as men, they won the trust of others, then betrayed them, sucked them dry and cast their bodies to the hunting dogs.

The monster-men were closing on him now, three figures, two of them with thunder sticks. He gripped the stone knife tighter, knowing they wouldn't come close enough for him to cut them, but the gesture was enough.

Before they killed him, they'd realize that he hadn't surrendered. They'd never own his soul.

He heard them talking with their human tongues, in words the elders of his village understood. Mawulan hissed and let them see the knife, evoking only laughter for his pains.

The first shot caught him in the chest and pitched him over on his back. He never felt the next three rounds, a waste of ammunition in the circumstances.

"Should we take him back?" one of the hunters asked.

"What for?"

"Forget about it. He'll be gone by morning, anyway."

They trooped back to the waiting helicopter, climbed aboard and lifted off.

Behind them, in the darkness, came the dingos, following the heavy scent of blood.

# CHAPTER ONE

The rugged peaks of the Blue Ridge Mountains of Virginia were thick with trees and steeped in history, soil hallowed by the blood shed in an epic civil war. A forty-minute flight from Washington, D.C., the wilderness stood fast against encroaching "progress," keeping precious secrets to itself.

One such secret was Stony Man Farm, situated in the Shenandoah National Park, off Skyline Drive. A bird's-eye view revealed a rich man's hideaway, perhaps, or the executive retreat of some well-heeled conglomerate. The central house was large, three stories, with a tractor barn and other outbuildings nearby, but even satellite or infrared photography wouldn't reveal the secrets locked away inside. Due north, a private airstrip took advantage of the natural terrain; constructed with an eye toward Lear-size jets and helicopters, it could handle all the latest fighter planes, as well.

Approaching from the north, Mack Bolan scanned the ridge line, following the highway with his eyes. A single car was moving in the opposite direction, sunlight glinting on its polished chrome. The sleek Bell helicopter's shadow flickered over the treetops and was lost.

The Farm felt more like home than any other place that he could think of at the moment. Friends and family, of a sort, were waiting for him there, but Bolan recognized the differences, as well. For he would never truly rest at Stony Man. The base would always be a launching pad to yet another battlefront in Bolan's endless war.

The chopper veered offtrack, skimming low above the trees. He saw the narrow access road below, a stretch of barbed-wire fence and open ground beyond.

A jeep was waiting at the helipad, with Barbara Price behind the wheel. Deplaning from the chopper, Bolan caught her smile and gave one back.

The lady looked terrific—honey blond, athletic, with a cover-girl complexion that belied her thirty-something years. Her clear blue eyes had a disturbing tendency to look beneath the surface and discover any secrets hidden there.

"You made good time," she said as Bolan slid into the shotgun seat beside her.

"Kansas City wasn't happening," he told her. "Someone needs to reevaluate Intelligence before we take another shot."

"Can do."

She put the jeep in motion, wheeling toward the house.

"What's happening?" the warrior asked.

"He wouldn't say. We're waiting on the sit-down."

"He" was Hal Brognola, out of Washington, the Justice honcho who was tapped to oversee the Sensitive Operations Group—a.k.a. Project Phoenix—based at Stony Man Farm. The Executioner had worked with the big Fed, in one way or another, since the early battles of his one-man war against the Mafia. In time, as Bolan's war expanded, their alliance had been formalized, dissolved and reassessed. Through all of it they had remained good friends, committed to a common cause.

They parked around the back and entered through the rear. A steel door offered coded access to the house, and Barbara punched the buttons, Bolan trailing in her wake. The dining hall was empty, but they caught Brognola just emerging from the security headquarters, followed closely by Aaron Kurtzman in his wheelchair.

Brognola was Bolan's height and then some, broad across the chest and shoulders, softening a little at the waist. His face was deeply lined, and there were gray flecks in his hair these days. He'd been riding shotgun on a desk for years, but he kept himself in fairly decent shape and never left his gun at home.

Beside him, Aaron Kurtzman's meaty face was broken by a winning smile. You didn't have to test his grip to know how he'd earned the nickname "Bear." The short sleeves of his shirt were strained by biceps that would make a big-time wrestler proud, a striking contrast to the legs, which had been paralyzed by gunfire in the one and only hostile raid on Stony Man Farm.

Brognola pumped Bolan's hand and asked, "What's happening in Kansas City?"

"Zip, as far as I could see. You'd better double-check your source."

"Can do. Right now we've got another problem on our plates."

They trailed Brognola into the computer room and rode the elevator down to basement level. Lights were burning in the War Room when they got there, and seats were arranged around the conference table, swiveled toward the broad north wall.

Kurtzman took the console as they settled in, his fingers tapping buttons to reduce the lights and key a slide projector mounted at his back. The first shot was a topographic map of Southeast Asia, with the borders etched in red. Brognola's small electric pointer beamed a white dot at the screen, and he maneuvered it around the point where Burma, Laos and Thailand meet.

"The Golden Triangle," Brognola said. "You know your history, but let's review it, anyway. Before the start of World War II, this region produced an average of forty tons of raw opium per year, most of it smoked legally in various parts of Asia. Nowadays the yearly haul runs better than a *thousand* tons. That's seventy percent of the world's illicit opium supply, give or take, and the refined China white has been outselling Mexican and Middle Eastern heroin for twenty years."

"You're right," Bolan stated, staring at the map. "That's history."

"Okay, let's try this morning's news." The blip of light moved north, across the Burmese border and into the People's Republic of China. "This is Yunnan Province, indistinguishable from the northern part of Burma, Laos and Thailand if you want to talk geography and climate. Poppy country."

"And?"

"According to our latest information from the drug-enforcement people, China's most important export crop right now is opium. They grow more rice and grain, but most of it stays home. Some of the opium goes into medication, but the rest—I'm told it runs to three, four hundred tons a year—all for export. They refine it on the spot and ship the powder into Bangkok via Laos. From there, after another month or two, it winds up on the streets."

"There was a rumble," Kurtzman offered, "years ago..."

"Correct," Brognola said. "When Mao gave Chiang Kai-shek the boot in 1949, rumors started filtering through Treasury, the Bureau of Narcotics and Dangerous Drugs. Of course, in those days, right on through the sixties, it was stylish to suspect the Red Chinese of everything from moving drugs to plotting Third World revolutions left and right."

"You're saying that they weren't?" Barbara Price asked.

"I'm saying Richard Nixon changed our outlook with his trip to China and the push for UN recognition in the early seventies. From 1972 till the trouble at Tiananmen Square, we were supposed to be the best of friends. It wasn't prudent to discuss the traffic from Yunnan."

"And now?"

Brognola faced the Executioner directly as he answered, "Now we're looking at a war on drugs that can't be won until we start to recognize the enemy. With so much focus on cocaine and South America, we've almost made it easy on the traffickers in heroin. It's nearly twenty years since DEA and NYPD cracked the so-called French connection, and we're looking at a brand-new plague of heroin from coast to coast. Seizures have more than doubled since 1980, and we estimate that barely ten percent of the imported China white is being intercepted."

"Which means?"

"Ten tons slipping through, in any given year."

"We can't be everywhere," Kurtzman growled, scowling at the map.

"We're not required to," Brognola replied. "In fact our best shot at the operation may not even be in the United States."

"How's that?"

Brognola nodded, Kurtzman pressed a button on the console, and Australia took the place of Southeast Asia on the screen.

"You think we've got a problem—let me tell you what the Aussies have to deal with. As of 1971, they had no significant drug problem at any level. Eight years later the federal police were officially describing heroin as 'a deeply rooted tree with branches that continue to grow and cast their sinister shadows farther across the country.' In concrete terms, that means yearly imports of six hundred to one thousand tons, with a street value between fifty and one hundred million dollars."

"That ain't hay," Kurtzman commented.

"Not when you consider that the average price in Bangkok runs around eight thousand dollars a ton, and it brings ten times that much in Sydney. It's a goddamn gold rush for the syndicates, and everything they see is China white."

"Who's moving it?" Price asked.

"Street dealers are predominantly native, but the smuggling is a Triad operation, with some Yakuza involvement on the side."

"Which Triad?" Bolan asked.

"The Yi Kwah Tao," Brognola said.

"So what's our angle?"

"DEA has no one in Australia at the moment, but the government has asked for help. The White House sees it as a golden opportunity to score one for the good guys, maybe do a favor for our ANZUS allies in the bargain.''

''When you say the Aussies asked for help—''

''It's strictly off the record. Anything we do is unofficial. They don't want to know about it in advance, and they won't cover for us if we drop the ball.''

''That sounds familiar.''

''Even so, they've given us some hard Intelligence that jibes with what the DEA has put together out of Hong Kong, Singapore and Bangkok. Bits and pieces that we didn't have before. It just might be the edge we need.''

''The players?'' Bolan asked.

At another nod from Brognola, Kurtzman ran his hand across the keys.

''Let's take it backward, from the bottom up. You'll have to work it that direction, anyway.''

The first face on the screen was thin and tan, surmounted by a mane of sandy hair. It was a candid photo, snapped discreetly, and it caught the subject in the middle of a smile.

''Meet Beamer York. According to the federal police in Sydney, he's become *the* man to see for China white. They know it, but they haven't got a thing worth laying out in court. Seems like their witnesses are prone to suffer from amnesia, when they don't drop dead or disappear.''

''We've heard that tune before.''

''Damn straight. York's not the only Aussie dealer with a major bankroll, mind you, but he's putting Sydney's other scumbags in the shade.''

''Connections?''

''Nothing but.''

The next face on the screen was leading-man material for Hollywood, a classic nose and jawline, with a hint of Asia in the eyes.

"York's backer since he switched from strong-arm robbery to dope, one Michael Lee. He's a war baby, Australian father, Chinese mother, born in 1946. The parents never married, but he traced his father back and wangled citizenship. It was the last time anybody really pinned him down. Since 1960 something he's been in and out, all over Asia, and he doesn't seem to have a fixed address when he's at home."

"Is he a Triad?"

"That's affirmative. He's what the Yi Kwah Tao call an 'incense master'—that's a territorial commander, roughly equivalent to a Mafia *capo regime.*"

"Some territory," Kurtzman muttered.

"Yes, indeed. Australia has around three hundred thousand Asian residents. If even half of one percent are Yi Kwah Tao sympathizers, that gives Lee fifteen hundred soldiers he can count on in a pinch."

"We know he's dealing smack?"

"The DEA says positively."

"But the Aussies haven't got a case."

"Same thing as York," Brognola said, "except they have a hard time even finding Lee. He's like some kind of hermit. Now you see him, now you don't."

"Which makes it tough to prosecute," Price stated.

"In spades."

"If DEA has eyes on Lee," Bolan said, "they should know his source."

"That's plural," Brognola replied as two Chinese faces showed up on the screen. "The beauty on your left is Chou Sin Fong, the Yi Kwah Tao incense master out of Bangkok. He's suspected in a couple dozen drug-related murders that we know about. One of his latest victims was a DEA investigator named Mc-Millan. He was getting close to one of Fong's grass sandals—that's a messenger, liaison man between the leadership and ordinary members—when he disappeared last March. They found his body floating in the Chao Phya River, but they had to send it home without a head."

"Terrific."

"He's a sweetheart," Brognola agreed. "The other hunk is Chiang Fan Baht, the incense master for Rangoon. According to the word I get, he's spent the past two years rebuilding drug routes into Burma from Yunnan. It's more direct and economical for all concerned. Without a stop in Laos, the Triads pocket six or seven million worth of bribes they'd have to use to grease the Pathet Lao."

"That leaves the source," Bolan said, keeping both eyes on the screen.

An older face replaced the other two, but age appeared to have no softening effect. The eyes were flint, the lips a bloodless gash that had forgotten how to smile.

"Lee's boss," the big Fed commented. "In fact the whole damn Yi Kwah Tao belongs to this guy. Sun Jiang Lao's his name. In Triad parlance, he's the 'Elder Brother,' which equates to number one. Sun snaps his fingers anywhere from Burma to the Philippines or Indonesia, and someone dies. His Triad's not the largest one around, but no one else comes close to him at payback time. When he was younger, working out of Hong Kong as a 'red pole'—the enforcer for a territory—someone started calling him The Cobra. It's The

*Great* Cobra, these days, and nobody has to guess who you're talking about."

"Headquarters?" Bolan asked.

"He's got a home in Bangkok and another in Macao, but no one's seen him much in either place for two or three years. He gets around, but rumor has it that he's spending lots of time up north these days, around Yunnan."

"Red China?" Price couldn't keep the skepticism from her tone. "I understood they purged the Triads back in 1949 or '50."

"So they say. And most of the illegal opium produced in the Golden Triangle is owned outright by nationalist Kuomintang—or KMT—exiles. That doesn't leave a revolutionary dealer lots of room to breathe."

"So they've invited Sun Jiang Lao to stay awhile?"

"Why not? He has the distribution network they require to move their product, and he pays in cash. It's perfect symbiosis, when you think about it. Down in Burma, even Thailand, you get outbreaks of morality from time to time, troops burning out the poppy fields and blitzing rural villages. Up north the Yi Kwah Tao have found themselves a hideaway where they can plant and harvest till the cows come home, no interruptions from authorities."

"They're greasing someone," Kurtzman said.

"Or maybe cashing in on unofficial policy. Beijing refuses to discuss the problem, so we have no way of knowing whether Yunnan Province has a rogue in charge or if the government has been exporting revolution in the form of China white."

"Who *is* in charge up there?" Bolan asked.

"General Li Zhao Gan," Brognola replied, his words accompanied by the appearance of a new face on the screen. "A hero of the People's Revolutionary Army, decorated for his courage in some border clashes with the Soviets a few years back. Since then he's been suppressing crime and rooting out revisionism in Yunnan."

"He works with Sun Jiang Lao?"

"Let's say the two of them cooperate. You won't find any of his soldiers harvesting the crop, but they ride shotgun on the shipments down as far as Burma, where the Yi Kwah Tao take over. Nothing happens in Yunnan of any consequence without a nod from General Li."

"It's hard to picture anything this size escaping the attention of Beijing," Bolan said.

"You got that right."

"So what's the plan?"

"We want to shut the pipeline down...or shake it up, if that's the best that we can do."

"An inside job?"

"It seems the only way to go."

"I'll have to have a word with Beamer York."

"At least."

"Work back from there, through Lee, and up the ladder to Yunnan."

"We're sharing eyes with DEA in Bangkok and Rangoon," Hal Brognola told him, "if you get that far. The Aussie end, you're on your own."

"As usual."

THE RUNNING SHOWER covered the sound of Barbara Price's footsteps as she entered Bolan's room and latched the door behind her. Standing there, her shoulders pressed against the door, she wondered whether this was a mistake. They hadn't been alone for months, and they had barely had a chance to speak since he arrived.

It would be easy to slip out and never let him know that she was there. A chance encounter after dinner, possibly, and see where that might lead.

No way.

She didn't want to wait.

Undressing on the move, discarding items of apparel on the floor, she caught herself reflecting on the other times they'd been together. There had never been a "date," per se, and never would be while their lives revolved around the covert world of Stony Man. Except when he was working on a mission from the Farm, she rarely knew where Bolan was from day to day, and that was probably a saving grace.

If she'd known each move he made, each time his life was on the line...

She draped her blouse across an empty chair, stepped out of her jeans, unsnapped her bra and let it fall. The air-conditioning was turned down low enough to make her nipples pucker and raised goose bumps on her skin.

A nice hot shower was the ticket, better yet with someone big and strong to scrub her back.

And when he finished that, she'd let him scrub her front as a reward.

The bathroom door was cracked an inch or two, emitting steam. She slipped off her bikini panties before she placed one hand on the knob and eased her way inside.

Bolan's silhouette through frosted glass was tall and lean. She couldn't see the too-familiar scars of battle yet, but she knew each and every one of them by heart.

Her fingers found the sliding door and drew it back. She saw him tense before he turned to face her, understanding that it couldn't be an enemy, not here.

"You want some company?"

His hungry eyes devoured every golden inch of her before he said, "I thought you'd never ask."

The frosted door slid shut behind her, and she stepped into his arms. Their lips met in a soulful kiss, tongues flirting for an instant, growing bolder as their passion flared. His hands began to trace the outline of her body, sleek and wet, the educated fingers pausing here and there to make her gasp.

"The soap," she told him, feeling breathless, dizzy now.

He palmed the bar and worked a lather on his hands, beginning at her collarbone and working downward, lavishing attention on her jutting breasts, the nipples burning in his palms. He soaped her rib cage, lathered gently curving hips and knelt to do her legs.

The first touch of his lips and tongue electrified her, making Barbara tremble where she stood. Her fingers tangled in his hair and drew him closer.

The spasm rocked her, making her head swim. She would certainly have fallen, but his hands cupped her buttocks, held her upright as he continued to lash her with his tongue.

It took her several moments to recover, riding out the storm, before she drew him upright, facing her. One arm around his neck, she raised her legs, encircling his hips, her free hand guiding him inside. She felt his heartbeat almost merging with her own, as if they had become one flesh, one blood.

The surge of Bolan's power was enough to push her over one more time, the steamy bathroom spinning wildly, until she was certain they'd fallen in a heap beneath the shower's spray.

It took her by surprise, long moments later, when she realized that they were standing upright, more or less, her shoulders pressed against the sweaty tile. She couldn't make herself relax; the muscles jumped underneath her skin as if she were connected to a live electric wire.

"They'll wonder where we are," he said at last, his deep voice sounding breathless.

Barbara pictured Hal Brognola and Kurtzman together in the dining room.

"Do you care?"

"Not really. No."

She kept one arm around his neck, her legs around his waist, and reached behind him, turning off the shower.

"So what are we waiting for?"

# CHAPTER TWO

The pilot's name was Stuart Hogan, and he hailed from Oodnadatta. He was short and sandy haired, mid-twenties, game for anything provided that the price was right. The single-engine Cessna had seen better days, but it would do the job.

"So where we going, mate?" the pilot asked as they began negotiating price.

"I'm not exactly sure."

"That makes it bloody difficult."

"I have a map, for what it's worth."

He spread it on the cluttered army-surplus desk. The map came courtesy of Beamer York. The warrior had leaned on the dealer, and the guy had told him everything he'd wanted to know. A wrong move toward shoulder leather had taken Beamer permanently out of play.

"Not much," the flyer said after a quick scan. "Your X looks small enough on paper, I'll admit, but it's a different story on the ground. Without coordinates, we could be searching two or three hundred square miles."

"I'm looking for a fair-sized ranch, or something similar. It shouldn't be that hard to spot."

"The only thing they're raising on a ranch in those parts, mate, is a pack of dingoes and goannas. It's a bleeding hardpan desert where you want to go."

"I'm not concerned about the crops or weather," Bolan replied. "There's someone on the ground I need to see."

"No worries, then. You call your chum and get coordinates. I'll drop you on his doorstep, nice and proper."

"That's the problem." Bolan held the pilot's gaze for several heartbeats, finally deciding he'd have to share at least a measure of the truth. "He's not supposed to know I'm on the way."

Stu Hogan frowned and glanced back at the map, his fingers drumming on the desk.

"I make it right around six hundred miles, one way," he said at last. "And that's without a bloody search. We'll have to stop at Barrow Creek for fuel, and likely more than once."

"The money's not a problem," Bolan said.

"I'm more concerned about this friend you're trying to surprise," the pilot said. "If *he* has friends, they may come looking for you. Meaning *us*. Up north my prospects for refueling are a trifle limited, if you get my drift. I wouldn't want to find a welcoming committee at the pump when I come rolling in on fumes."

"It shouldn't be a problem," the Executioner told him. "I'll need an overflight to check the layout, then you drop me well away. You should be safely home before the people on the ground get wise."

"With any luck, you mean."

"If you don't want the job—"

"I didn't say that, mate, now did I? I believe that I'm entitled to some information going in, that's all."

"The less you know, the better off you'll be."

"That's your opinion. Anytime I put my ass and aircraft on the line, I like to know the reason why."

It would be easier to walk away and find another pilot who was more concerned with cash than questions. Hogan's name had come up half a dozen times when he was shopping for a set of wings, but there were others in the game. Less scrupulous about their cargo or their passengers, perhaps, which simply meant a higher price without the questions going in.

But he had a feeling as he studied Hogan's face, almost a sense of déjà vu, reminding him of Jack Grimaldi when they met in Vegas in another life.

If he was wrong, a careless word could cost him everything. Stu Hogan was a dead man if he tried to turn the game around and offer Bolan to his enemies.

"I'm looking for a man named Michael Lee," the warrior said at last.

The pilot shrugged. "Can't say it rings a bell."

"No reason why it should. He likes his privacy."

"I'd say he must do, if he's living where you say."

"He deals in heroin, importing by the ton."

The pilot's eyes went hard. "God's truth?"

"I'm telling you enough to cost your life, if Lee finds out."

"Sod Mr. Michael Bloody Lee. I had a sister down in Adelaide who got mixed up with that shit. It cost *her* life, and no mistake."

"She's not alone."

"You don't look much like a policeman."

"No."

"Which tells me that you're either looking for a story, or you're out to kick somebody's ass."

"I've never been much good at writing."

Stu Hogan nodded thoughtfully, then cracked a smile. "Five hundred dollars for a one-way trip, plus any fuel I use for up and back."

"Sounds fair."

"Bring anything you need tomorrow morning, five o'clock. You'd better get some sleep."

TWELVE HOURS LATER they were airborne, flying over craggy mountain ranges, grassland fading into arid desert as they traveled farther north. The outback was a place of legendary contradictions and extremes—dry months that left the soil bleached pale and cracked, offset by weeks of pouring rain that sparked flash floods, deluging frontier settlements and wiping out their scattered, narrow roads. It was a land that time forgot, marsupials in place of mammals, and the only land on earth where deadly snakes outnumbered harmless species ten to one. The common spiders packed more venom than a full-grown copperhead in the United States, and scored a higher yearly body count. Wild dogs and vultures squabbled over the remains.

But Bolan's first and foremost enemy would be the desert sun. It reached them even in the aircraft, a blinding glare off chrome and convection currents tugging at the Cessna every time they left a mountain range behind and leveled out above the desert floor. Down there he knew the heat could kill a man within hours if he ran out of water and was miles from nowhere.

They stopped for fuel at Barrow Creek, a twenty-minute interruption of their journey, and pushed on from there with Hogan's charts in place of Bolan's nearly worthless map. It wasn't quite like looking for a needle in a haystack, since there was no hay and no place to hide. The trick would be to discover a ranch or compound in the middle of the wasteland, insulated from the outside world by miles and miles of barren, sun-baked earth.

They crossed the fence at half-past two, swung back and followed it for several miles before they gave it up and aimed the Cessna north again. After another twenty minutes, they spied the central compound, off to Bolan's right. A ranch house, something like a barn, outbuildings and a pair of Quonset huts that Bolan took for barracks from a distance.

"Want a closer look?"

"Not now. The less concerned they are about intruders on the property, the better off I'll be."

"Your choice, mate."

"Double back in the direction of that wash we saw with all the trees, and find a place where you can drop me off."

"You're sure?"

"It's why I'm here."

"From what I see down there, your friend won't be alone."

"I never thought he would be."

Hogan turned the Cessna back, proceeding south, but he was clearly less than thrilled.

"You have a plan for getting back?" he asked.

"I'll think of something."

"I could kill some time at Barrow Creek, come back tonight or in the morning if you need a lift."

"Too risky. You were right about somebody looking for you if you hang around too long."

"It don't feel right, somehow."

"Forget it," Bolan said. "It's what I do."

"I hope you're good."

"We'll see."

The Cessna touched down on a flat strip of desert about fifty yards southwest of an arroyo flanked by straggly, stunted trees. It wasn't much in terms of cover, but it seemed to be the best available.

"Good luck, mate."

"Same to you."

Bolan checked the gully for snakes and scorpions before he settled in and started sorting through his gear. There was a decent chance that Hogan's Cessna had been spotted from the house, and the Executioner meant to be prepared.

He waited out the daylight hours shaded by a tarp of desert camouflage, sipped water sparingly from one of three canteens while he prepared his weapons for the night ahead. He heard no sound of aircraft, vehicles or voices as the scorching day wore on.

At sundown Bolan shed his camouflage fatigues and donned a blacksuit for his nighttime hit. He buckled on his combat harness, with the heavy Desert Eagle Magnum automatic on his hip and the sleek Beretta 93-R in its armpit sling. Spare magazines for both filled pouches on his web belt, and his chest was crossed with bandoliers of ammunition for the Colt Commando that he carried on a shoulder sling. His face and hands were blackened with combat cosmetics to eliminate the risk of glare beneath a brilliant desert moon.

Four miles back to his target over open ground, and Bolan took his time, alert for any sign of motorized patrols or sentries covering his angle of approach. If Michael Lee was sweating out the possibility of an attack, it didn't show.

The compound lights were visible when Bolan came within a mile of contact, homing on the glare.

A thousand yards out, and the warrior started to circle, using compact glasses to survey the house and its surrounding structures. One shed obviously housed a generator, while the open barn was home to several jeeps and flatbed trucks. The Quonset huts were dark and silent, but he marked a guard outside, with some kind of long gun tucked beneath his arm. Three other sentries were visible around the compound—at the barn, outside the generator hut and along the south side of the manor house.

Bolan concentrated on the house, where he would find his quarry, if the man was currently in residence. It was a doubt that plagued his mind, but there had been no way of checking up on Lee without forewarning him of an attack.

So be it.

He was here, and it was time to move. If fate had spared his target, Bolan would deliver a resounding message to the dealer in his absence. Foul his nest and set him running, hoping for a chance to find his trail again.

The Executioner closed in from the west, a gliding shadow on the moonlit landscape. A hundred yards and closing, with the Colt Commando primed and ready, Bolan let his combat instincts take control.

How many hostile guns against him here?

If both the Quonset huts were barracks and both were full, he made it thirty hardmen underneath the metal domes. The house could hold another dozen easily, but he suspected Michael Lee would get along without an occupying army in his living room. Three sentries visible, say three or four staff in the house, and he was pushing forty.

He crept up on the blind side of the generator hut and left a satchel charge, its timer running down to doomsday as he circled toward the house. Strategic floodlights cauterized the open ground on every side, and he would have to wait until the generator blew before he made his move on Lee.

The engine sounds distracted Bolan, and he swiveled toward his flank. A pair of headlights rapidly approached from the empty flats, the driver holding to a rough collision course, still unaware of the intruder in his path.

A jeep.

The headlights found him, and Bolan dodged to his left, but someone in the jeep had registered his presence and shouted in a high, excited voice. The driver swung his vehicle to follow Bolan, high beams sweeping out to catch him on the run.

The warrior swung around to face the jeep and raised his carbine as the shotgun rider opened fire. The Colt Commando stuttered, 5.56 mm tumblers shattering the windshield of the vehicle as bullets from a submachine gun kicked up dust to Bolan's left. The floodlights let him see his target slump back in the seat, the driver throwing up one hand as if his flesh would stop steel-jacketed projectiles short of lethal impact on his chest and face.

A sudden deadweight on the wheel swerved the jeep, and as the starboard rubber dug in, the jeep flipped, expelling bodies on the way. They hit the ground like rag dolls, limp and boneless, one of them immediately flattened by the rolling jeep.

A siren began whooping from the general direction of the house. The warrior spun in that direction, charging, hearing shouted questions on his flank.

The sentry on the generator hut was nearest at the moment, with a good, clear shot.

Bolan stumbled, almost falling as the shotgun pellets slapped against his thigh. Momentum kept him on his feet a heartbeat longer, twisting toward the source of danger. His ears picked up the blast a moment later. There was movement near the generator hut, a man-shape standing tall and lining up another shot.

Bolan stroked the trigger on his Colt, and a line of tumblers spurted dust a full yard short of his intended target.

This time Bolan saw the muzzle-flash and threw himself aside. He struck the hard-packed ground with force enough to empty out his lungs, but kept his death grip on the carbine, rolling as the second charge of pellets swept past overhead.

He had perhaps two seconds to respond before the gunner managed to correct and find his range.

The satchel charge exploded, blacking out the compound even as it crushed his adversary under several hundred pounds of smoking wreckage. Bolan scrambled to his feet despite the protests of his wounded leg, and headed toward the house.

In front of him the live-in hardforce came streaming off the porch, automatic weapons covering the night. He dropped the first two in their tracks before the others saw his muzzle-flash and opened up, converging streams of fire like angry hornets buzzing in the night.

He jettisoned the carbine's empty magazine and snapped a fresh one into place, retreating as the facing windows of the ranch house suddenly exploded, more guns hammering the darkness from concealed positions. Bolan dropped another pair of gunners with a parting burst before he took off toward the barn.

The sentry there was on his own and pacing nervously when Bolan burst upon him, striking out with the Colt Commando's stock. The gunner went down, choking, and a second blow was all it took to finish him.

Inside the barn the moonlight revealed half a dozen jeeps, three flatbed trucks and one with canvas arched across the back. The jeeps had keys in the ignition, and Bolan slid behind the wheel of the first one, stifling a groan as white-hot pain flared through his wounded leg.

The blood was soaking through the warrior's clothes and made a squelching sound as he settled in the driver's seat. He turned the key, relieved to hear the engine come alive without delay, and put the stick shift in reverse. He made a short half turn lined up with the open door, as dark shadows raced toward his sanctuary from the house.

He palmed a frag grenade and yanked the pin, released the safety spoon and rolled the bomb underneath the second jeep in line. That done, he stood on the accelerator and gunned toward the open doors, flicking on his high beams in a bid to blind his adversaries momentarily.

The jeep was taking scattered hits before the warrior cleared the threshold. He fired the Colt one-handed, driving with his left, uncertain whether he was scoring with the short, sporadic bursts. A bullet grazed Bolan's side—fresh blood, fresh pain—and he swerved to clip a running soldier with his right-front fender, knocking him aside.

The frag grenade went off beneath the jeep in the barn and blew the twenty-gallon fuel tank, shooting plumes of burning gasoline in all directions.

He killed the headlights in case a spotter was tracking his retreat. Using the brake lights would be unavoidable, but he'd do it as sparingly as possible.

The arroyo where he'd started was four miles from the house, another nine or ten miles farther to the barbed-wire fence on the perimeter. He wasn't going back, but distance was important. Once beyond the wire, he had a better chance of giving them the slip.

He couldn't read the jeep's odometer by moonlight, and it wouldn't help him anyway, since he had made no point to check it when he started out. The readout on his wristwatch told him it was going on six minutes since he cleared the barn, and most of that had been a flat-out run across the desert, making forty, forty-five miles an hour. If he held that pace, he should reach the fence in another twelve or thirteen minutes.

His leg hurt like hell, and he was sitting in a pool of blood. Bolan hoped that the flow would clot before he lost enough to make him dizzy, start him driving aimlessly in circles until the jeep ran out of gas.

It struck him that he should have jumped at Hogan's offer for an airlift out, but it wasn't a part of Bolan's code to jeopardize the innocent unnecessarily. Besides, there would have been no way to keep the rendezvous the way he was, shot up and running for his life. You could forget about coordinates and strategy when it began to fall apart in combat and your ass was in the fire.

Still, there were things he had to think about, and soon.

Like fuel.

The jeep had been a godsend, but it wouldn't run on prayers. If he ran out of gasoline before he reached a settlement, it would be worse than useless, tracks behind him like a guilty finger pointing to the spot where he was dumped on foot.

He found the headlight switch, experimenting briefly, twisting it until the dashboard came alive. Speedometer. Tachometer. Odometer. The fuel gauge.

He was running for his life with half a tank of gas.

They had to have had pumps and tanks around the ranch, but that meant nothing to him now. He tried to estimate the mileage for the jeep, approximating speeds, allowing for the raw terrain. Assume a standard twenty-gallon tank, and he was good for ten. At fifteen, eighteen miles per gallon on the average, he was looking at one hundred fifty to one hundred eighty miles.

With any luck at all, he had enough to make a run for Tennant Creek, provided that he didn't lose his way. The moonlight was deceptive, and he couldn't read his pocket compass well enough to navigate with any kind of real assurance.

Damn it, he would *have* to use the lights and keep his fingers crossed that his assailants missed the distant glimmer, overlooked him in the midst of all the chaos he'd left behind.

He pulled the knob for lights and cursed. The steep-walled gully was less than fifteen feet in front of him as Bolan hit the brakes. He felt the tires dig in on sandy soil, but they were losing it as a void of empty space appeared beneath the front tires.

The vehicle dropped ten feet, with Bolan twisting in the driver's seat and kicking backward, plummeting through darkness as the lights went out. There was a rending crash, then his skull struck something solid, deeper blackness flooding in to quell his pain and banish conscious thought.

He never heard the walkers coming, never felt their strong hands as they lifted him and carried him away.

# CHAPTER THREE

The first pale light of dawn revealed the full extent of damage to the compound in a way that flashlights never could. They'd been working through the night to clean things up, bring order out of chaos, but Michael Lee's first broad view of the destruction caused him to snarl.

The house was relatively clean—some broken windows at the front and ten or fifteen random bullet scars, but it could all be put to rights without much difficulty. Elsewhere, they'd lost the generator hut and all that it contained, which meant no power tools to speed the cleanup. The barn-garage was badly damaged, and several vehicles destroyed.

The single greatest injury was that inflicted on the incense master's pride. Someone—a total stranger—had the sheer audacity to trespass on his land, assault his home, kill eight of his soldiers and escape in one of Lee's own vehicles. The very notion made him tremble with frustration.

His people knew enough to stay away from Lee when his handsome features bore a brooding scowl. It didn't happen frequently, but each of them could reel off stories of the gruesome fate that lay in store for men—or women—who provoked the Triad incense master. Such brutal violence, sparingly applied, helped Lee maintain a sense of discipline among his troops and

spread fear in the ranks of those who were his enemies.

At the moment he wished that there was someone he
could kill bare-handed, to defuse the headache building up behind his eyes. But first he needed to identify
his enemy. No easy task, when friendly corpses and
some shattered, burned-out buildings were the only
evidence in hand.

The aborigines had been dismayed and frightened by
the firefight, but his people had them working now. As
always, they were slow to start, reluctant to cooperate
until his foreman used the cattle prod a time or two.

The final cleanup would be time-consuming, but the
worst of it was reconstruction. They'd have to do
without electric power for the best part of a day, at
least, until the ruined generator was replaced. He'd
dispatched a man to Alice Springs by air—the helicopter had returned from night patrol, too late to do them
any good—but there was still a chance that they might
have to wait another day or two, despite his promise of
a healthy bonus on delivery.

Meanwhile, he had some time to watch his men at
work and puzzle over who was brave—or ignorant—
enough to challenge him.

Before the thought was fully formed, Lee had
amended it. If they were simply ignorant, his enemies
couldn't have found his home, nor would they have
begun the fight by killing Beamer York.

At first Lee had believed the execution of his man in
Sydney was a simple bid for power by some rival gang.
It was unusual for York to be caught napping. The
marksman's medal found on Beamer's desk held no
immediate significance for Lee—some trinket York

admired, perhaps—but he'd filed it in his mind for future reference.

This morning, with the smell of charcoal in his nostrils and the aborigines digging graves to bury his casualties, Lee understood that York's death hadn't been a simple gang-related hit at all. Instead, it was the opening volley in a war against his family, against himself.

The thought of waging war against a ruthless foe was nothing new to Michael Lee. He'd been fighting all his life, it seemed, from the beginnings in Macao, when he was just a half-breed orphan running in the streets and living hand to mouth.

Lee's father was Australian and a serviceman who'd fought the Japanese in China during World War II. Lee knew that much because his mother kept a faded snapshot of the man who'd made her pregnant and abandoned her when he'd finished serving time in uniform. She bore the child alone, rejected by surviving members of her family for bringing shame upon their heads, and gave her infant son his father's Christian name. She never tried to get in touch with Michael's sire or "bother" him in any way, because it would have been unseemly. She would rather sell herself to strangers as a prostitute and spend her meager earnings on the rice and fruit they needed to survive.

She couldn't stretch the money far enough to cover decent lodgings, clothing or medicine when she was ill. Her son had just turned nine years old when he was orphaned; Yuan Lee fell victim to a virulent strain of influenza that swept the poorer quarters of Macao. Alone, with nothing but the clothes he wore, a pocketknife and snapshot of his father with some English scribbling on the back, he'd become a street urchin.

In those years—as today—the children of Macao's disreputable slums were loosely organized in gangs that stole to eat or clothe themselves and fought for territory they could call their own. Police ignored the problem until merchants filed complaints, at which time they'd sweep the streets in force, assaulting any scruffy child they found outside of home or school. The beatings were intended as a lesson, but a homeless, starving child was slow to learn.

In time the gangs became more militant and better organized. The leaders fought to stay on top, selecting their lieutenants from the ranks by choosing those with courage, daring and initiative. Among the Shadow Dragons, Michael Lee had earned a reputation as a wicked fighter, no holds barred, and he absorbed the beatings from police without complaint, intent of finding quiet ways to even up the score. His first known murder, of a street patrolman in Macao, had been committed at the tender age of fourteen years.

Two years later, following a bloody rumble with a rival gang, the Shadow Dragons found themselves without a leader. In the circumstances it was natural for aspirants to challenge one another, fighting for the honor and respect that came with heading up a major gang. Within three days Lee challenged—and defeated—eight pretenders to the throne. One of the larger, older boys was killed and another permanently crippled in the face-offs, leaving Michael Lee in charge.

By that time members of the Shadow Dragons had begun to pick up pocket money working part-time for the local Triads, coveting the tailored suits and jewelry, flashy cars and women of the adult gangsters. Under Michael Lee, the teenage gang progressed from running errands to running drugs and other contraband. They pulled off daring robberies and gave a portion of their loot back to the Triads as a form of tribute, for protection from the law. Some of the older members took on murder contracts, gaining easy access to selected targets, slipping in and out of places where an adult would have been suspected.

Among the several Triads operating in Macao, the 14K was the largest, but the Yi Kwah Tao was unsurpassed in terms of militance, the status of its arsenal and the sadistic punishments it meted out to enemies. Impressed with Michael Lee's performance as the warlord of the Shadow Dragons, Chiang Shun Tak, the incense master for Macao, invited Lee to join.

In olden times his mixed blood would have been a detriment to Triad membership, but Chiang Shun Tak already had a plan in mind for Michael Lee. Consulting with the Triad's dragon head, he raised the prospect of expansion onto foreign shores, where Chinese emigrants were waiting to be organized, exploited, used. Along the way, if they could make a living from the white man, what would be the harm?

Lee's initiation to the Yi Kwah Tao followed the cumbersome, time-honored structure of Triad ritual. Conducted to a secret chamber, he stood silent while the incense master asked the vanguard—his recruiter—a total of 333 prescribed questions, assessing the new initiate's fitness to serve the Triad. The white sash Lee received would be his badge of membership throughout his three years of probationary service with the family.

Three years had seemed forever at the time, but it had passed with lightning speed. Almost before he knew it, Michael Lee was standing in the presence of his incense master, hearing of the leader's plan to launch a quiet infiltration of Australia. There were Triad members on the island continent already, to be sure, but Lee would be the "red pole"—the enforcer—if he managed to achieve his goal of settling in without his syndicate affiliation being known.

The photograph of Lee's father was the key to everything. With help from Chiang Shun Tak, he managed to obtain a birth certificate and promptly filed an application for Australian citizenship. Initial hesitation by the government was overcome when auditors perused Lee's banking records in Macao and verified that he appeared unlikely to become a burden on the welfare rolls.

There would be no reunion with his father, dead since 1964, but Lee wasn't concerned with family ties. He had a mission in Australia, and he set about performing it with energy that made his masters proud. When cancer claimed the life of Chiang Shun Tak a short year later, Lee had been elevated from the rank of red pole to become the incense master for Australia, building up a fresh new territory of his own.

The key was heroin, a blight still largely unfamiliar to Australians as the 1960s faded into history. Before another decade passed, however, China white would take its place among the leading law-enforcement problems of the nation, and a major share of the imported poison had been introduced by Michael Lee. He rarely handled drugs himself, but in a few short years he'd become immensely rich.

That wealth wasn't acquired without some cost, of course. There had been competition on the streets, which he was called upon to overcome by force of arms. There would be more, inevitably, as the years went by. Drug money looked too "easy" for the jackals to resist a power play.

But this was different. Lee could feel it in his educated bones.

Someone had already gone beyond the norm for poaching on another salesman's territory. Beamer York might possibly have been a gang-related hit, but this was much too...

Yes. Professional.

He still had no idea how many men had been involved in the attack on his home, but all of them had managed to escape. His sentries might have done their best, but it was far from good enough. As for the foolish rumor spread among his troops that said a single man had done all this, Lee shook his head, dismissed it out of hand.

Impossible.

With all the fire his men were laying down the previous night, the worst of shots would certainly have bagged a solitary prowler. Someone who could do this on his own would have to be a one-man army, superhuman or the next best thing.

Retreating toward the house, he flagged down Chou Tse-tran. His red pole was assigned to keep the aborigines working and repair the breaches in security, but one of his subordinates could to the job as well. Lee had more pressing business for his chief enforcer.

Inside the house he moved directly to his study, leaving the door open as he walked around his massive desk and took a seat. Chou followed moments later, closed the door behind him and didn't sit until he was invited to.

"They still insist one gunman was responsible?"

"Some do," the enforcer answered. "The rest still don't know what to think."

"We must suppress such foolishness," Lee said. "It's enough to lose eight men, but we must not elevate our enemies to mythic status."

"No, sir." Chou was silent for a moment, thinking, then he asked. "You see a link between last night and York?"

"I don't trust coincidence. If the events had happened months or even weeks apart, perhaps. But hours?"

"We can rule out the Sicilians," Chou informed him. "They don't have the strength or nerve enough to make a war these days."

"Perhaps with reinforcements from America?"

Chou shook his head. "I would have known."

"The Yakuza, perhaps?"

The enforcer thought about it for a moment, frowning, "Possibly, but they're in a building phase, still putting down their roots. For them Australia is as much a source as marketplace. They move more contraband through Sydney, back to Tokyo, than in reverse. Predominantly guns from the United States."

Lee's frown seemed etched in stone. "The native gangs are small and relatively weak. They lack the quality Americans call grit."

"If they were desperate enough for cash—"

"They also lack the talent," Lee reminded him. "Which leaves . . ."

The enforcer shifted slightly in his chair, becoming more erect, if possible. A scent of danger in the air had put him on his guard.

"Another Triad, then."

"It's the logical conclusion. They're jealous of our great success and fear increased expansion at their own expense."

"In other words they fear the truth."

"Fear often leads to desperate actions, Chou."

"Which family do you suspect?"

"The 14K have most to lose in terms of dollars, but the Chiu Chou have a longer history with drugs. They've been dealing heroin to the United States and Canada since Vietnam. The poppy is their bread and butter, so to speak."

"Both, then."

"They wouldn't act in unison, though one might well agree to let the other do his dirty work."

"Suppose that it's neither one? No other Triad?"

"Then we have a mystery," Lee said. "And I hate mysteries as much as I mistrust coincidence. I won't tolerate a question begging answers."

"Understood."

"The key might lie in Sydney. You must go as soon as possible and do whatever's necessary to determine who killed York and why."

"Yes, sir."

"The marksman's medal might turn out to be important, after all. Some sort of sign, perhaps. A link to something in the past."

"A military link, perhaps?"

"I'm considering the possibilities."

"A thought, sir."

"Yes?"

"The Chiu Chou buy their opium predominantly from the Kuomintang in Burma. As we know, the Kuomintang are staunchly anti-Communist. They might regard our intercourse with General Li as nothing short of treason. Thus, a military medal at the scene of Beamer's execution, and..."

"It's a prospect worth investigating," Lee responded, "but the medal's brief inscription was in English."

"A deliberate misdirection. Symbolism with a twist."

"Investigate *all* possibilities."

"Of course, sir."

"In the meantime, I must break the news to Elder Brother."

"Ah."

"It would be better if we had an answer to the riddle. Better still, if I could let him see the heads of those who have dishonored us."

"It shall be done."

"And quickly, Chou."

"Yes, sir."

"One other thing before you go. The blacks."

"I fear their work will never be the best, sir. Something in their constitution seems to self-destruct if they are not at liberty."

"I mean the *other* blacks," Lee said. "The runaways."

"I've had the helicopter searching for their camp. The pilot was involved in such a mission just last night, when we—"

"I know," Lee interrupted him, hands raised for silence. "I imply no criticism of your orders, Chou. If anything, the need to root them out and punish them is more acute than ever."

"I understand."

"For all we know one of them might be informing on us, to our enemies."

"They shall be found."

"Without delay."

"As you require."

"If it's possible to bring some back for questioning, they might prove useful."

"Sir."

"But they must still be rooted out in any case."

"Yes, sir."

"That's all."

Chou closed the door behind him as he exited the study, leaving Michael Lee alone. The incense master of the Yi Kwah Tao resisted an urge to pour himself a double Scotch whiskey. Reliance on a crutch like alcohol was proof of weakness in a leader, and he would allow no questions to arise concerning his abilities or clarity of thought.

Not now, of all times.

One thing that the enemy had spared him, for the moment, was the grim necessity of touching base with Sun Jiang Lao. The blast that wrecked their generator had deprived the camp of all communication, save for half a dozen hand-held walkie-talkies that would soon be dead if they weren't recharged. Bad news would have to wait a bit, which gave the incense master time—a day or so, at least—to put his house in order and regain some face.

Lee closed his eyes, imagining his enemies. They were a group of faceless men so far, but he'd know them soon enough. Chou made good sense about the KMT, but there were other possibilities, as well. Worldwide there were at least a dozen Triads with sufficient nerve and numbers to attempt a coup against the Yi Kwah Tao. Together, the official estimates suggested that their membership might top one hundred thousand—more than five times that of the Sicilian gangsters in America.

The worst of all scenarios would be a union of other Triad families in opposition to the Yi Kwah Tao...but it would also be unprecedented in the thousand years of Triad history. His mind flashed back to one of the oaths that every new initiate pronounced before he was accepted into the society: I Must Not Trespass Upon The Territory Of My Sworn Brothers.

And yet Lee understood that money was the one sure means of cutting family ties. Where profit was involved—especially in the amounts that poured in to the Triad coffers from the sale of heroin abroad—there seemed to be no room these days for brotherhood.

He understood the urge of other Triad syndicates to trespass on his claim, and it didn't offend him morally. A war between the families would be a complex undertaking, and he knew that Sun Jiang Lao would be reluctant to proceed. But Lee still had a few tricks up his sleeve.

The first step had to be identifying his assailants, working out their names and number so that he could move against them swiftly and efficiently. He had two strikes against him now, as the Americans would say, and he couldn't afford a third.

The marksman's medal came to mind again and made Lee frown. He thought that there was something lurking in the shadowed corner of his mind, but he couldn't extract the bit of information he required. Perhaps if there was someone he could ask...

Enough.

It was a problem to deal with later. In the meantime he had a product to protect and runaways to punish. Enemies to kill.

# CHAPTER FOUR

In Bolan's dream, he dragged himself along a narrow tunnel, moving toward a speck of light that could have been a hundred yards or several miles away. Behind him, in the darkness, sounds of close pursuit were growing louder, but he didn't recognize a human voice. Instead, the scraping, snarling sounds reminded him of something from a zoo, but couldn't recall the creature's shape or name.

The pain was worse now, costing precious time as Bolan wriggled down the narrow passageway, a sense of earth and rock above him, great tons pressing down and bent on crushing him to death. He swallowed rising panic and continued on his way.

The light was closer now, no doubt about it, and he found fresh energy. Arriving at the tunnel's end, he was surprised to find the opening no larger than his head. He'd be forced to dig, and quickly, if he meant to save himself.

His fingernails were cracked and bleeding by the time he finished, spilling from the tunnel into blazing sunlight. Safe at last, he thought, until he struggled to his feet and saw that he had come out in the middle of a barren wasteland, stripped of trees and any other landmark for as far as he could see. The sun was merciless, the desert breeze a draft from Hell itself.

In front of him the narrow tunnel was emitting angry sounds, almost reptilian in nature. Bolan glanced around him for a weapon or a place to hide, found neither, and prepared to fight against his enemy bare-handed. Any second now...

A dark, squat shape exploded from the tunnel, streaking after Bolan with a snarl, too fast for him to recognize its shape. The hurtling body struck his chest and slammed him backward to the brown, parched earth, fangs straining toward his throat.

His eyes snapped open, blinking in the glare of sunlight, but he caught himself before he screamed. A movement on his left brought Bolan's head around, and even that was painful as daggers lanced deep inside his skull.

A girl was kneeling in the shade beside him, studying his face. Her skin was chocolate brown, and she was naked, with the sole exception of a narrow, plaited belt around her waist. She made no move to hide herself from Bolan's gaze, but watched him for a moment longer, then finally rose and disappeared.

The lean-to was a simple one, dry brush piled up against a wooden pole with forked supports at either end. The shade it offered couldn't be described as cool, but Bolan understood that it was better than exposure to the broiling sun.

He lay still for another moment, checking out his body, measuring the pain. His memories were jumbled, falling into place haphazardly, but he recalled the raid on Michael Lee, the firefight and escape, his stolen jeep nose down in a ravine.

He raised one hand to feel around his aching skull, encountering dry blood, but nothing that appeared to be a major wound or fracture. The discomfort in his side was relatively minor, nothing but a graze. His flank was something else—the shotgun blast—but Bolan soon discovered that his pant leg had been split, some kind of poultice molded to the wound and bound with tattered cloth.

He struggled to a sitting posture and reached for the bandage. He had started to untie it when voice distracted him.

"Too soon."

He turned to find a young man crouching at one corner of the lean-to. He was as naked as the girl, who stood behind him, but a wooden boomerang was tucked inside his thin belt on the left. A leather pouch hung on the right.

A score of questions crowded Bolan's mind at once, and he was sorting through them for a place to start when the naked man turned and spoke to the girl, his language a mixture of grunting and clicks of the tongue. The girl replied in kind and disappeared.

"Minmara, Joseph," the man said in English, pointing to himself.

"Mike Belasko," Bolan said. "You brought me here?"

"Found jeep," Minmara answered. "You fall on head."

"How long?"

"Last night."

"I had some gear."

"Guns put away. Not needed here."

"There might be others, coming after me."

"Your friends not find you."

Bolan frowned. "They aren't my friends."

"Men hurt you, there?" Minmara pointed to his wounded leg.

"They tried their best."

"Bad men." It didn't come out sounding like a question.

"Do you know them?"

Minmara frowned. "You feel okay to walk?"

"Let's try and see."

Minmara helped him from the lean-to. Once on his feet Bolan calculated that the wounds weren't as serious as he'd thought. Still weak from loss of blood and the concussion that had knocked him out, he stood beside Minmara and surveyed a makeshift village. About a dozen lean-tos were scattered in among some rocky crags to take advantage of the meager shade. He didn't recognize the landmark and could only risk a guess at where they were.

"The jeep," he said. "Which way?"

"No good," Minmara said in answer to his question. "Jeep all broken."

"If it's nearby—"

"Not close. Bad men look other places first."

"There'll be trouble if they find me here."

"Come trouble, anyway," Minmara replied. "My people, the Arunta. Not speak English language. I learn some from go away to city, time ago."

Beneath one nearby lean-to an older woman was communicating with the girl that Bolan recognized, sign language standing in for the accustomed clicks and grunts. By this time he wasn't surprised to see that she—and all the other people in the village—wore no clothes beyond the simple decorative belts.

Minmara followed Bolan's gaze and said, "She may not speak one year. Her son be killed. She is in sadness."

"Mourning," Bolan said.

"The grief for one who dies. Her son killed by the bad men, for he run away."

His guide was moving, and the Executioner fell into step beside him.

"How many of you are there?"

"What you see. The others . . . gone."

"Gone where?"

"To serve the bad men. Be dead soon."

They passed two children playing in the dust, their blond hair shocking in the sunlight. He remembered reading somewhere that the younger aborigines were often blond until they passed their sixth or seventh year.

"They go by choice?" Bolan asked, concentrating on Minmara's last remark.

"Men come at night with trucks and guns. Take people off to work. A few try run away. Most don't come back."

They passed the cold remains of last night's cooking fire and shortly passed beyond the limits of the camp. Minmara climbed atop a giant rock, and Bolan followed him with difficulty, working out a measure of the stiffness in his leg. His head felt better now, as if no more than half a dozen men with hammers had been trapped inside.

"Work where?" he asked.

Minmara swept the flat horizon with his eyes, half turning toward the east, and pointed off at nothing.

"That way," he responded. "In the hole."

A frown creased Bolan's face. He'd surmised that they were both discussing Michael Lee, although Minmara didn't know his name. How many "bad men" could there be within a few square miles, equipped with jeeps and guns? And yet, just when he thought he had it figured out, Minmara changed the rules.

"Which hole is that?" he asked.

"Great hole in earth. The bad men send my people in, bring out again."

"You've seen this place?"

Minmara shook his head. "Bulwayo sees and runs away at night. We find him, hurt like you, but more. Can't fix. He talk about the hole before he dies."

"Did he explain what he was doing in the hole?"

"Dig some," Minmara replied. "Move boxes in and out for trucks."

Some kind of bunker, Bolan thought, or possibly a mine. The latter possibility appeared to make more sense, all things considered. He recalled that portions of Australia were renowned for gold strikes, plus a host of other minerals. It wouldn't be surprising if the acreage now occupied by Michael Lee and company should have a shaft or two on-site.

And if the mine wasn't in use, per se, what better place to store supplies? Imported heroin, perhaps?

It was a leap of the imagination, granted, but Minmara's reference to trucks and boxes helped him get there. And if Lee was looking for a low-cost, silent work force, he'd find it in a troop of captive slaves.

"If someone meant to find this hole, where would he look?"

"No good," Minmara said. "Bad men are all time watching. They kill you quick."

"I might not have a choice."

"Get well. We leave here soon. Need meat."

Below them, in the boulder's shade, two women dug the ground with pointed sticks. As Bolan watched, one of them pulled a speckled lizard from the hole that she had excavated, snapped its neck and dropped it on the ground as she began to dig again.

"For food," Minmara told him, pointing at the lizard. "Also honey ants, some roots we find."

The soldier heard his stomach growl, in spite of him.

"Sounds great."

As RED POLE for the Yi Kwah Tao, it was the lot of Chou Tse-tran to follow orders from his incense master. The chief enforcer of the family had responsibilities—security throughout the realm, protection of his boss, suppression of the Triad's enemies—but he wasn't expected to consult on policy. If Michael Lee instructed him to hunt for blacks around the desert, he would do as he was told.

It worried Chou, when he considered that they might be facing war against the 14K or Chiu Chou Triads over heroin. Both groups were larger, more widespread and had greater cash reserves. The Chiu Chou had been dealing heroin to the United States for twenty years, and they had overcome resistance there by one means or another, alternately buying off or killing off competitors, depending on their needs. Lee was convinced the Yi Kwah Tao would triumph if it came to war, but Chou Tse-tran wasn't so sure.

It would have been a grave mistake—perhaps a fatal one—for him to voice his doubts before the incense master. Lee was under pressure at the moment, working overtime to save his territory, and he didn't need his second in command disputing each decision that he made.

In one respect the search for blacks made sense. It would enable Chou to sweep the desert and determine whether any of their enemies from the previous night's raid were still at large in the vicinity. Of course, they could have hopped on board a bush plane or a helicopter, winging out of the area.

It was the speed and scope of hostile operations that concerned Chou most. He was accustomed to a fair amount of bungling and confusion when it came to violent competition in Australia. Random shooting incidents weren't unheard-of, but an orchestrated and precise campaign, with two destructive raids within as many days, six hundred miles apart...

He heard the helicopter coming back from Alice Springs, with news of the replacement generator. Chou Tse-tran was more concerned about the compound lights than anything. His men could do without hot showers for a day or two, but he didn't look forward to the prospect of a pitch-black desert night with lurking enemies abroad.

He waited for the helicopter, first a speck on the horizon, growing rapidly until it took the general outline of a giant, prehistoric insect. Patiently he stood and waited for the dust to settle. The messenger emerged in a crouch and ran forward to report.

"They say tomorrow."

"So be it. Go and help the others with the truck barn. There's much work to be done."

"Yes, sir."

Chou snapped his fingers and another Triad member was beside him instantly. "Refuel the helicopter," he instructed. "Tell the pilot we're going out again at once."

The soldier bowed and ran to do his bidding.

At least, Chou thought, the raiders hadn't touched their fuel supply. The tanks were buried underground, but open flame or an explosion could ignite the pumps and spread from there, with disastrous results.

It took them fifteen minutes to refuel the helicopter, and they were airborne moments later, a lookout with an automatic rifle in the shotgun seat, while Chou Tse-tran staked out a place in back.

"What are we looking for?" the pilot asked.

"Stray abos," Chou replied. "We must find and punish runaways."

The pilot shrugged, accustomed to obeying orders. In the absence of directions from his passengers, he picked a compass point at random and proceeded north-northwest. If someone else was paying for the time and fuel, he'd be glad to fly all day.

Chou watched the desert skimming past beneath the helicopter, the immeasurable open space contrasting sharply with his mental images of home. In Hong Kong people jammed together in a crush that left no room for privacy, pollution choked off the air, vehicles jammed the streets. Australia was a different world, outside the major cities, where a man could walk beneath a crystal sky and blazing sun for days on end without encountering another human being.

At a glance it would have seemed impossible for anyone to hide in such a wasteland, where the stunted trees were often miles apart or simply nonexistent, waterholes so few and far between that men and animals would often die of thirst between one pit stop and another. Even so, Chou knew from personal experience how difficult the search for aborigines could be on such a hunting ground, where his intended prey had lived for generations and would know the land by heart.

He wouldn't fail, but it might take some time to carry out the incense master's orders. By their very definition, runaways would be elusive, hiding out, exerting every effort to avoid recapture. Chou would spare them that, all right, except for one or two to satisfy the incense master's need for someone to interrogate. As for the rest...

The thought of killing someone in the next few hours brought a smile to Chou Tse-tran's face. It was a chance to start repaying some of the indignities his family had suffered in the past two days. And if the first to die were simple abos, ignorant of a conspiracy against the Yi Kwah Tao, so be it.

They would be the appetizers, meat served up to the incense master on a silver platter to prepare his palate for a feast of blood.

THE LIZARD WASN'T BAD, as such things went. In training for the Special Forces prior to shipping out for Vietnam the first time, Bolan had been forced to dine on worse as part of the survival course demanded by the Green Berets. He could remember snakes and insects, grubs and swamp rats from the marshland near Fort Benning. On the whole he thought that desert roots and roasted lizard were the way to go.

The honey ants were something else.

His hosts had found a nest beneath some straggly trees a half mile out, and dug down deep enough to raid the chamber where a thousand workers hung suspended from the ceiling, sacrificing everything they had to give the colony a living food supply. Each day the hunters brought them seeds and insects, drops of sap collected from the roots of living plants. The stationary drones consumed it all, their rudimentary digestive tracts converting it to an equivalent of honey, storing it inside their abdomens instead of building hives, and bloating up to six or seven times their normal size. Upon demand, the living honey pots regurgitated sweets to those who fed and bathed them through the day, a queer link in the desert food chain, where each speck of nourishment and drop of moisture was preserved against the coming time of need.

And to the aborigines, the honey ants were living candy, favored for dessert. Collected live, they were consumed by pinching off the head and jaws before the rest was swallowed whole. The Executioner decided that they weren't half-bad once you got past the tiny, wriggling legs.

Around the fire Minmara's people spoke about the "bad men" who had terrorized the region for the past two years, their spokesman paraphrasing for the soldier's benefit.

From what he gathered, Michael Lee and his marauders made a habit of collecting slaves approximately twice a year. A "sky beast" did the spotting—probably a helicopter, from the rough description—and a flying squad of jeeps and trucks converged to spring the trap. Sometimes old men and children would be left behind, and sometimes they were shot down on a whim. When stragglers managed to escape, they were pursued and killed unless they found themselves a hiding place.

Among the dozen members of Minmara's shrunken tribe, one woman and a teenage boy had managed to escape from their abductors, both before they ever saw "the hole" Bulwayo had described before he died. The others had been rejects—smaller children and the elderly—or fleet enough to dodge the raiders when they came in search of slaves. Minmara had become their leader by default, when he'd returned from Darwin eight months earlier, possessed of broken English and a working knowledge of the white man's ways.

"The government should be informed," Bolan said, as the round of stories petered out. "Lee's men have broken ten or fifteen major laws that I can name offhand."

"The white man's state cares not for us," Minmara said. "The bad men have much money, many guns and many friends."

"Has anybody tried to turn them in?"

Minmara shook his head, a frown of inbred fatalism carving furrows in his cheeks.

"No use," he said. "If the police come here, the bad men kill our people still alive, hide bodies. This way, one or two escape, come back to us."

"And more get taken in the next raid."

"Finished now," Minmara said. "We leave here soon, walk far away. The bad men do not find us there."

"They'll find somebody else," the Executioner replied. "Another tribe."

"May be. We all Arunta here."

The simple logic canceled any argument that Bolan might have offered, and he gave up trying. What would he accomplish if he did convince Minmara and the others to report Lee's raids for slaves? They would be forced to flee from their ancestral lands, in any case, before they could report the crimes, and there was every chance that Lee would use mass murder to erase the evidence of any crime.

Experience had taught the soldier not to rope civilians in on thankless missions in his everlasting war. Minmara's people had been volunteers, but only to a point. The act of saving Bolan's life didn't commit

them to a broader role, nor was the Executioner entitled to expect support when he went looking for his
enemies again.

If anything, he owed the tribe a debt of gratitude,
which would be best repaid by leaving them alone, allowing them to slip away without the shadow of his
personal decisions darkening another aspect of their
lives. They had been through enough already.

He sat and listened to the desert night, a soft breeze
playing in between the rocks, while bats swept overhead and pinged their sonar beacons at the darkness,
seeking prey. The rest was ringing silence, save for
muffled conversation in the pale ring of the camp fire.
Overhead the deep blue velvet sky was bright with
stars.

How long before his enemies came searching for him
here? Minmara's confidence in their ability to lose "the
bad men" carried little weight with Bolan, even granting that the aborigines knew their native land and held
a few tricks back against their adversaries. If the system was a perfect one, Lee's slavers would have gone
home empty-handed every time instead of whittling
down the tribe with periodic raids.

And if they fled tomorrow or the next day, what
would Bolan do? He hadn't pressed the point about his
weapons, but he couldn't afford to put more ground
between himself and Michael Lee when he would only
have to double back on foot and do it all again. With
some allowance for his wound, he thought that he
could pull it off... but not if he was forced to hike an
extra twenty miles or so to do the job.

He let himself relax a bit, the fire's warmth seeping
into him.

It would be difficult, if not impossible, for Lee's men to surprise the camp by night. Tomorrow would be soon enough for him to make his choice, and he would think about the weapons then.

Just now he had Minmara's people and the desert night to keep him company.

# CHAPTER FIVE

They rose at dawn as the first pale blush of daylight glowed on the eastern skyline. At first the Executioner was stiff, but as he moved about the camp, he was relieved to find the pain receding in his wounded leg. As for the headache, it was gone. Some tenderness around the crust of blood on Bolan's scalp was the sole reminder of his crack-up in the stolen jeep.

The women spent an hour digging roots and lizards on the far side of the rock pile, throwing in some juicy insects for variety, and they sat down to breakfast with the sun a red-orange ball on the horizon. As the day wore on, it would begin to lose its color, bleached white as the earth began to simmer from its unforgiving heat.

When Bolan asked which way the tribe was traveling that day, Minmara pointed west. It was the quickest way to put more ground between the bad men and themselves.

"I won't be coming with you," Bolan said at last.

"Must come," Minmara told him, putting on a frown.

"I've still got work to do. It isn't finished yet."

"You hurt. The bad men kill you next time, maybe."

"It's a chance I'll have to take."

"Come safe with us. Be strong and come back later."

Bolan shook his head in an emphatic negative. "I haven't got the time."

"Arunta not for fighting. Spears and boomerangs no good against the guns."

"I'm not recruiting," Bolan said, and saw the blank look on Minmara's face. He tried another tack. "I think you should go. The Arunta should be safe, away from here."

"You, also. No one here to help you next time, when you fall from jeep."

The warrior smiled. "I like your confidence. I'm staying, anyway."

"I think—"

The distant sound of rotors cut Minmara off, and Bolan never found out what he thought. The whole tribe rose as one, their eyes turned eastward toward the sun, whose glare concealed their enemy.

Minmara scowled and spit. "The sky beast comes."

"A helicopter," Bolan said. "I'll need my gear."

Minmara hesitated for a few more moments, watching as a tiny speck on the horizon grew before their eyes and took on the silhouette of an exaggerated dragonfly. Around him the Arunta scattered, kicking over lean-tos, seeking cover in the shaded nooks and crannies of the rock pile.

If it maintained a steady course, the chopper would have passed due north by perhaps a quarter mile, but you could almost feel the pilot checking out the rugged heap of boulders planted in the middle of a barren wasteland. Cover was the second-hardest thing to come by in the desert, after water, and the searchers wouldn't miss an opportunity like this.

"They're coming," Bolan said before the helicopter even veered off course. A heartbeat later it was banking, running on a new diagonal that put the hunters on a dead collision course with Bolan and the tribe.

"Get down!"

"Too late," Minmara answered fatalistically. He held his ground, bare-headed, waiting for the chopper with a sad expression on his face.

Behind him Bolan found a crevice in the rocks and wormed his way inside, upsetting several smallish lizards as he did so. This would be a scouting run, he calculated, and the one small hope they had lay in deceiving the pursuers, letting them believe that the Arunta were alone and few in number, lightly armed with wooden spears and boomerangs. They could preserve a measure of surprise if he convinced Minmara to return his guns. Outnumbered they might be, but it was still the only chance they had.

The helicopter circled once around the rock pile, faces in the cockpit studying Minmara where he stood. It would have been an easy shot, but neither of the chopper's occupants seemed so inclined. The second time around, from his concealed position near the crest, the Executioner saw one of them dictating coordinates into a microphone.

After another moment the airship roared away, receding in the eastern distance. They were going back to meet the earthbound hunters, Bolan thought, and guide them in. The aborigines were on foot, and there could be no question of a dozen naked people outrunning modern vehicles.

Minmara turned to face Bolan as the warrior rose from hiding, shrugging off the fresh discomfort in his wounded leg.

"My gear."

"We go," Minmara said.

"Out there?" Bolan jerked a thumb across his shoulder toward the empty desert. "How do you expect to lose them on the open ground?"

"We do our best."

"Not good enough," Bolan said, knowing that the time for tact was past. "Those chopper jockeys were the scouts, and reinforcements won't be far behind. They'll run you down with jeeps or shoot you from the air. It's no damn choice at all."

"And what is your way, white man?"

"Stay right here," he said, "and make them come to you. We've got the only cover for a mile or more. They'll have to root us out, and that could be expensive."

"They have guns."

"And so do we."

Minmara hesitated for another moment, but finally turned and tossed an order to the naked girl who had been Bolan's nurse the night he first arrived in camp. She disappeared around the far side of the rock pile, coming back moments later with his Colt Commando, bandoliers and combat harness. Both his side arms had survived the crash, and there was still one frag grenade on Bolan's web belt.

"We're in business," Bolan said, and pointed to the spears a couple of Minmara's people carried. "Are you any good with those?"

THAT MORNING Chou Tse-tran had chosen not to take the helicopter out. It wasn't flying he disliked, so much as being airborne in the middle of a wasteland where the barren ground stretched out as far as he could see in all directions. It was like patrolling hell, and he'd passed the job to his subordinates, remaining with the lead jeep of a tiny caravan that left the compound shortly after dawn.

It was already hot, but they were carrying canteens. Chou's broad-brimmed hat would shade his face, and never mind if it made him resemble something from a cheap Italian western. He was hunting men today, and it was deadly serious.

The Ruger Mini-14 braced against his right leg was his favorite weapon, sighted accurately to a hundred yards. He always used it when they hunted aborigines, but it wasn't suitable for the occasions—more infrequent now—when he was called upon to work in Sydney or the other cities where the Triad's influence and drugs had spread. On those occasions, when he did the dirty work himself, Chou leaned toward silenced automatics or the compact Ingram submachine gun if he had to execute a contract on the fly.

Behind him, in the jeep's backseat, one of his soldiers manned the radio. They'd been driving for the best part of an hour when it crackled into life and an excited voice reported contact somewhere up ahead. The scout called out coordinates, but they were Greek to Chou Tse-tran. He turned and snapped an order for the helicopter to return and lead them in.

The round trip would require ten minutes, more or less, and there was nowhere for their targets to run or hide out here. Their fate was sealed, but they were all too ignorant to recognize the fact.

They sat and waited, engines idling in the heat haze, for the helicopter to return. The sound came first, and then a flyspeck appeared, growing larger by the moment until it circled overhead and blew a dancing sandstorm around their vehicles. Chou cursed and grabbed the radio away from his subordinate.

"Lead on!" he snapped. "Stop wasting time!"

"Yes, sir!"

He glanced behind him at the second jeep and the flatbed, which brought up the rear in case they captured any aborigines for the incense master to interrogate. Three vehicles, ten guns, and it would have to be enough.

Chou felt a fleeting doubt, as they began to move. Suppose it was a trick, somehow? Suppose the enemy who struck their compound had arranged a trap?

Impossible.

The blacks were fugitives, a ragtag band of nomads from the Stone Age, shunned by everyone they met. Chou had a superficial knowledge of their customs, and he knew they mutilated growing boys at puberty to the extent that fathering a child required more luck than passion. If you visited one of their villages it was fifty-fifty that the chief would offer you his wife to keep you warm at night.

Barbarians.

It was a pity that they lacked the stamina to work as slaves for any length of time. A few months here and there before a creeping apathy combined with malnutrition to destroy them in captivity. Someday, Chou reckoned, they would find themselves devoid of local tribes to raid, but by the time that happened, they would all be filthy rich and living in an air-conditioned penthouse somewhere, with the godforsaken desert fading into memory.

The helicopter ran ahead of them, a hundred yards or so, but it was still in sight when Chou picked out their destination rising like a pimple on the barren skyline, something like a hill or rocky outcrop.

No wonder, Chou Tse-tran mused, that the aborigines were so primitive, existing like Neanderthals, with nothing but the simplest tools and weapons. They'd never dreamed the wheel or sought to clothe themselves against the sun. They had domesticated dingoes, but they couldn't teach the dogs to hunt or fetch. In terms of agriculture, they were wholly ignorant, content to eat the roots they managed to collect by chance.

As far as Chou was concerned, they should be grateful for a chance to learn from their superiors, instead of running off and hiding in the desert. It was time for them to grasp that fact, and he was well prepared to drive the lesson home.

Five hundred yards until they reached their target, and he felt the old excitement thrumming in his veins. The kill was coming, human prey delivered to his hands at virtually no risk to himself. It was the way Chou liked it, with a winning edge.

He set the Ruger in his lap and flicked off the safety. The dust and heat meant nothing to him now, when he was focused on his prey. Tomorrow or the next day, after he had carried out the incense master's orders, he'd be off to Sydney in pursuit of other enemies.

But first some sport.

The thought of fresh blood made him smile.

THE ROCKS wouldn't provide great cover, and they offered no real sanctuary from an airborne burst of fire, but they were definitely an improvement on the open desert floor. Out there the Executioner and his Arunta comrades would have been encircled in a moment, cut to pieces by converging gunfire.

As it was, he lay in wait and watched the vehicles approaching with the helicopter swinging wide around their stony fortress. He hadn't shown himself as yet, and they'd be expecting something in the nature of a few stray spears—if the Arunta ventured to resist at all.

The chopper did its scouting job and fell back, hovering, some fifty yards due north. He marked the vehicles—two jeeps and what appeared to be a half-ton truck—approaching from the east. He counted ten members of the opposition team, undoubtedly all armed, plus anything the helicopter might contribute once the shit came down.

He shifted his position, kept a boulder on his left to screen the chopper as he sighted down the Colt Commander's barrel at his targets. They'd pulled up forty yards away, jeeps on either side of the half-ton like bookends. As the gunmen clambered from their vehicles, he spotted submachine guns, shotguns and here and there a rifle.

They had definitely come prepared.

Three white men, and the other seven were Chinese.

Surprise was still the key, and Bolan palmed his one frag grenade, working out the safety pin as he prepared to start the party with a bang. There was a subtle shifting in the rocks as a number of the aborigines hefted stones or boomerangs, preparing to make a final stand against their enemies.

Bolan waited for the first few rocks to fly, some falling short, a couple bouncing off the vehicles with loud metallic clanging sounds. One of the hunters laughed, and then another, all of them involved within a few short seconds.

It would be an easy kill.

Bolan pitched his lethal egg as half a dozen stones took flight. It struck the ground behind some gunners on his right and wobbled as it rolled.

The blast was like a thunderclap, more startling because the sky was crystal clear, no sound but engines idling, mocking laughter and the pattering of stones to break the morning stillness. Shrapnel and the shock wave slammed three gunners off their feet forever, flaying rubber on the nearest jeep and blowing out its windshield.

At once the other gunmen scattered, shouting back and forth or cursing as they raced for cover. Two retreated toward the vehicles, one ran in the direction of the helicopter and the last four charged directly toward the rocks, already laying down a screen of automatic fire.

Bolan had discussed procedure with Minmara, trusting the Arunta spokesman to interpret for his people. They were meant to keep their heads down when the shooting started, staying under cover, out of the warrior's way if possible. Confronted with the opposition one-on-one, they should defend themselves, but otherwise refrain from giving Lee's commandos any targets for a turkey shoot.

It was a simple plan, and Bolan watched it go to hell within the first few seconds of the clash. He had a running target in his sights, his index finger tightening around the automatic carbine's trigger, when Minmara and a couple of the other males stood up among the rocks and started hurling wooden spears at their attackers. One struck home, a glancing blow that knocked the runner off his stride for just a heartbeat, but the rest were wasted, and the Arunta painfully exposed.

Lee's gunners took advantage of the opportunity, redoubling their fire. Minmara dropped behind a giant boulder, seemingly undamaged, but the other two were cut down where they stood, one dead before he hit the ground, the other screaming as he fell.

Bolan tracked the nearest runner with his Colt and fired a short, precision burst. The man spun, a full three-sixty on the run, before he pitched face-foward in the dust.

And that left six.

The helicopter's crew was finally reacting, circling for position at a hundred yards, and Bolan put them out of mind for just a moment. He'd found himself another open target, scrambling over weathered rocks and hampered by the Uzi he toted.

A 3-round burst erased his target's interest in the battle, blowing him away. His nearest sidekick found some cover in the shadow of a boulder, popping up to spray the higher rocks with shotgun pellets now and then.

He should have varied his technique.

The third time he showed himself, Bolan caught him with a burst that opened up his face and dropped him backward on the sand.

Six down, and that left four, plus the helicopter crew. As if in answer to his thought, the chopper came in low, more noise and nuisance than a lethal risk. Bolan wondered if the scout crew had been dumb enough to make the run unarmed.

The chopper circled back and made another pass, still nothing in the way of hostile fire, but gunners on the ground were taking up the slack. The one who tried to reach the helicopter had retreated to the nearest jeep now, and was helping two of his companions spray the rocky crags with automatic fire. A fourth had gone to ground within the rocks themselves, short bursts from what appeared to be a mini-Uzi chipping stone on either side of Bolan's sniper nest.

The warrior saw Minmara moving like a shadow and dared not shout a warning that would put the hostile gunner on alert. Instead, he fired a short burst toward his other enemies, avoiding damage to the vehicles as best he could.

Minmara made his move some thirty seconds later, lunging from the cover of a rocky outcrop, falling on his target with a short stone knife. The gunner tried to throw him off, his Uzi spraying aimless fire around the landscape, but Minmara's blade was at his throat by then. A gout of crimson flew from the jugular before they toppled out of sight. Moments later Bolan saw Minmara's grinning face, blood smeared across his chin.

It didn't seem to be his own.

The helicopter circled overhead, attempting to distract him, until the Executioner unleashed a short burst from his carbine, etching a tattoo across the fuselage. The pilot got his message, swinging out of range before a second burst could find the rotors or the engine block.

Downrange two submachine guns and a rifle tried to pin him down, their owners firing from the cover of the jeeps and truck. He hoped to save the vehicles—or one of them, at least—for transportation back to Lee's estate, but they were useless to him if he couldn't take out the three surviving gunners.

One man was firing at him from the flatbed of the half-ton truck, concealed behind the cabin when he dropped down. The other two were huddled in the shadow of the jeep on Bolan's left.

His best hope for a kill would be the gunner on the truck. Each time the man popped up to fire, a portion of his body was exposed to Bolan, looking through the windshield and out the small back window of the cab. It would be tricky and would require precision timing, but he wasn't going anywhere until the job was done.

He fed the Colt a brand-new magazine and waited, covered by the rough face of a boulder from the gunners at the jeep. If they had any thoughts of rushing him, it would have been a perfect time.

His target rose to fire again, a rifle poking out across the flat roof of the half-ton's cab. He squeezed the carbine's trigger, held it down and hosed a dozen tumblers through the windshield, striking flesh with at least half of them.

The shooter vaulted backward with a cry of shock or pain, no telling which. His body struck the flatbed of the truck with a resounding thud and didn't rise.

And that left two.

The gunners at the jeep were wishing they were somewhere else, but getting out meant letting down their guard, emerging from the cover they had found. Their only option seemed to be a long wait in the sun, until the helicopter pilot radioed or ran for help—assuming there were still more working vehicles in camp.

When they decided on their move, they wasted no more time. Both firing, one man came up on each side of the jeep. They tried to pin down their adversary with random fire, uncertain of his actual position in the rocks. The brief delay had granted Bolan time to shift positions, ready for them when they made the break.

He caught the would-be driver with a rising burst that zippered him from crotch to throat and punched him over backward in a lifeless sprawl. The dead man's trigger finger clenched in reflex, and his submachine gun emptied out its magazine, some of the bullets ripping through the truck beside him, hammering beneath the dusty hood.

One was left, and Bolan faced the shooter eye to eye across his gunsights, squeezing off before his enemy had any real chance to react. The Colt Commando's 5.56 mm tumblers cut a fist-sized pattern on the gunner's chest and spun him in his tracks, a whirling dervish with his arms outflung in death.

All done... or was it?

Bolan rose from cover, standing where the two-man helicopter crew could see him clearly, ready if they had a move in mind. When nothing happened after several seconds, the Executioner brought the carbine to his shoulder, sighting for a kill shot on the pilot. It was enough. The chopper swerved away, its rotors whipping at the air in swift acceleration, swinging out of range.

And gone.

The news would get to Michael Lee before the helicopter did, but they'd bought some time, at least. As for the price...

Three members of the tribe were dead: the men cut down by early hostile fire, as well as the grieving woman who had done her talking with her hands. The latter victim had been taken with a lucky head shot, possibly by accident, when she looked out from cover in a move to find out what was happening. The enemy had suffered greater losses, but the death of three Arunta meant a significant loss among the tiny nomad tribe.

He left Minmara's people to their chief and went to check the vehicles. The jeep on Bolan's right had two flat tires, plus shrapnel damage to the steering column, while a final burst of point-blank fire had finished off the truck. That left a single jeep in working order, keys in the ignition, with a spare fuel can in back.

With the assorted weapons scattered on the field, he thought it just might be enough.

But he'd have no time to waste.

# CHAPTER SIX

The Triad hardman stammered through his brief report like someone who expected to be cut off at any moment, and his fears weren't misplaced. The incense master stood before him, scowling, hands clenched into hard, white-knuckled fists behind his back. Lee's eyes were chips of flint, as dark as night and sharp enough to shave with.

"And you ran away," he said when his subordinate had finished speaking.

"There was no choice, Master. I had a pistol, nothing more. The other men were dead."

"Including Chou Tse-tran?"

"All dead. I saw them fall."

An elbow in the ribs evoked the pilot's shaky nod of confirmation.

"You made no attempt to help them?"

"But we did, Master. As I explained, the white man nearly shot us down. You may inspect the bullet holes, if you don't—"

"I may do anything I wish!" Lee snapped, his anger raising blotches on his cheeks. "Just now I choose to speak with you."

"Of course." A wise note of humility had entered the observer's voice.

"You say there was a white man with the runaways?"

"Yes, sir. Well armed, he was. Chou's soldiers would have overrun the blacks without a problem, otherwise."

"*One* man?"

"If there were more, they didn't show themselves."

"Describe him for me."

"He was tall, dressed all in black. Dark hair, I think. He had some kind of automatic weapon and grenades."

"One man defeated Chou Tse-tran and nine of your blood brothers?"

"Sir, as I explained—"

"The blacks did nothing?"

"They were throwing rocks and spears at first . . . perhaps as a diversion."

"And the vehicles?"

The man shrugged and looked confused. "We had no way to bring them back," he said, nonplussed at being forced to state the obvious.

"Were any of them damaged?"

"Who can say, Master? There was a blast beside one jeep, much firing all around. It might be possible to drive them still, but we couldn't find out. I thought that it was best for you to hear the news without delay."

Lee bit his tongue to keep from cursing at the man. He was correct, of course. It was a stupid oversight to send out the helicopter unarmed, but there was nothing he could do about it now. As for the truck and jeeps, one man could only drive a single vehicle, no matter if he *was* a one-man army on his feet. The aborigines could no more drive a jeep or truck than they could build a shuttle craft and fly it to the moon.

One vehicle to watch for, then, assuming any of them had escaped the clash unscathed. If all of them were wrecked beyond immediate repair, it meant his enemies were still on foot.

He waved the scout and pilot off, a gesture of dismissal, while his mind raced on ahead.

A white man with the aborigines, well armed with automatic weapons and grenades. The point where Chou Tse-tran had come to grief was several miles north of where the stolen jeep had been discovered, wrecked in a ravine. No sign of any occupants, aside from muddled foot tracks in the dust that told his hunters nothing worth the trip.

It was a riddle Lee would have to solve before it killed him, and his instinct told the incense master he was running short of time, as well as able-bodied troops. Ten dead this morning, eight the night before last, and his live-in force was nearly cut by half. It would take time to summon reinforcements from the streets of Adelaide and Sydney, once the generator was installed. In the meantime Lee was on his own.

It challenged credibility to think one man could conquer ten, no less that he was somehow allied with the aborigines. Lee had dealt with the Arunta long enough, in predatory terms, to know they trusted few men with a lighter skin than theirs. Experience had taught them that the white and yellow men were happy to ignore them when they couldn't be exploited for a selfish purpose, and the nomads took considerable pride in living on their own. It was ridiculous to think they had the means for signing on a mercenary warrior, much less pay him when he'd done his job. There had been no attempt to find the other members of their tribe when Lee's home was attacked, no bid to set them free.

And yet . . .

There might just be another explanation if he looked for one.

A raider running for his life. A stolen jeep. The desert tricks him with a gully and he crashes. Stunned, perhaps unconscious, he is helpless when the nomads come along.

Lee shook his head. No matter how this thing had happened, he was looking at a situation that could blow up in his face. He still had much at stake beyond the wasted lives of soldiers, and he had to salvage what he could.

Beginning now.

The generator would arrive that afternoon, but it could be installed without him. Michael Lee had more important business waiting.

At the mine.

IT TOOK THEM ninety minutes, digging in the sand with sticks, stones and fingers, to prepare three graves. In keeping with tradition the Arunta would be buried in a sitting posture, knees drawn up against their chests, each facing some ancestral landmark that would signify their spirit fathers and the totems that had guided them in life. The women wept and sang, but there was nothing Bolan could have singled out as prayers or eulogies.

"We're out of time," he told Minmara when the simple service was complete. "For all we know, they might have other vehicles. The helicopter works, regardless, and they won't be coming back unarmed."

"You come?"

The warrior shook his head. "I'm going back. Lee's mine. I still have work to do."

"Minmara, too."

"That's not a good idea."

"Have jeep. Have guns. What else we need?"

"A couple dozen soldiers would be nice."

"And still you go alone?"

"I've done this kind of thing before," the Executioner replied.

"With leg hurt?"

"I'll get by."

"Minmara know this country."

"But you haven't seen the hole."

"Don't have to see. Minmara *knows.*"

"I'll take directions, but I've told you that I'm not enlisting volunteers."

"My people there. The bad men find us here, kill more. What difference if I go with you or run and hide in desert, if they kill Minmara either way?"

"If I distract them, you might have better odds."

"With two, your job is easier."

"I won't take that responsibility."

"Minmara go without you, maybe. Kill the bad men by myself."

"With those?" He nodded toward the slender spears Minmara carried in his hand.

"And this."

He raised his flat stone knife, still dark with blood.

"You wouldn't stand a chance."

"Teach guns, then."

Bolan glanced in the direction of the captured weapons, stacked on the floorboards of the jeep behind the driver's seat. Five submachine guns, three pump shotguns and a pair of automatic rifles. Six or

seven handguns. Magazines for different weapons lay
on the floor beside a box of 12-gauge shotgun shells.

He considered the odds of survival, his and the
Arunta's, and made a decision.

He strode to the jeep and picked out an AK-47 with
a bandolier of magazines that he'd lifted from a corpse.
If nothing else, he could prepare the few survivors of
Minmara's people to defend themselves.

There would be time.

There had to be.

He briefly showed Minmara how to load and cock
the rifle, how to aim it, when and how to fire. They
used up half a magazine on semiauto fire, the other
half on automatic, leaving seven in the bandolier.

Returning with an Uzi, he repeated the instruction,
watching as Minmara's eyes lit up, a broad smile on his
face as he held power in his hands. The shotguns were
a snap, compared to automatic and selective fire.

The warrior knew what he was doing, and he didn't
do it lightly. Some would say that he was playing
God—or Satan—by corrupting innocence and teaching simple men to kill as they'd never done before. He
took another view, regarding it as every victim's right
to stand against his enemies on equal footing, with the
finest tools and weapons readily available.

If something happened and he missed again with
Michael Lee, at least the few Arunta he'd armed today
would stand a fighting chance against the bad men next
time out.

"Minmara ready now."

Mack Bolan wore a solemn smile. He didn't plan to
undermine the man's confidence by telling him his enemies were still light-years ahead of him in lethal skills.

"I've shown you all I can with these."

"Go with you now."

"I told you—"

"You say Minmara cannot fight with spear. Have guns now, just like you. We stay or run, the bad men come and kill us. Only chance to find them first and finish."

Bolan couldn't fault Minmara's logic, but he didn't want to think about the consequences of enlisting aborigines for his second raid against the Triad camp. Three dead already, and the stakes were only getting higher as the day wore on.

And yet, he thought, who had a better right to claim a shot at Lee? Minmara's people had been murdered and enslaved to serve the Triad's needs. He could deny them for the moment, take the jeep and simply drive away, but he couldn't prevent them following in time.

"What happens to the others?" Bolan asked.

Minmara pointed to the west.

"Go that way. Five, six miles along, find caves. Safe there, I think."

"I ought to have my head examined," Bolan muttered.

"Please?"

"Forget it." Glancing at his watch, he noted that the best part of another hour had elapsed since they'd filled the graves. He started for the jeep, Minmara on his heels, and said, "Let's find that hole."

THE OLD, ABANDONED MINE was ten miles north of Lee's main compound, at the dead end of a dusty, unpaved road. It was, in fact, his chief inducement toward the purchase of the property, but it had seemed unwise to plant his home directly on the site. Too great a risk in the event that he should ever be surprised by the police.

The mine had once produced a meager crop of gold, or so he was informed, but that was in the early 1940s, and the vein was quickly spent.

But it was still a useful piece of real estate. With almost two hundred feet of tunnels, forty feet below the surface at its greatest depth, it was a cool, dry storehouse whittled from the sun-baked earth. The entrance had been boarded over, hung with warning signs that Lee preserved for the sake of appearances, but he had strung new lights inside and reinforced the beams that kept the walls and ceiling in their proper place.

These days the mine produced a different kind of gold, more valuable than the grains and nuggets it had coughed up during World War II. Lee used it as a temporary storehouse for the China white he bought from Chou Sin Fong in Bangkok, and a separate chamber was converted to a modern laboratory, where the 99.9 percent pure shit was "stepped on" several times—with sugar and baking soda—to get it ready for the streets of Sydney, Melbourne, Adelaide and Perth.

Inspection from the air would show a long-abandoned dig site, with some newer tire tracks where the owner of the land had sent employees to inspect the mine and guarantee that it was safe. Police would never give the shaft a second glance, unless someone should tell them where to look.

A runaway perhaps, whose only means of striking back was by revealing what he knew to the authorities.

Police corruption in Australia was improving, from the incense master's point of view, but it had a long way to go before he felt as secure as his brothers were in Hong Kong, Singapore and Bangkok. Even the

United States had more policemen "on the pad," and it would take more time for Lee to plant his seeds among municipal and federal agencies.

The very time he might not have, if enemies revealed his stash of heroin and thus exposed his true identity, his purpose.

Which meant that it was time to move his product to a safer place.

The Sydney warehouse would suffice in the short term, and he'd find a better place from there. Lee's first priority was speed, and he was counting on his soldiers, plus the twenty-odd black slaves, to have his lethal inventory and the lab equipment packed for shipment by that afternoon.

The two remaining flatbed trucks were rolling by the time that his mechanic finished checking out the helicopter. There were seven bullet holes across the fuselage, but none of them had damaged anything vital to the aircraft's operation.

"Let's go," he told the harried-looking pilot. On the sidelines Yuan Ju Lin, his new lieutenant, waited with an Uzi submachine gun slung across one shoulder, muzzle pointed toward the ground.

The pilot nodded, scrambling for his seat, and Yuan climbed in behind him, giving Lee the shotgun seat. A moment later they were airborne, following the trucks across the desert flats.

A few more hours, and the worst would be behind him. With the merchandise secure, he could proceed from strength to crush his enemies.

IT WAS MIDAFTERNOON when Bolan reached the fence and paused to cut a makeshift gate. He didn't close the flap behind them, but rolled on without delay in the direction Minmara pointed out.

There was a decent chance that they would miss their target, even in the daylight. They were navigating on a secondhand interpretation of a dead man's unsupported word, with no way of knowing whether he'd been delirious with pain or fever when he gave directions to "the hole."

If they found nothing, he'd wait for nightfall, turn back toward the compound and inflict whatever havoc he could manage with Minmara's help. Kill Michael Lee this time, if possible, and shut the pipeline down, however briefly.

But the hole had his attention now, and he was pushing on.

Ironically the trucks and helicopter helped him get there in the end. Minmara saw the half-tons' dust trail first, and moments later they could see the flyspeck of the helicopter following, headed due north.

The Executioner hung back, unwilling to reveal himself the way his enemies had done. His track was a diagonal, to intercept the column farther north, without alerting those whom he pursued.

"The sky beast," Minmara said, pointing.

"Men in a machine. Any luck at all, and you'll get to see one when it's dead."

He cut their speed, a compromise between discretion and pursuit. Another twenty minutes passed before they met the unpaved, hard-scratch road and fell in line behind their prey. From that point on he checked the rearview mirror frequently to verify that they hadn't become the middle float in a parade of death.

There was a second chain-link fence around the entrance to the mine, a circular perimeter a hundred yards across. The warrior's compact glasses showed him that the gate was closed, but neither chained nor locked. A single member of the gang was on watch. Two flatbed trucks were parked outside the dark mouth of the shaft, more guns in evidence as naked blacks fetched wooden crates and cardboard boxes from the tunnel to the waiting vehicles. Lee's helicopter sat to one side, separated from the other vehicles by fifty yards or so, its rotors drooping in the sun.

Minmara took the glasses, let the warrior focus them and scanned the compound for himself.

"My people."

"So you're clear on how to use those guns?"

"Shoot straight. Kill bad men only."

"That's the plan. Okay, we're going in."

He put the jeep in gear and aimed it toward the distant gate, accelerating slowly.

At forty yards he stood on the accelerator, aiming for the unlocked gate instead of the man. Lee's sentry scrambled clear, a shout of warning on his lips. Bolan hit him with a sweeping burst that flattened him before they struck the gate and kept on going, veering toward the half-ton trucks beside the entrance to the mine.

He counted six guns right away, all startled by the crash and sudden burst of firing, momentarily uncertain what to do about the speeding jeep. Minmara helped them work it out, the captured AK-47 blasting as he stood in his seat, his rifle braced across the windshield's frame.

His first burst killed one gunner where he stood and sent another spinning with his arm in bloody tatters. Bolan dropped a third before their adversaries scoped out what was happening and started to return the fire.

"Hang on!"

He hit the brakes and nearly lost Minmara as the jeep slid sideways in a rolling cloud of dust. They used the drifting screen for cover, leaping clear and firing on the run, Minmara shouting to his people in the language only they could understand.

A Triad soldier lunged at Bolan from around the tailgate of the nearest truck, thrusting out an automatic pistol. The Executioner responded with a butt stroke from his carbine, emptying the hardman's hand before he had a chance to fire. A 3-round point-blank burst was enough to finish it.

Minmara had his people moving, clustering behind the trucks while one man disappeared inside the mine to fetch the rest. Outside, two gunners plus a third that Bolan hadn't seen on arrival were laying down a steady cover fire.

He risked a glance around the half-ton's fender, just in time to see two figures sprinting for the helicopter. Nothing like a firm ID at that range, with the dust and bullets flying, but it stood to reason that the chopper was reserved for Triad VIPs.

Before he had an opportunity to wing a burst in their direction, his assailants rushed the trucks, three streams of fire converging on the point where Bolan's head had last been seen. He went to ground, the bullets pinging off metal, raising spurts of sand where they slipped underneath the truck.

Minmara saw the Triad gunners coming, and he met them with a corkscrew burst of automatic fire that pitched one over backward in the dust. The other two split up, still firing as they ran in opposite directions to avoid Minmara's fire.

Too late. The man had his target fixed, and he was tracking as the Triad gunner scuttled to his left, the AK-47 spitting death. He caught the guy with his last few rounds and knocked him over in a boneless sprawl.

The final gunner had to know that he was dead, but there was no such thing as giving up in contests with the enemy. He kept on coming, straight at Bolan's gun, absorbing half a dozen 5.56 mm tumblers on the way before he missed a step and tottered forward, finally collapsing on his face.

Erupting from his hiding place, the Executioner sprinted back in the direction of the makeshift helipad, but he'd missed his chance. The ship was airborne, rising out of range and circling northward.

What lay in that direction? Daly Waters, Birdum, Borroloola, maybe half a dozen other towns whose names the Executioner couldn't recall. It made no difference, since he had no way of giving chase in time to catch them, nothing in the way of contacts on the ground he could alert to head them off.

A bust.

And, then again, not quite.

Minmara's people flocked around him, laughing as he spoke with them. On the flatbed of the nearest truck, a pile of wooden crates had taken several hits and they were leaking snow white powder from the bullet holes.

"This truck should run," he told Minmara, pointing toward the half-ton that hadn't begun to load yet, scars of combat concentrated in a cluster on the driver's door. "We'll push the other one inside the mine and let it blow."

"Close hole?" Minmara asked.

"I wouldn't be surprised."

A victory of sorts, but he was only getting started on the long road to Yunnan, and he'd missed the fox his first time out. It was an oversight that Bolan would be working full-time to correct.

Beginning now.

# CHAPTER SEVEN

The Qantas flight to Bangkok circled once before approaching the airport north of town. It was an easy touchdown, more or less on time, and Bolan was relieved to stretch his long legs after seven hours in the air. He took his carryon from underneath the seat in front of him and got in line to leave the plane.

The teeming concourse was a change from Western airports he was used to. The security was fair, increased in recent months with threats of anti-U.S. terrorism linked to Operation Desert Storm, but the airport still lacked the feeling of a military outpost evident at many European airports in the past few months. He claimed his luggage from the carousel and passed through customs with a brief examination of his passport and his health certificate. The Thai inspectors seemed to have no interest in his suitcase or the shockproof camera case that had survived their journey in the belly of the plane.

He left the terminal and found a taxi, opting for the fifth one back in line. It was a simple trick, but if his enemies were on alert somehow, and waiting for him at the airport, it was doubtful they'd spend the time or cash required to buy off every driver waiting at the curb.

His hotel was the Montien, directly opposite the Snake Farm, facing toward the Patpong district with its countless nightclubs, massage parlors and live-sex shows. A bellboy waited to assist him with his bags and followed Bolan to his suite of rooms when he had finished checking in. The soldier tipped him and received a smiling thank-you before the door swung shut and he was on his own.

His first stop was the padded camera case, which opened with a key. He lifted out the camera, spent five minutes with a small screwdriver and revealed the sleek Beretta 93-R automatic pistol tucked inside. The custom silencer was safe inside a separate telephoto lens, and extra magazines were slotted into dummy videocassettes. A tug removed the thick egg-carton padding from the broad lid of the case, exposing Bolan's shoulder holster in its secret hiding place.

The bag and contents had been scrutinized by customs officers in Brisbane, but they weren't interested enough to try the camera out once Bolan demonstrated how to load the flat cassettes in place. The silent auto was his only weapon at the moment, but he planned on picking others up from local sources prior to moving on.

A shower first, before he hit the streets. It was the middle of the afternoon, and Patpong nightlife wouldn't start to simmer for a few more hours. His contact, set up in advance from Stony Man, wouldn't be ready or receptive if he showed up too far in advance.

He stripped and padded naked to the bathroom, turned the shower on as hot as he could stand and slipped beneath its stinging spray. It helped to open up his pores and sweat the smell of travel out, relaxing muscles stiffened by long hours in a flying cattle car.

World travel might be something to anticipate if you were privileged to take your time and go first-class, but rushing for a seat in tourist class was something else entirely. On the rare occasions when he traveled to relax, the Executioner preferred to dawdle over favorite places, savor the approach and what came after, but his trip to Bangkok was the furthest thing from traveling for pleasure.

He had come to meet one man and kill another, if he could. The difficulty of his task might be compounded by the fact that he had let one target slip beyond his sights already. There had been no word of Michael Lee since Bolan's final raid, but that could only mean that he hadn't been seen. It didn't tell the warrior where his quarry was.

For all he knew the Triad incense master could be hiding out in Bangkok at that very moment, plotting his revenge. Lee wouldn't know his enemy by name, nor why he'd been singled out for punishment, but he could still advise his brothers of the Yi Kwah Tao concerning Bolan's style and method of attack. Surprise could often make the difference in a game of life and death, and every moment Michael Lee remained at large potentially reduced Mack Bolan's chances for success.

He switched the shower onto icy cold and stood there until the cobwebs of fatigue were washed away. A few more hours, and he'd be moving toward the meeting with his contact, a Thai named Prem Koh Bangsaen, who'd worked with DEA from time to time and shared his information with Brognola's SOG. He wasn't part of Stony Man Farm or any other agency, per se, but neither was he strictly what he seemed to be.

According to Brognola's briefing, Prem Koh Bangsaen dealt in contraband, and it was known that he'd moved narcotics in his time. But an arrest for smuggling prescription medicine had left him faced with twenty years hard time in one of Thailand's jungle prison camps, where getting out alive was all a prisoner could hope for, and retaining any vestige of his former life—much less his health—was frosting on the cake. Prem made a deal, and he'd been supplying information to assorted law-enforcement agencies the past three years.

It was a dicey way to live, with no way of telling when a careless word or someone else's error would precipitate a contract from the people you did business with—and then informed on—day by day. One slip meant certain death, but so far Prem had managed to maintain his footing on the razor's edge. His local contact with the DEA had recommended him as someone who could brief a "new kid" on the Bangkok Triads and perhaps supply an introduction to the family.

He turned off the shower and reached outside to pull a fluffy towel down from the rack. As Bolan dried himself, his mind was racing forward, weighing odds and angles, sorting out advantages and disadvantages in preparation for the next phase of his deadly game.

It was a disadvantage, certainly, that he'd missed the tag on Michael Lee, but he had also salvaged something in the fact that Lee had never seen his face. The Triad incense master might or might not be in Bangkok, but aside from intuition and suspicion, there was nothing he could use to burn the Executioner.

Not yet.

Prem Koh Bangsaen was something else, a man who made his living in the murky twilight zone between the dealers and the law. He played both ends against the middle to protect himself and make a profit in the bargain, which told Bolan that there could be times when information flowed both ways. Prem wouldn't know his mission going in, but he would obviously know that Bolan represented some authority from the United States. That information in itself would be enough to put a price on Bolan's head.

And in the streets of Bangkok, life was cheap.

He took his time dressing, selecting items from the "up-scale dealer's" wardrobe Barbara Price had put together for him back at Stony Man. She knew his sizes and she knew the look, from thousand-dollar suits and Gucci leather to the high-price jewelry and monograms on shirts of virgin silk.

The jacket he selected had been cut, like all the others, to accommodate the 93-R automatic in its shoulder rig. A close inspection would reveal that he was armed, and that was fine. No self-respecting dealer in narcotics walked the streets of Bangkok—or Los Angeles—without his trusty shooting iron. It was a badge of office, like the flashy diamond on his pinky and the thick roll of currency he carried.

There was only so much you could do to prep yourself for combat with a new, untested enemy on hostile ground. Reaction was a part of it, and playing with the cards that you were dealt, but any soldier worth his salt was also conscious of the need to use initiative and keep the pressure on.

As ready for the Bangkok game as he would ever be, Mack Bolan hit the streets.

BANGKOK GENERALLY—and the Patpong district in particular—enjoyed the reputation of a place where any pleasure known to man or woman was available for patrons with the ready cash in hand. The face of Patpong burned with neon after sundown, advertising go-go clubs and bars where customers could rent a "hostess" by the drink or by the hour, tattoo parlors in the classic Oriental style, massage emporiums that offered hands-on therapy for the libido and selected "theaters" that offered live-sex shows on stage. It was Las Vegas with an Eastern twist and no holds barred.

Beneath the surface, though, there was another Bangkok. In defiance of prevailing law and human decency, some merchants catered to the darker side of human nature, dealing drugs and other forms of misery. In Patpong, for a price you could obtain a child of tender years to pamper or abuse at your discretion. Psychopaths and drugged-out losers bet their lives on semipublic games of Russian roulette. Snuff films weren't unknown, and patrons with a taste for hands-on drama were permitted to participate in their production if the price was right.

Mack Bolan knew the underside of Bangkok, its ability to swallow victims whole and spit them out in twisted forms their mothers wouldn't recognize. Some disappeared entirely and became the stuff of fading memories or grisly legend.

Bolan, for his part, intended to survive at any cost.

When the warrior left his room, the crowds were shaping up in Patpong, jamming sidewalks, spilling over to the streets where traffic made life interesting. The uniforms he saw were mostly U.S. Air Force and Marines, civilian tourists from the West intent on showing off the kind of gaudy flowered shirts you normally associate with beach resorts in Honolulu. Here and there tight knots of Japanese—all male, most of them middle-aged—were locked in earnest huddles, trying to decide which live-sex club or whorehouse seemed to offer greater value for their money.

The nightclub Bolan sought was called the Golden Dragon, and a neon likeness of the title reptile coiled around its otherwise mundane facade, the wide jaws spilling cherry-colored flames that framed the entryway. A doorman roughly Bolan's height and ten pounds heavier relieved him of the standard cover charge and flashed a smile carved out of ice.

Inside he found a "hostess" waiting to receive him, taking Bolan's hand before his eyes adjusted to the murky atmosphere. It was the same in almost every Patpong club—as well as in the fleshpots of Macao, Hong Kong and other stops on what some travelers described as the "Far Eastern sex-tour circuit." Hostesses in Patpong bars would sit with customers and order watered drinks at beefed-up prices all night long, or they might whisper in your ear and mention that they had a room upstairs, perhaps a friend to lend a hand if you were so inclined. The house received a cut, and Patpong kept its reputation as a neighborhood where sex was not only available, but damn near inescapable.

The hostess steered him to a corner booth, where Bolan disengaged his hand before he took a seat. She made as if to sit beside him, but the warrior blocked her way and shook his head in an emphatic negative. She seemed inclined to argue, but about that time a group of fresh-faced sailors crossed the threshold, and the hostess burned him with a parting glare before she hurried off to try her luck with better prospects.

Bolan ordered beer and made it last, examining the smoky room before he focused his attention on the stage. The audience was mostly male, the bulk of them paired off with hostesses who kept the barmaids hopping with their orders. On the smallish stage, blue spotlights framed a stripper who was down to bare essentials, writhing through a "dance" of sorts that looked more like the prelude to a gynecologist's exam. Despite her youth and looks, the exhibition seemed more automated than erotic, more depressing than conducive to arousal.

His wait was complicated by the fact that Bolan didn't know who he was waiting for. He had a name and a description that would fit most Thais between the age of twenty-one and forty-five, a password and a question that would theoretically confirm Prem Koh Bangsaen's identity if there was any doubt.

And all of it boiled down to squat if Prem decided that the meet was too risky.

It was a risk that Bolan recognized before he caught the Qantas flight to Bangkok, and it hadn't put him off. If Prem bailed out, he would devise another method of connecting with the local Triad under Chou Sin Fong...but he'd give this method every chance before he hung it up.

A woman entered Bolan's field of vision, brushing past the hostesses who looked her up and down with thinly veiled disgust at competition on the hoof. It was unusual, though not prohibited, for unescorted women to patronize bars like the Golden Dragon, where the business of pleasure was basically monopolized by hostesses at the door and the dancers onstage.

This one was flashy, easily a cut above the staff and most of the seductive talent working the street outside. She held herself erect and poised, not looking down her nose at anyone, but letting no one doubt the fact that she was here on business and wouldn't be turned away.

She spent a moment checking out the room, then veered toward Bolan's booth. His stomach tightened, and he hoped he hadn't misjudged the lady, that she wasn't one more hooker to be brushed aside.

And on the other hand...

"You are American?" she asked him, standing over Bolan's table, an expression on her face that could have been amusement or mistrust.

"Red, white and blue."

"Your name is Mike Belasko?"

"Have we met?"

She answered with a question of her own. "May I sit down?"

"That all depends."

"On what?"

"On what you're selling, and the price attached."

He caught a flash of irritation in her eyes. "I'm not a whore!" she snapped.

"I don't know what you are," he countered. "I don't even know your name."

"Mai Lin Lakhon," she said. "Is that enough?"

"Not quite."

"I bring a message from your friend."

"Which friend is that?"

"Prem Koh Bangsaen."

"I guess you'd better have a seat."

Her recitation of the name meant nothing—less than nothing if his contact had been blown somehow—but Bolan watched her take a seat across from him. Even in the murky darkness of the club, her eyes were bright. Her dress was cut provocatively low in front, and shadows gathered in the valley of her ample cleavage.

"Prem does not share the nature of your business," she assured him.

"There's no reason why he should."

"You are expecting him, I think."

Bolan shrugged noncommittally. "I've been checking out the nightlife, taking in the local sights."

"I am instructed to retrieve you. Prem is waiting at a nearby place."

"That's it?"

The lady looked confused. "Excuse me?"

"Just like that, you waltz in here and I'm supposed to follow you outside? No thanks."

"You do not wish to meet with Prem Bangsaen?"

"*He* set the meeting place. I'm here. Now, if he wants to change the rules..."

"Of course," she said, embarrassed at the knowledge of her oversight. "You wish the password, yes?"

"It wouldn't hurt."

"Prem told me I should ask if you have seen the eastern star. And your reply...?"

"That it shines brighter in the spring."

"Such games." She frowned. "Are you a spy?"

"Not even close."

"Then shall we go?"

Outside, the street was teeming. Taxis, private cars and three-wheeled *samlors* flowed both ways and jockeyed for position in the narrow lanes. Along the sidewalk prostitutes were showing off their wares and hailing customers at random, and barkers for the sex shows leaned out of neon doorways here and there to snag an elbow, whisper something hot and juicy in an unsuspecting ear.

Mai Lin moved off to Bolan's left, away from his hotel and deeper toward the pulsing heart of Patpong

Road. He fell in step beside her, rubbing shoulders with the wide-eyed tourists and the denizens of Bangkok's seamy underside.

When they had covered close to fifty yards, a voice hailed Mai Lin from the doorway of a tattoo parlor. Turning, Bolan matched it to a slender ruffian with one bad eye and a long scar running down the left side of his face. The cyclops had a partner with him, taller, heavier, and both of them were clearly drunk.

Mai Lin seemed torn between continuing along her way and speaking to the men. She finally made up her mind and doubled back past Bolan to confront the one who called her name. Their conversation was in Thai, too fast for Bolan's meager knowledge of the language to relieve his curiosity, but there was anger in the raised voices.

It all boiled over in a ringing slap that rocked Mai Lin back on her heels and raised a scarlet palm print on her cheek. Before the punk could take a second swing, his arm was caught in Bolan's fist and wrenched back to the level of his waist.

"That's not a good idea," he said, uncertain whether any of his words were getting through.

The hoodlum tried to pull his arm away, his free hand coming up and looping in a sweep toward Bolan's face.

Not good enough.

Another twist, some pressure, and his adversary squealed, the elbow separating with a muffled *crack*, the radius and ulna snapping from the strength of Bolan's grip. The cry of pain from Scarface was a muffled, bleating sound, reminding Bolan of a frightened barnyard animal.

He shoved the man away and turned to face his friend, who was already moving forward with an open razor in his hand. The brawler's first swing should have done it, but he aimed at Bolan's face and missed. The shiny blade sliced empty air as the warrior went beneath his arm and slammed a solid right into unprotected ribs.

He bored in, crowding his attacker as the blade man staggered backward, looking desperately for room enough to take advantage of his weapon. Bolan dodged another swing and caught him with a rising knee between the legs, enough to finish it as his assailant gasped and slumped against the wall. His last move, cupping one hand on the razor wielder's face and slamming him against the plaster wall until his eyes rolled back, was for the woman's benefit.

He didn't know if she'd set up the confrontation, but he'd shown what he could do when it was two-on-one and hand to hand. A test, perhaps, or simply one of the occurrences that make the Patpong district risky for the uninitiated tourist.

Either way, Mai Lin put on a grateful face as they proceeded on their way. A small crowd gathered near the fallen thugs, hands darting into pockets after cash or credit cards.

"You saved my life," she said at last.

"It didn't look that bad."

"You don't know Yam Salim. The one-eyed man."

"He's one arm short right now. A perfect match."

"He won't forget this insult."

"I should hope not," Bolan said. "A man who slaps women on the street and tries to take a stranger out should remember everything he learns from the experience."

"This way."

Their track led down a narrow side street, barely wide enough to qualify for alley status in the States. It smelled of urine, uncollected trash and cats gone wild. For all he knew, it might turn out to be a death trap, but he had to play the cards as they were dealt.

"Let's go."

# CHAPTER EIGHT

There was no traffic on the side street, which wouldn't accommodate a car, and even beggars shied away, preferring lights and crowds with better prospects for a handout. Bolan followed Mai Lin halfway down and stopped when she did, turning toward a dingy flight of steps that served the nearly hidden entrance of a basement room.

"Down there," she said, directing Bolan with a nod.

"You first."

"No trust?"

"We'll have to work that out," he said. "Right now we're strangers standing in the dark."

"Of course."

She took the lead and pressed a bell beside the plain, unpainted metal door. It seemed to Bolan that she pressed it twice, then waited for a heartbeat, tapping it twice more. The lock came open with a snap, and Mai Lin stepped across the threshold.

He had his jacket open, with instant access to the automatic slung beneath his arm, as he passed through the open doorway. Passing by, he gave the door a shove and bounced it off the wall in case some member of a welcoming committee was sequestered there.

No dice.

The entryway was no more than the short end of an L-shaped corridor, with light showing from around the corner up ahead. Mai Lin was watching Bolan curiously as she closed the door. No knob on either side, although there was a handle in the middle of the door, for pulling inward. Bolan heard the heavy lock engage and knew that he was trapped, if trap it was.

"This way."

He followed her around the corner and discovered that the corridor was relatively short. Some twenty feet in front of them was a door, with blank walls on either side.

The door was closed, and Mai Lin knocked. Behind her, Bolan felt the fingers of his right hand tingling, imagining the weight of the Beretta and its recoil on a point-blank killing shot.

A desk and plain black filing cabinets were inside the room. Behind the desk a slender Thai was on his feet and waiting, hands behind his back, regarding Bolan with suspicious eyes.

"Mr. Belasko?"

Bolan heard Mai Lin slip out and the door ease shut behind him.

"Prem Bangsaen?"

A narrow smile was Bolan's only answer. He would have to verify his contact now before they went ahead.

"Your friend from Washington discussed my coming?"

"James McAllen, yes. It is agreed."

The name was false, but it conformed to Bolan's information from Brognola, via DEA. So far, so good. At least he knew he had his man.

"May I sit down?"

"Please do."

He hooked a simple wooden chair in front of Prem's desk and sat, his hand remaining in proximity to the

Beretta. Even with the password ritual complete, the Executioner wouldn't relax his guard.

"They've told you why I'm here?"

Prem nodded. "It is dangerous to play games with the Triads."

"I understand that you've been doing it for years."

"A different game, perhaps. The information I supply to certain agencies is used elsewhere, in Hong Kong or the Philippines, sometimes in the United States. The distance is a form of insulation, shall we say."

"It's like you say, a different game."

"More risk for all concerned."

"I need two things from you—supplies and information. No one needs to know where I laid hands on either one."

"In Bangkok there are many secret eyes and ears."

"You trust the girl?"

"Mai Lin? Implicity. She was my brother's wife."

"Past tense?"

"He is deceased. You mentioned some supplies?"

"Munitions and the necessary transportation. Can you handle it?"

"That would depend upon your needs."

He rattled off the deadly shopping list as Prem memorized it without resorting to notes of any kind. When Bolan finished, Prem was silent for a moment.

"It will not be cheap," he said finally.

"It never is. Cash on delivery?"

"Acceptable. I should have something for you by tomorrow morning. You're an early riser, I assume?"

"I'm flexible."

Prem tore a piece of paper from a notepad, wrote down a number and passed the slip across his desk.

"Tomorrow call this number between 6:00 and 6:30 a.m. A car with rental papers shall arrive at your hotel within the hour. You are staying at the Montien?"

"That's right."

"There will be luggage in the trunk. Inside, the items you require. The driver will be someone else I trust."

"I pay him, then?"

Prem nodded. "Forty thousand baht," he said.

Two thousand dollars, give or take. It was a decent price, and Bolan made no effort to negotiate.

"Sounds fair."

"The information next."

"You work with members of the Yi Kwah Tao?"

"From time to time. They are a selfish lot and generally do business with their own. The 14K and Chiu Chou families are much more generous."

"Are you familiar with a man named Michael Lee?"

"By reputation only," Prem replied. "He is the incense master for Australia, I believe."

"No word on whether he's in town right now?"

"In Bangkok?" Prem Bangsaen's expression showed surprise before he shook his head. "Did you expect to find him here?"

"We missed connections earlier this week," the Executioner replied. "I'm not sure where he might turn up."

"Inquiries can be made, if you desire."

"It couldn't hurt."

"And if you find him?"

"We've got business to discuss."

"I see. As for the Yi Kwah Tao?"

"I'm interested in their connections with Yunnan and General Li."

"The links you speak of are not generally known."

"Let's say I got a lucky tip."

Prem leaned back in his chair and made a steeple of his fingers, taking on the aspect of a lecturer.

"The Yi Kwah Tao are not diversified as other Triads. To be sure, they operate casinos, trade in flesh wherever possible, but they do not concern themselves to any great extent with the legitimate investments. Drugs provide the bulk of family revenue, and nearly all of that is opium or heroin."

"Whatever happened to the Golden Triangle?"

"It still produces heroin in massive quantities," Prem said, "but there are finite limits to the crop, and most of it is spoken for by Chiu Chou traders or the 14K. For members of the Yi Kwah Tao, there was a simple choice—ignore the trade in drugs, or find a way to share the wealth."

"No choice at all."

"Precisely. Having made the only choice their appetites allowed, they faced another problem—where to find the product when existing crops are virtually monopolized by other Triad families. Their sacred oath bars stealing from their brothers, and they did not have the necessary troops, in any case. A war between the families, ten years ago, would almost certainly have doomed the Yi Kwah Tao."

"And what about today?"

Prem shrugged. "Their strength and numbers have increased. Myself, I think they have more guns than soldiers, but who knows? In any case they do not need to steal. They have discovered outlets of their own."

"Yunnan."

"It is ironic, don't you think? More than a hundred years ago the British empire fought a war with China to insure that sales of opium among the Chinese people would continue, for the benefit of European traders. Now the Chinese are in business for themselves, and white men launch another war to halt the trade.''

"Times change."

"Indeed. You are alone?"

"So far."

"It will be difficult to deal with General Li, much less the Yi Kwah Tao."

"I'm counting on it."

"How would you begin?"

"The less you know up front, the better chance you have of coming out of this in one piece."

"You seek my help," Prem said. "I cannot work in total ignorance."

"Agreed. I mean to shake up the Triads a bit before I move along. The Yi Kwah Tao, specifically, but if the 14K and Chiu Chous take some heat along the way, I wouldn't mind. The more they snap and snarl at one another improves the odds."

"What is it that you want from me?"

"Besides the hardware," Bolan said, "I'll need a list of targets. Places I can hit to make them squeal the loudest in the least amount of time. Including Chou Sin Fong, if he's available."

"Americans are always so ambitious."

"If it's more than you can handle..."

"Not at all. A list will be included with the other items in your luggage. Seven thousand baht."

"Affirmative. And if I need to get in touch?"

"Same number for the vehicle," Prem said. "A message in my name will be relayed at any hour of the day or night."

"I'd say we're finished, then, for now."

"Take care in Bangkok, sir. The city has a different face for every visitor, and it is always dangerous."

Bolan hesitated in the doorway, turned to Prem and answered, "So am I."

Mai Lin was waiting for him in the hallway, watching Bolan's face as he emerged.

"All finished?"

"For the moment."

"I shall walk you back to your hotel."

"I'll find my way."

"You are not lonely in a city far from home?"

"It never crossed my mind."

The warrior spoke the truth, for he couldn't have said where home was anymore.

"You think about it, though?"

He smiled, and Mai Lin fell in step beside him as he said, "I might, at that."

PREM KOH BANGSAEN wasn't opposed to taking risks, per se. His life had been a risk, in one way or another, from the time that he began to run the streets, around age nine.

Bangkok was still the "Venice of the Orient" in those days, with the bulk of city transportation handled by a network of canals, which were the city's streets and first line of defense. Flat barges served as market stalls, and water taxis bore their passengers to almost any destination they desired.

Times change, as the American had pointed out.

In Thai, Bangkok was called Krung Thep, the "City of Angels." Its name derived from the three hundred religious monuments that dotted the city map. Statues of Buddha were everywhere, some of the finer ones sculpted from emerald and gold, attracting more tourists than devout worshipers on any given day.

But Bangkok also had another side, as Prem well knew. The temples faced on streets where life was cheap and licensed taxi drivers had been known to work in league with gangs that robbed and killed their paying customers. Prostitutes of both sexes and all ages catered to the tourist trade, and Bangkok had replaced 1960s Marseilles as the world capital of heroin traffic.

At forty-three, Prem Bangsaen was a product of his environment. A born survivor, he had outlived his parents and four siblings, clawing his way up from the vast, untidy orphanage of the streets to live in relative security and luxury. He wasn't wealthy, in comparison to Chou Fong or the other Triad leaders based in Bangkok, but he made a decent living for himself and meant to keep on living while he had a choice.

It was a simple fluke that put him in cooperation with the DEA and other U.S. agencies. His first attempt at smuggling prescription drugs had been successful, even lucrative, and Prem Bangsaen wasn't a man to spit on golden opportunity. If he could double his investment once, why would he shun the opportunity to do the same again? It didn't seem so terrible, when all around him evil men were dealing in narcotics, killing or enslaving thousands every day with the illicit product of their poppy fields. What harm was there in penicillin, streptomycin and other medicines that healed the sick?

The answer came with his arrest on smuggling charges, followed by a criminal indictment that would take him off the street for years . . . unless he made the sensible decision to cooperate. The local officers had introduced him to Americans, then more Americans, and the rest was history.

These days Prem still did business as before, but he had one more operation on the side. Along with gold and diamonds, stolen jewelry and endangered species for the pet shops of America, he also traded information. The narcotics officers were generous, delighted to retain a source of such reliability and proved contacts on the wrong side of the law. They never put Prem's life at risk by making any moves directly traceable to him.

Until tonight.

He didn't trust the tall American who called himself Belasko. Not that Prem Bangsaen suspected him of doubling for the Triads or informing to his enemies. If anything, the opposite was true. He looked inside the tall man's eyes and saw a zealot's soul. Afraid of nothing, he would challenge any power, throw his life away in the pursuit of goals that no man could achieve. And in the process, he might drag down those around him when they sought no part of his campaign.

Still, Prem shared some of the American's distaste for Chou Fong and the Yi Kwah Tao. His brother— Mai Lin's husband—had been working for the Triad as a runner, moving parcels, when it suddenly became expedient for them to cut their overhead. A sacrifice was called for to assuage the egos of authorities, and Prem Lan Sing was chosen by the incense master.

Given drugs to carry and a pistol to defend himself, he was dispatched upon an errand much like any other, unaware that narcotics officers were waiting at the other end to lock him in a cage. He panicked in the face of badges and was killed, a debt that Prem Bangsaen placed squarely on the doorstep of the Yi Kwah Tao.

Repaying such a debt could take a lifetime, planning carefully against the day when even the most lowly had an opportunity to strike a telling blow against the rich and powerful. It happened, now, that the Americans had granted him a golden opportunity to even up the scales, but Prem Bangsaen was also interested in making sure that he survived to savor his revenge.

Thus far the tall man had asked nothing that would place his life in jeopardy. The weapons were a simple thing in Bangkok, easier than drugs and less expensive at the going rate. As for the targets, he could reel off several dozen names and addresses from memory, without consulting any of his "special" files. They weren't generally published in brochures for Western tourists, but they weren't classified. There were a thousand different ways in which a raider could acquire the name and street number of this whorehouse or that opium den. As for the homes of ranking Triads, any one of several thousand people could—and would—reveal the information for a price.

Prem's tracks were covered at the moment, barring some mistake on his part or a new, more dangerous request from the American. In such a case, he'd be forced to contemplate the risks and weigh them in his mind. If this Belasko pushed too far, appeared unbalanced in his move against the Triads, Prem would make connections with his local contact and demand relief. It certainly wouldn't be in the DEA's best interest to sacrifice their prime informant to a stranger's one-man holy war.

And if they turned him down?

Prem didn't like to borrow trouble when his daily life produced enough to keep him occupied. In Bangkok things were rarely what they seemed, from the exalted halls of government down to the city streets. Self-styled reformers worked in league with dealers of narcotics, and religious spokesmen held controlling interests in the fleshpots of the Patpong district. Working whores aspired to lives of luxury, and filthy beggars would be kings, if they could only find the wherewithal.

And what did this Belasko want from Bangkok?

He had mentioned Michael Lee, a heavy Triad from Australia, as if Lee should have been expected in the city. Prem Bangsaen had no news from Australia yet, but he'd definitely ask around. If there was turmoil in the Yi Kwah Tao, it could affect his business at a multitude of different points, and he'd have to be prepared for anything.

Belasko's words came back to him: "I mean to shake up the Triads a bit before I move along." His actions could have a devastating effect on Prem's world.

The worst part of informing for the DEA or any other agency was the restriction it imposed on the informer. If he chose to undermine Belasko's effort and report him to the Triads, Prem would be required to spell out how he knew the tall American and where his information came from in the first place. Giving up Belasko would be tantamount to signing a confession of his role as a police informer... and signing his own death warrant in the process.

He'd seen the way that Triad soldiers dealt with those who talked. The severed tongues and mutilated genitals were standard forms of punishment. A skillful torturer could keep his man alive and conscious for a period of days, dismantling his body and his mind until the final product bore no close resemblance to humanity. It was a point of pride among the Yi Kwah Tao that traitors died a thousand times before their bodies were surrendered to the ground.

No, thank you.

Prem hadn't survived this long, against the odds, to volunteer for a position on the Triad operating table. If he had to lose Belasko as a means of self-defense, he'd devise some way to keep the sacrifice anonymous, with no links between Prem's business interests and the stranger with the graveyard eyes.

God willing, it would never come to that.

He thought about Mai Lin and wondered whether he was placing her at risk by having her run interference with Belasko. She was still his brother's wife, at least in spirit, and he had no wish to see her killed. Of course, she knew the risks, and Prem suspected that a chance of striking back at Chou Fong's family had motivated her as much as any cash that might change hands.

He made a private, solemn vow to pull her out the moment he anticipated any danger to the tall American. Meanwhile, her contact with the stranger would be minimized, for Mai's protection. She wouldn't be present when the weapons were delivered in the morning, and he wouldn't call her out again in any case, unless another meeting was required.

The office that he occupied this night was one of several premises employed by Prem from time to time. He didn't own the building or the furnishings, had no idea of what—if anything—was slotted in the filing cabinets to his left. When he required a private place to meet with strangers, he'd make a call, agree upon a rental price and it was done.

Next time he met Belasko, if there was a next time, they'd use some other place. And he'd call Mai Lin once more to act as guide for the American, avoiding conversations on the telephone that might betray them both. Meanwhile, he'd attempt to meet Belasko's needs without another face-to-face, for both their sakes.

He wanted no part in the tall man's private war, if it could be avoided. Prem was still a businessman, and he preferred to pass his days without the threat of lethal violence stalking every moment of his life.

But now, he gloomily reflected, there might be no choice.

One thing was clear enough for anyone to see—the stranger had brought death to Bangkok, in his heart and in his eyes.

*Whose* death remained a question only time could answer.

And the answer would be scrawled in blood.

# CHAPTER NINE

The Bangkok blitz began at half-past ten on Tuesday morning, when the Executioner had scanned his list of targets and arranged them on a city map for personal convenience. He wouldn't observe a pattern in his strikes to let the enemy predict his moves, but it was helpful to observe which major streets were closest to his targets to facilitate approaches and retreats.

His vehicle had been delivered to the Montien precisely on the stroke of seven, and he paid Prem's driver after briefly checking out the "luggage" in the trunk. The little Thai had counted Bolan's money, stuffed it in a pocket of his shiny sport coat and was last seen walking east on Patpong Road.

So far, so good, but there was still the possibility of treachery, and Bolan drove a few miles out of town before he found a rest stop and began to check the weapons he had purchased. In addition to the Uzi submachine gun with its loaded magazines, he had grenades—incendiary, fragmentation and stun— together with a two-pound cake of C-4 plastique and assorted fuses in a separate bag.

He counted fifteen targets on the list from Prem Bangsaen, including Chou Sin Fong's home address and the downtown office where he stopped in several times a week in his capacity as "businessman."

It was enough for now.

He started with a house off Sathorn Road, a half mile from his own hotel. This house wasn't a home, but there were children on the premises, some purchased from their families in the countryside, some others simply picked up off the streets. In the United States their faces might have decorated billboards and milk cartons. In Bangkok they were captured in explicit Polaroid shots, circulated by pimps and taxi drivers in a search for customers who craved a taste of youth.

It might not be the sickest game in town, but it was close, and Bolan meant to shut it down before the day got any older.

Parking was a problem everywhere in Bangkok, but he found a place outside the nearby boxing stadium and walked back through a drizzling rain.

In the past his lightning strikes against specific enemies had often carried messages—a deadline for release of hostages, for instance—but he had no message for the scum who ran this "house of joy." Some members of the staff might manage broken English, but the Executioner could think of nothing they could say to save themselves.

For years they'd been storing up bad karma, betting everything they had that judgment day would never come, and it was time for them to pay the tab. With interest due.

The hit itself would be the message, and his Triad targets were at liberty to make their own interpretations as he went along.

The house had doors in front and back. He chose the latter, passing two preadolescent boys as they removed great sacks of garbage to a bin in the yard. They looked at him with hollow, haunted eyes, as if expecting him to make a choice and snap his fingers, taking one or both of them upstairs.

The back door opened on a kitchen, where a woman with a lean and sallow face was heating up some kind of greasy stew that looked worse than it smelled. Around the dining table seven girls and four young boys sat waiting, silently, in front of empty plastic bowls.

The cook was speaking in angry tones when Bolan entered, his appearance causing her to miss a beat. She found her voice again and blurted out a question Bolan neither understood nor cared to answer. The woman reached toward a rack of kitchen knives when he began to cross the room in her direction.

Bolan let her see the Uzi then. He could have shot her, but he was thinking of the children when he swung the stubby barrel against her skull and dropped her to the floor.

"Get out!" he told the staring children. *"Pai!"*

As one, they bolted for the door. He didn't watch to see how far they ran, but it would make no difference. If they doubled back in time, they'd discover that the "house of joy" was gone.

He cleared the kitchen, entering a sort of parlor with a spiral staircase on his left. A chunky man with pockmarked cheeks was halfway down the stairs when he saw Bolan, recognized the weapon in his hands and froze. He made a perfect target, standing there, and Bolan took advantage of the moment, squeezing off a burst that dropped him in his tracks.

The sound of gunfire raised a startled shout from somewhere on the second floor. An older man, half-dressed, appeared in seconds, rushing towards the stairs and brandishing an automatic pistol in his hand.

He sized the situation up too late, and tried to wing a shot at Bolan as he ran.

The Uzi stuttered, parabellum manglers chewing up the banister, the wall behind him and the soft flesh in between. He staggered, reeling for a moment, triggering a wild shot toward the ceiling as he fell.

No other sounds of life came from inside the house, but Bolan had to check before he burned the place down.

He took the upstairs first. Eight bedrooms, all unoccupied. Downstairs, more empty rooms, including one that had been soundproofed for the privacy of paying customers who liked their action rough.

He left one thermite canister inside a closet, backing out before it detonated and spewed white-hot phosphorous around the room. He lobbed another toward the upstairs landing, trusting it to do the job, and cleared the kitchen swing door before it blew. He gave the prostrate cook a glance in passing and decided she could make it on her own.

Or not.

The two boys he'd passed on entering were waiting for him in the yard, a small girl sandwiched between them like an afterthought. They stared at Bolan, saw the smoke come rolling out behind him.

Slowly, hesitantly, one boy raised a hand and waved the warrior on his way.

THE HEROIN that made its way to Bangkok was refined outside the city to reduce the risk of handling opium or morphine base in major quantities. Ten pounds of raw opium produced one pound of morphine base, that bulk reduced still further by refinement into heroin.

The warehouse on the Chao Phya River wasn't large or well maintained by Western standards, but its stock of merchandise, by weight, would fetch a higher price than gold. A ton of China white, in the United States, would earn the best part of a billion dollars for its dealers on the street. No calculator or computer Bolan ever saw could tabulate the cost in terms of human lives and misery.

He left the car near the Thieves Market, locking it and tipping a pair of rough-looking teens to watch over it for him, showing them his pistol in case they had a sudden urge to go in business for themselves.

His drive-by had revealed two sentries on the outside of the warehouse, stationed on the loading dock. He let them see him coming, curious about a white man walking on the riverside, but more or less accustomed to the ways of Western tourists in a foreign land.

No guns were in evidence as Bolan closed the gap, but they wouldn't be far away. His own hand was tucked inside the pocket of his raincoat, wrapped around the butt of his Beretta.

According to the list supplied by Prem Bangsaen, this warehouse and its contents were the property of Chou Sin Fong, the local incense master of the Yi Kwah Tao. Fong's soldiers stayed on the loading dock, alert as Bolan veered off course and moved in their direction, feigning rapt preoccupation with the guidebook that he carried in his hand.

At twenty yards he felt them shifting nervously and knew that it was time. The warrior dropped the guidebook and withdrew the 93-R from his right-hand pocket, squeezing off four silenced rounds in rapid fire.

The gunner on his left took both slugs in the face and flew backward, sliding in his own blood on the concrete loading dock. His partner had one hand inside his nylon windbreaker, digging for hardware, when a triburst of 9 mm parabellum rounds punched him through a sloppy pirouette, dropping him beside the lifeless body of his comrade.

Bolan took the stairs in a rush, circling the corpses to reach a metal door behind. He slipped inside, returning the Beretta to its shoulder rig and bringing up the Uzi.

He strode silently down a sterile corridor before a left-hand turn put him in the warehouse proper. Crates and boxes had been stacked in rows, with aisles between them wide enough to take a forklift. On his right a makeshift office was separated from the storage area by waist-high plywood, glass on top.

Three men were huddled in the office, all of them Chinese. Two more were just emerging from the farthest aisle away from Bolan, lost in conversation, one of them consulting figures on a clipboard that he carried in his hand.

One of the Triad members in the little office spotted Bolan, getting out a shout before the Uzi opened up and drowned his words of warning. Going in, the Executioner had known that everybody on the premises was dirty, and he took no prisoners.

A long burst from his submachine gun raked the office cubicle from left to right and back again. The dead men fell together in a jumble, on or near the desk, invoices shredded in the hail of parabellum rounds. The two survivors broke for cover, both intent on reaching hidden guns, and Bolan tracked them with the Uzi, holding down the trigger in a blaze of sound and fire. The impact lifted both men off their feet and sent them sprawling, twitching as they died.

The heroin was labeled as machine parts, plastic kilo bags concealed among the hardware. If a customs man was blind—or bought and paid for—it would stand a decent chance of getting through. More was stashed in bolts of silken fabric, and he gave up looking after that. There were too many places for the smugglers to hide their poison.

No choice, then. He'd have to destroy the whole place.

The warrior used the C-4 plastique, shaping fist-sized charges, planting them at intervals where they would have the ultimate destructive impact. Staggered fuses gave him time to clear the loading dock and cover half a block along the riverside before the first charge blew.

He stood and watched the warehouse self-destruct, a ruptured gas main kicking in around the third or fourth explosion, bright flames pouring through the shattered roof and walls. He had no way of telling how much heroin had been destroyed, but he was satisfied to estimate the burn at several hundred kilos, give or take.

Enough to make the Yi Kwah Tao take notice, any way you ran it down.

A crowd was gathering to watch the fire, some of them risking death or painful burns to run in close and try the doors on the expensive cars outside. The warrior left them to it, retracing his steps toward the Thieves Market and finding his own vehicle intact, the teenage watchmen looking grave as he approached. More shoppers from the market were already drifting toward the river, following the sounds of the explosions. The Executioner saw a flash of understanding in the young men's eyes as he doled out an extra hundred baht.

The word would spread in no time, but the Executioner expected that. The presence of a foreigner with weapons, at or near the scene of the disaster, would confuse his enemies and keep the Triads guessing. In the circumstances every little bit of chaos was a benefit to the offensive team.

Two targets down, and there were plenty left to go, but Bolan had an urge to touch base with his local contact first. By definition lightning war was limited in scope and time. There were provisions to be made for moving on when he had done his work in Bangkok.

How long?

He shrugged off the question and concentrated on his driving, looking for a public telephone.

Not long, but he'd have to soften up his enemies before the final stroke. The rules of covert warfare were the same, no matter where the enemy was found.

Identify.

Isolate.

Exterminate.

He had identified his opposition in the City of Angels, and his blitz was aimed at breaking down their links with other Triad families. They weren't isolated yet, but he was getting there.

A few more stops, and then he'd pay a call on Chou Sin Fong and let the Triad incense master feel a touch of cleansing fire.

Not long.

But for his enemies, the next few hours would be a lifetime.

CHOU SIN FONG despised the telephone. It interrupted him when he was meditating, sometimes even when making love, and the majority of calls that reached his private line brought more bad news.

It had begun three days before, with a report of the disturbance in Australia. Michael Lee had been attacked and nearly killed by unknown enemies, his operation left in shambles. Scheduled shipments to the island continent would be delayed indefinitely, and the product earmarked for the streets of Sydney, Perth and Adelaide would have to remain in the Bangkok warehouse, gathering dust.

Fong sympathized with Lee, but only to a point. The man was young to be an incense master in the Yi Kwah Tao, promoted over older veterans because the Elder Brother liked his style and "fresh" approach to moving heroin. It troubled Fong, departing from tradition so, but it wasn't his place to challenge Elder Brother on his choice.

Not yet.

If Lee was driven permanently from his territory, it would be a different matter. Such a man wouldn't be fit to hold the honorable title of an incense master in the Yi Kwah Tao. His "new" ideas would count for nothing if an enemy could suddenly appear from nowhere and defeat him on his own home turf.

And if the younger man were ousted, then what? Fong had all the work that he could handle in Bangkok, but he would be happy to select a member of his staff to take Lee's place. With loyal subordinates in charge of the Australian territory, he could easily enhance his profit margin, while improving traffic for the family as a whole.

It would require some salesmanship, of course, convincing Sun Jiang Lao to validate the move, but Fong had confidence in his ability to win the Elder Brother's ear. They'd been friends for decades, fighting side by side to make the Yi Kwah Tao a force to reckon with among the other, larger Triads. They'd been successful so far, and Fong's loyalty had to count for something when he asked a simple favor.

Unless the trouble in his own house brought him down.

An outbreak in Australia was one thing, with the white men still in charge and local street gangs fighting for a place within the overall narcotics trade, but Bangkok was supposed to be secure. The yearly murder toll, around ten thousand dead, meant nothing in the final scheme of things, for no one but a lunatic would stand against the mighty Triads in their own backyard.

Until this morning.

Fong sat staring at the hated telephone, his dark eyes almost daring it to ring with more bad news. His mind was racing, trying to anticipate the next move of an enemy whom he could neither touch nor see.

The first strike had been bad enough, with the destruction of a valued joy house that had earned Fong better than one hundred thousand baht per night from wealthy pedophiles. Three small-time members of his staff were dead, the house reduced to ashes and the captive children gone.

All things considered, Fong was less concerned about the monetary cost and loss of life than by potential damage to his self-respect. Subordinates were easily replaced, and children were among the cheapest of commodities available in modern Thailand. Fong could send his agents out to buy a dozen more by sup-pertime, and never feel the pinch. Likewise, he could acquire another house and set up shop before the day was out.

The damage to his reputation would be something else, if he allowed the hostile action to go unavenged. And then, on top of everything, had come the second raid, much worse this time, with the destruction of his river warehouse and the fourteen hundred-kilo bags of China white inside. Another five men lay dead but they were nothing—less than nothing—in comparison to the narcotics.

Fifteen tons lost would mean another trip to General Li, and this time well ahead of schedule. There would be no bargaining on price when customers were screaming for the product they had bought and paid for.

He gave up estimating the expense and concentrated on the damage to his reputation now that he'd been assaulted twice within a single day. He had his soldiers on the street, intent on turning up a lead to the identity of those who had challenged Fong, but there was little he could do to speed up the process.

If patience was a virtue, it could also be a pain.

He felt it in his stomach, gnawing at him, the desire to get up from his desk and take an active role in tracking down his enemies. In younger days Fong would have done exactly that, but he was older now and wiser, with a standing in the Triad to protect. It wouldn't do for him to be seen scrambling on the street when he had legions of subordinates to do such things.

If he had been a praying man, Fong would have asked the gods for help, but he didn't trust anyone or anything outside the Triad family. His problem would be solved when he identified his enemies and watched them die. Until that time—

He flinched involuntarily, recoiling as the telephone began to ring.

THE FIRST TIME Bolan called, a soft voice on the other end had asked him for a call-back number, which he instantly refused. His option was to wait for twenty minutes, try again and hope that Prem Bangsaen would be available.

He did.

Prem was.

"Good morning."

"Coming up on afternoon," the Executioner responded.

"You have had a busy day so far."

"It's heating up."

"Indeed. Your subject is responding as expected. There are soldiers everywhere."

"With any luck they just get in each other's way."

"As to the reason for your call..."

A measure of impatience tinged Prem's tone, as if the more time spent in conversation with this stranger from the West, the greater his own risk of jeopardy. It was, Bolan thought, an entirely healthy attitude.

"I need another contact."

"In Bangkok."

"In Rangoon. I'm not sure when I'm leaving Thailand, but there won't be any time to spare on introductions when the clock runs down."

"I understand." Prem mulled over the question for a moment, finally replying, "I would trust my life to Ne Tin Kyat. He is a guide by trade."

No point in asking what that meant, when caravans of heroin and other contraband blazed well-known trade routes through the northeast quarter of the country. There were ways to double-check if Prem was jerking him around, but for the moment he'd take the name and file it in his memory.

# CHAPTER TEN

The best thing about pain, thought Yam Salim, was its effect upon the memory. Without the nonstop throbbing of his broken arm inside its heavy cast, he might have wiped his chance encounter with the tall American from his mind. A simple thing, and yet it should have ended very differently, with pain inflicted on his enemy.

It sometimes struck him as bizarre, the way things happened when you least expected them, but Bangkok was the kind of town where something happened every day, and you got used to it, took things in stride. It had been much the same when he was slashed across the face, long years ago, and lost the use of his left eye.

But he had paid that insult back, with interest. His attacker had been blind when Yam Salim last saw him, and the chances were that he was dead by now.

It was as it should be.

He nursed his drink and thought about the chance encounter with Mai Lin Lakhon. A choice piece of ass if ever there was one, but she paid no attention to men who worked for a living. Given the chance, Yam would have reminded her that her own husband had been a working man—died working for the Triads, as it happened—and it wouldn't hurt for her to take some comfort with another, after all this time.

Perhaps the tall American was more her type.

Yam's mind was turning over like a small but well-oiled engine, sorting bits of information, putting them together here and there in different ways until a few of them began to fit.

Mai Lin was known to spend time with her brother-in-law, Prem Bangsaen. And Prem, in turn, did business with the families. Sometimes, the rumors had it, he did business with Americans and Europeans if they asked him nicely and showed up with cash in hand.

It was entirely possible, therefore, that Mai Lin had been leading the American not to her bed, but to a business meeting when she met Yam Salim and his companion on the street.

A business meeting with . . . who else?

Yam frowned and sipped his drink. The theory, even if correct, did nothing to assist him in his quest for ultimate revenge. Prem had connections, and if he was dealing with the American, that meant other men of power were involved.

The sudden thought lanced through Yam's brain like summer lightning, straightening his spine and clenching both hands on his glass, white knuckled.

An American.

A stranger.

Many came to Bangkok every day, of course, and most of them wound up on Patpong Road before they caught a plane back home, but few—if any—found themselves in Mai Lin's company, conducted to a meeting with the likes of Prem Bangsaen.

Suppose, just for a moment, that the tall American wasn't a businessman. What then?

Like every other denizen of Bangkok's streets, Yam knew about the violent action that had taken place that morning. Someone had reportedly abducted children from a Triad house of joy and killed some members of the staff before they burned the building down. A short time later an attack upon a river warehouse operated by the Yi Kwah Tao had managed to destroy a fortune's worth of contraband, believed to be the purest China white.

Coincidence?

Or could it be conspiracy?

Yam smiled, relaxing, as he felt the pieces falling into place. A tall American arrives in Bangkok and is met by—or introduced to—Mai Lin. She, in turn, conveys him to a meeting with her esteemed brother-in-law, the very night before persons unknown launch their violent assault on Triad operations in the city.

It was curious, and there was no way he could document the link, but Yam Salim didn't believe much proof would be required. He knew some members of the Yi Kwah Tao, one of them a "grass sandal," or messenger, and Yam was sure that he could win an audience with someone in authority if he applied himself.

And tell them what?

His story, suitably embellished, would cast Mai Lin, her American and the rest of her family in the worst possible light. No matter if the tall man was involved with the disturbances or not. He owed a debt of pain to Yam Salim, and Yam would save much energy and avoid much risk by having soldiers of the Yi Kwah Tao collect that debt on his behalf.

Yam pushed his glass away and left some money on the bar. He must be sober for his meeting with the Triads, or they'd dismiss his information out of hand, perhaps even punish him for wasting their precious time.

A first impression was important, and it wouldn't hurt his case if they remembered he had run some minor errands for the family in the past.

A sudden thought came to him: what if they listened to his story and, instead of acting outright, chose to question Prem Bangsaen? Suppose Prem told a different tale and managed to convince the Triads of its truth?

No problem. Yam Salim would offer most sincere apologies for his mistake, explaining that he only wished to help the family in time of need. They surely wouldn't punish him severely for an innocent mistake, especially when his motives were the best.

Case closed.

He found a pharmacy and shelled out twenty baht for breath spray to disguise the telltale smell of liquor, moving swiftly toward a tavern where he knew that members of the Yi Kwah Tao spent leisure time. They wouldn't have such time this morning, but the owner of the tavern was a member in his own right, and he had the means of passing on an urgent message to important leaders of the family.

Revenge was sweet, and Yam Salim could taste it even now.

THE "STUDIO" WAS SITUATED ten miles south of Bangkok, off the Sukhumuit highway, leading to Pattaya. Privacy was guaranteed by the surrounding forest and a narrow access road that could be covered easily and quite efficiently by one or two men hidden in the trees.

In lieu of risking it, the warrior drove on by and found a sheltered turnout half a mile downrange. An ancient bus rolled past while he was changing into tiger-striped fatigues, but no one seemed to give his car a second glance. He left it locked, the extra weapons out of sight, and struck off through the jungle, following his instinct and his compass.

He had no way of knowing whether there were lookouts posted in the woods, though he was counting on a gun or two along the access road. No problem there, if he maintained a straight course toward the house. They would be watching out for nonexistent vehicles when Bolan made his move.

The studio wasn't well-known to members of the public, even though the films that it produced on shoestring budgets earned impressive figures every year. The "stars" received no billing on the screen— there were, in fact, no credits whatsoever—and they gave no interviews. It was unlikely that a fan would ever recognize them on the street, because the men wore leather masks on camera, and the actresses were never seen on film a second time.

It was a cutthroat business, making snuff films for an audience of ghouls around the world, but the producers never came up short of talent. Teenage prostitutes were always glad to turn some extra income on a porno gig, and they were seldom missed by anyone of consequence. If periodic warnings circulated on the streets and hookers grew more cautious for a while, it was a simple matter to arrange abductions or to buy some peasant's daughter in the countryside. As for the men, they were recruited from the scum of Bangkok and paid off with baht or bullets, based upon their attitude and their ability to keep a secret.

Bolan knew the studio was only one of four or five producing snuff films in the Bangkok area, and that taking out one source of filth would barely cause a ripple in the marketplace.

But it would have an impact on the local Triads, and at the moment Bolan's goals were limited.

One project at a time.

He reached the tree line, scoping out the ranch-style house. No sentries were visible, but there were two cars parked in front and a panel truck around the side. Curtains were drawn across the windows, and no video cameras were visible.

He crossed the open ground with long, swift strides and paused beside the panel truck. With one quick twist the gas cap came free, and Bolan used a strip of handkerchief to make a wick. It caught the lighter's flame at once, and a moment later he scuttled back around the house, with the Uzi primed and ready.

The explosion, when it came, was even louder than he hoped. A shock wave smashed windows on the south side of the house, and the spray of burning gasoline ignited shrubbery, walls and shingles on the roof.

He hit the back door as a pair of gunmen cleared the front, and it was a short sprint down a hallway to the sparsely furnished bedroom where the day's extravaganza was in progress. A naked woman in her early twenties lay spread-eagle on the bed, bound hand and foot. Her costars were together on the sidelines, likewise naked, smoking through the mouth slits of their leather masks. A cameraman was huddled nervously with the director, shooting glances toward the door as Bolan entered.

The warrior didn't speak Thai fluently, but there was no mistaking the director's shocked expression as he caught a glimpse of grim death on the threshold. Bolan hit him with a burst that punched him to the floor. The Uzi kept on tracking, parabellum manglers taking down the cameraman and two masked "actors" in a spray of blood and strangled screams.

Reloading on the move, he crossed to stand beside the bed, retrieved a wicked-looking dagger from the nightstand and used it to slit the woman's bonds. She cringed from him at first, perhaps uncertain what was happening or just how close her brush with gruesome death had been.

He found her clothing folded in a corner and returned to drop it on the bed. He removed cash and car keys from the director's pockets, both of which he left beside the clothes. By that time she could smell the smoke and was dressing hastily as Bolan left the set.

He met one of the gunners coming back and stitched him with a burst that dropped him in his tracks. Outside, the other lookout from the house was joined by one assigned to watch the driveway, trying hopelessly to quench the spreading gasoline fire with a garden hose.

One of them saw the Executioner emerging from the house and tapped his comrade on the shoulder, shouting urgently in Thai. They both forgot about the house and scrambled for their weapons, but it was too late. A blazing figure eight from Bolan's Uzi swept them both away, and ringing silence settled on the clearing, broken only by the hungry crackle of the flames.

He saw the woman clear the house and head toward the cars before he moved back toward the tree line. She could ditch the vehicle in Bangkok, even sell it if she had some contacts there, and maybe come away from her near-death experience a little wiser than she had been going in.

Or maybe not.

The Executioner had done his part to help the lady out, and she was on her own. His war was waiting for him in the city, and he still had several stops to make before he was prepared to play the final hand.

He turned his back upon the Triad funeral pyre and let the forest swallow him alive.

THE MORNING'S NEWS unsettled Prem Bangsaen. He'd expected trouble from Belasko when he set himself against the Triads, but for once reality exceeded his imagination. It was difficult for him to grasp that the American was still alive, much less proceeding with the steps of his audacious plan.

Of course, the day was young. How long could any single man elude the Yi Kwah Tao in Bangkok when his adversaries had two hundred soldiers on the street?

Not long.

Belasko deserved Prem's admiration for the courage he displayed in battle, but his plan was tantamount to suicide. With one man against an army, who could doubt the outcome in a struggle where the odds were so uneven from the start?

Their latest conversation, with Belasko's plan for an escape to Burma, had done nothing to relieve Prem's troubled mind. The American wouldn't live to see Rangoon, but he'd placed the call to Ne Tin Kyat as promised, following his private rule that one must never break a promise to a dying man.

Prem's greatest fear was that Belasko might be captured by his enemies instead of dying on the street. The Triads were adept at milking information from the most recalcitrant of sources, using methods that would make a die-hard sadist's blood run cold. If the American was taken, he would talk…and where would that leave Prem Bangsaen?

He thought of leaving Bangkok, and the prospect made him scowl. His life was here, although he maintained bank accounts in other cities under several different names. The act of leaving, in itself, wouldn't be difficult, but where would he discover yet another city so well suited to his needs?

And how could he avoid the long arm of the Yi Kwah Tao, no matter where he ran?

A life in hiding didn't suit his temperament, but it was better than no life at all. He still had friends in Indonesia, Hong Kong and the Philippines. If all else failed, he could request protection from the DEA, with relocation in America.

And moving to the States might not be such a bad idea. The Triads had their outposts in America, of course, and Prem knew that their strength was growing all the time. But the United States was vast in size, a world unto itself, where anyone with ready cash on hand could lose himself and find a new identity before the week was out.

He felt a need to leave the office, move among his people for a bit and push Belasko from his mind. His contacts on the street would keep him well advised of new developments, and he could flee the city on an hour's notice if it came to that.

Prem locked the office door behind him, pocketed the key and started down the stairs. His driver would be waiting in the car, and they could select a destination as they went along. It was enough right now for Prem to be in motion, going somewhere. Anywhere.

He reached the landing on the second floor and hesitated, feeling more than recognizing something out of place. He heard a scuffling footstep on the floor below before he saw the Triad soldiers coming for him, three men racing up the stairs.

There could be no mistaking their intention, and he seized the only option readily available: he turned and ran.

The stairs seemed steeper now that he was in a hurry, gravity conspiring with his enemies to slow him down and help them overtake him. He raced past his office, lurching up the final flight until he reached the flat roof.

And where to go from there?

The building on his left was taller by a full two stories, with nothing in the nature of a fire escape or ladder to assist him. On his right an alley lay between his building and the next, although their rooftops were precisely level.

Could he make the leap?

There was no time for contemplation, as he heard the hardmen pounding up the final flight of stairs, mere yards from where he stood. Prem took a breath and held it, digging in with both feet as he sprinted for the meager sanctuary of the roof next door.

A hundred things could still go wrong, assuming that he got that far, but it was time to concentrate on first things first. A few more yards, the leap itself—

And he was airborne, pushing off with everything he had, the alley yawning underneath him like a hungry mouth.

He fell mere inches short, his desperate fingers clutching at the cornice of the roof, his shoulder sockets threatening to separate. His feet could find no purchase on the plaster, no means to support himself and scramble for the top.

Behind him angry voices changed into laughter as the Triads witnessed his predicament. It would be no great trick to shoot him now...or send a man around to hoist him up alive.

And then?

It would be *his* turn with the cruel interrogators, pleading ignorance until they went to work, then pleading for the privilege of telling everything he knew and more, his mind concocting stories to appease them, bargaining for life to no avail.

No one survived interrogation by the Triads, even if they started talking before the butchers had a chance to utilize their skills. It was a point of honor with the Yi Kwah Tao; interrogation was an art form and example to the world at large.

There was no choice.

Prem closed his eyes and offered up a prayer to Buddha as he pushed off from the roof and plummeted to the ground.

THE CASINO WAS LOCATED off Ploenchit Road, midway between the British and American embassies. It was too early for a major crowd, but that was fine with Bolan, who preferred to work without an army of civilians in the way. A simple in-and-out would suit his needs, and he could move on to another strike without delay.

The tiger-striped fatigues had been replaced by an expensive business suit, an outfit that required he leave his Uzi in the car. A couple of incendiary sticks and the Beretta 93-R slung beneath his arm would have to do the job.

He passed a pair of U.S. sailors and heard them grumbling about the money they'd lost. Inside, a dwarfish maître d' met Bolan with a smile and welcomed him to the establishment. A finger snap produced a foxy hostess, who immediately steered him toward the cashier's cage, but Bolan caught her by the arm when they were halfway there.

"Speak English?"

"Yes."

"I need to see the manager right now."

"For why?"

"We've got some business to discuss."

As Bolan spoke, he pulled the left side of his jacket back enough to let her see the pistol in its armpit sling. She stiffened, momentary fright reflected in her eyes, but she didn't resist.

The office lay upstairs. The sentry posted by the door saw them coming, went for his leathered hardware and stepped out to meet them with a question on his lips. Before the hostess could respond, the Executioner had drilled a silenced round between the gunner's eyes and dropped him where he stood.

"You get the picture now?"

"Yes."

"Let's do it, then."

She knocked and waited for an answer, speaking swiftly when she got the chance. The door was opened to reveal a dark, suspicious face.

"The manager?" he asked.

The hostess shook her head, and Bolan shot the sentry in the shoulder at point-blank range, the impact lifting him completely off his feet. The manager was gaping from his swivel chair as Bolan shoved the hostess toward a neutral corner, closed the door behind him and advanced in the direction of the tidy desk.

"I'm short on money," Bolan told him, counting on the manager of a casino to be competent in English. "I'll be taking yours."

"A robbery?"

"You're catching on. Don't worry, though. I'm also burning down the place, so your insurance ought to cover it."

The manager was looking desperate, glancing toward the top drawer of his desk, but if he had a weapon there, he didn't like the odds. Reluctantly he came around the desk and joined the hostess, moving out in front of Bolan as they led him back downstairs. He trailed them to the cashier's cage and waited while the manager delivered curt instructions, watching as brightly colored notes were loaded in a nylon duffel bag.

"Come out of there," he ordered when the bag was full. The cashier glanced at the manger, received a nod of confirmation from his boss and did as he was told.

The Executioner removed a slim incendiary stick from his pocket and primed it, flipping it into the open cash drawer as he turned away from the cage. He palmed the Beretta, disconnecting the custom silencer with a twist and dropping it into his pocket, and hefted the bag full of cash.

"We're leaving now," he told the manager and hostess, glancing toward the gaming tables, where a dozen customers were working overtime to lose their last few baht.

There was no time for subtlety. He triggered two rounds toward the ceiling, watching faces snap around in his direction as the echoes battered back and forth between the walls.

"Get out!" he shouted. "We're closing down."

As if to emphasize his words, the first incendiary popped behind him and smoke and flame erupted from the cashier's cage. He watched the stampede toward the door, a couple of the players grabbing eagerly for chips until he fired another round between them, knocking splinters from the roulette wheel.

He dropped two more incendiaries on his way outside, enough to guarantee substantial damage by the time fire fighters made the scene. It might not level the casino, but the joint wouldn't be doing business for a few nights, anyway.

The manager and members of his staff had vanished by the time Bolan reached the sidewalk. Fair enough. He walked back to his car, alert for any tails and spotting none. The first alarm bells rang inside his mind as he approached his waiting car.

Mai Lin was standing in the recessed doorway of a small boutique, some ten feet from the vehicle. Her hands were empty, no apparent weapons, but he marked the strained expression on her face.

"What is it?" Bolan asked as she fell in step beside him, moving toward the car.

"The Triads came for Prem this afternoon," she answered. "He is dead."

# CHAPTER ELEVEN

The worst part, Bolan thought, was that the news didn't surprise him. He regretted losing Prem Bangsaen, but it had all been too one-sided up until now, and he'd known the Triads would react somewhere, somehow, before he put the Bangkok game to bed.

So be it.

Mai had money of her own and means of fleeing Bangkok undiscovered. She'd waited this long, tracking down Bolan as he pursued the enemy, to warn him that the Yi Kwah Tao were moving closer, inch by inch. As they had killed her husband's brother, so the troops of Chou Sin Fong were searching for another target now to finish off their sweep and reassert control.

The "good" news was that Prem Bangsaen had died in flight, escaping from his enemies. They hadn't questioned him, so there'd been no time for drugs or torture to elicit Bolan's alias or mission. Prem's death left them in the dark and they'd stay there if Mai Lin could slip away before they had a chance to find her.

Bolan drove her to the airport in the car Prem had provided. Over her objections, he insisted that she take a portion of the cash from the casino for her airline tickets and expenses on the road. He waited with her in the concourse until her flight to Singapore was called and Mai Lin vanished through the loading gate. Gone.

And it was payback time.

He had considered rounding off the Bangkok blitz with several more attacks on Triad business fronts, but it occurred to Bolan that he'd be wasting precious time. Prem's death meant that his enemies were getting closer, even if the details of his plan were still obscure. Every moment he delayed gave Chou Sin Fong more time to strengthen his defenses, gearing up for an attack.

Fong's office was located in a downtown high-rise, one block west of Tri Petch Road. It would have been a relatively easy mark, but instinct told the Executioner his quarry wouldn't be remaining at his desk this afternoon. He might evacuate the city altogether, but it seemed more likely that the incense master of the Yi Kwah Tao would try to save face with a show of courage, standing fast against his unseen enemy and marshaling his troops.

Which meant that he'd be at home.

That morning, prior to launching any raids, the Executioner had driven past Fong's estate on the Phya Thai Road, a mile north of the Bangkok Victory Monument. He'd noted wrought-iron fences, trees and shrubs that offered fair concealment to the Triad guards inside. The house was barely visible, a single-story Thai traditional, but he'd seen enough to get a fix on its location, moving on before the sentries had had a chance to notice him.

Four hours remained until sunset, and he used the time to rest at his hotel. There was some risk involved in going back, but Bolan saw no reason why the Triads should be looking for him there. They had surviving witnesses from the casino raid, but several thousand Western tourists entered Bangkok every week, most of them male. Without a name or photograph, it would take days to scour each hotel in town, eliminating likely prospects, and the Executioner didn't intend to grant his enemies that kind of time.

Back at the Montien, he showered, ate a light meal in his room and slept until his wrist alarm went off at seven-thirty. Instantly awake, he threw the covers back and slipped into his nightsuit first, light slacks and sport shirt covering the combat dress. His webbing and the bulk of Bolan's hardware occupied one duffel bag, beneath the bed. The other duffel held a million baht in red and purple notes—some thirty-eight thousand dollars at the current rate of exchange.

He would be needing more in Burma, but the cash would take care of itself. His first priority was checking out, and moving on from there to keep his date with Chou Sin Fong.

A porter took his luggage down while Bolan tended to the heavy duffel bags himself. There were no spotters in the lobby that Bolan could see, and he kept it casual, settling his bill in cash and following the porter through revolving doors to reach the parking lot. His luggage and the duffel bag of currency filled up the trunk of the sedan; his military hardware occupied the shotgun seat as Bolan paid off the porter and drove away.

The Patpong district was as bright as day and more attractive, neon washout and the alternating shadows covering a multitude of sins. The prostitutes looked younger, slimmer after nightfall. Sleazy bars and sex clubs managed to acquire a certain ambience the light of day couldn't provide. If you kept both eyes on the traffic, it was possible to miss the homeless beggars, the addicts scrounging for a few odd baht to feed their habits, children offering themselves or younger siblings in exchange for food to eat, a place to spend the night.

The warrior wouldn't miss the City of the Angels, when he left.

He followed Raj Damri Road past the Sports Club, circling the Victory Monument, which memorialized Thailand's conflict with Cambodia in the early days of World War II. He made another drive-by of the Fong estate and kept on going, circling the neighborhood until he found a place to park his car two blocks away.

It wasn't perfect, but the extra distance gave him some security in case Fong had his spotters out. The downside was a two-block run through hostile fire if the penetration blew up in his face.

A trade-off.

In the circumstances Bolan thought it was the best that he could do.

He shed the slacks and sport shirt, tucking them beneath the driver's seat before he buckled on his webbing. Glancing left and right along the darkened residential street, he brought out the Uzi and double-checked its magazine.

He would have liked a chance to scan the grounds before he made his move, count heads and check for sensors, TV cameras, dogs—whatever. As it was, he wouldn't have the opportunity to do a recon of the target area. It would be do or die, with instinct, nerve and the advantage of surprise to see him through.

He made his way unchallenged through yards and gardens. Five short minutes found him at the wrought-iron fence, concealed in shadow as he scanned the grounds of Fong's estate.

Whatever happened next, a fighting man could only do his very best to stay alive.

He climbed the fence, avoiding sharpened spikes on top, and dropped on the other side.

THE DAY HADN'T GONE WELL for Chou Sin Fong. There had been fleeting hope, a glimmer in the darkness, when his troops brought word from Yam Salim. The man was a petty hustler on the Patpong streets, but he'd told his story with conviction and the overriding motivation of revenge.

Fong trusted honest hatred in a way that he'd never trust in friendship, love or any of the other soft emotions. Men possessed by hatred focused full attention on their enemies to the extent of sacrificing all that they held dear for one sweet taste of vengeance.

Yam Salim had sacrificed all that and more.

At first his tale of the anonymous American and Prem Bangsaen had been alluring, something Fong could chase to its conclusion, offering a hope that his accumulated problems might not be the work of brother Triads moving in to crush him. An American meant outside forces, round-eyed enemies whose interest in the Yi Kwah Tao would bring the other Triads into line, a solid front of all for one and one for all.

If only Prem Bangsaen had lived to give up the white man's name.

Prem's death—an accident or suicide, depending on your point of view—left Fong without a lead to the identity of one who might be the root of all his recent trouble. To be sure, the brief description of the man who looted his casino seemed to mesh with the report from Yam Salim, but it brought Fong no closer to his man. When soldiers were dispatched to fetch Mai Lin Lakhon, the woman was nowhere to be found.

In lieu of grilling Prem Bangsaen, Fong's experts had begun to question Yam Salim. The man had repeated his account of meeting the American in Mai Lin's company, and there was no more to be said. He lived three hours on the operating table, finally expiring from the shock and loss of blood, and Chou Sin Fong knew no more than he had when they'd begun.

A tall, anonymous American who stole Fong's money, shot his men and started fires. It was a riddle he'd have to solve, and soon, if he intended to maintain his grip on the Bangkok underworld.

Already there were rumbles from the 14K and Chiu Chou factions, rumors more than anything that Fong could put his finger on, suggesting that his Triad "brothers" would be pleased to see his territory up for grabs. It went against their oath of loyalty to say such things, of course, but who among the brotherhood of pimps and thieves had never coveted another member's power, wealth or influence?

Fong understood the call of human nature. He was ready to defend himself against the other families if it should come to that, but first he had to find out who was sponsoring the raids against his Bangkok enterprises.

Was it possible that jealous members of another Triad clan had picked the tall American to do their dirty work? The thought unsettled Fong, but having taken root inside his mind, it wouldn't go away.

Who else would have the nerve to move against the Yi Kwah Tao?

Fong thought about the Yakuza, and then dismissed the notion out of hand. The Japanese had problems of their own at home, and where expansion was concerned, their full attention focused on America, with all its bankrupt airlines, country clubs, hotels and shopping malls. The Yakuza might soon own California, but it had no grip on Thailand yet.

As for the British, they had no real syndicates outside their own pathetic islands, where the bullyboys of Liverpool and London concentrated on casinos, prostitution and distributing the drugs they managed to import. The Triads had a solid foothold on the British Isles, and if the Tommies weren't careful, they'd soon be playing second fiddle in their native land.

Which narrowed Fong's consideration down to the Americans, and where was one to go from there? Aside from the Sicilians, losing power in the face of widespread federal prosecutions since the early 1980s, there were countless gangs involved in the narcotics traffic. Some of them were foreigners who fastened on America like leeches on a water buffalo—the Latins, Orientals, some from the Caribbean—but there were native syndicates, as well. Most focused their attention on cocaine, but heroin was coming back in style these days, and cutthroat dealers would be quick to spot and take advantage of a changing market trend.

The question was, would any of them dare to face the Yi Kwah Tao in Bangkok with a shooting war when it was so much simpler to negotiate for price or try to steal the merchandise when it arrived in the United States? It was beyond the realm of plausibility for Yankee mobsters to believe they could defeat the Triads on their own home turf. The very notion smacked of madness...not to say that all Americans were strictly sane.

But if another family of the Triads was involved...

In Chou Sin Fong's opinion, it would be a clever plan for one of his devoted "brothers" to employ

American assassins in a move against the Yi Kwah Tao. By misdirecting Fong's immediate suspicion, his assailants gave themselves a chance to strengthen their position, even posing as his friends against the "common enemy." While they were "helping" Fong, his so-called allies would be in a prime position to unseat him and usurp all he'd fought and worked for through the years.

It was a clever ploy—and one Fong might have tried himself in other circumstances—but he knew the game too well for anyone to cloud his mind so easily. If there was treachery afoot among his brothers, Fong would be prepared to mete out punishment in kind. And if he had misjudged them somehow, none need ever know about his private doubts.

There had been no attempted strikes against his property since the casino raid that afternoon, and it was tempting to assume the storm was past, but Fong wasn't prepared to let himself indulge in wishful thinking. He'd seen his enemies at work, and they wouldn't be satisfied until they brought him to his knees.

Tonight his troops were on patrol throughout the Patpong district, watching over businesses and property belonging to the Yi Kwah Tao. Police were likewise on alert, some of them earning more from Fong than from the state, prepared to feed him any information they received.

With Fong's connections in the city, high and low, it was impossible for anyone to carry out a hostile operation on this scale and not leave something of themselves behind, some trace that he could analyze and use against his enemies before they struck again and made him look the fool.

The loss of face was worse in some ways than the critical financial loss he had sustained thus far. If Chou Sin Fong was made to seem ridiculous, a man who couldn't rule his own established territory, he'd soon fall prey to every small-time thug and hustler on the street. The situation called for an example, a dramatic lesson, and he couldn't put it off much longer.

Rising from his easy chair, the Bangkok incense master of the Yi Kwah Tao was moving toward his liquor cabinet, looking forward to a drink, when gunfire suddenly erupted on the grounds of his estate. He felt a hard knot forming in his stomach, threatening to take his breath away.

More firing, this time closer to the house. Fong was shouting for the guards before he reached the doorway of his study, fear and anger tightening his vocal cords. He scarcely recognized the high-pitched sounds emerging from his throat, but none of his soldiers seemed to notice as they took their orders, racing for the yard with guns in hand.

The enemy had made his first mistake by coming after Fong at home.

THE FIRST TWO SENTRIES went down easily. He found them smoking and talking quietly, their backs turned toward the dark perimeter of the estate. It was a careless move, and Bolan took them out with one shot each, the silenced automatic chugging twice and dropping both men facedown on the grass.

He had an AK-47 now to back up the Uzi and give him extra range. The dead man's pockets yielded two spare magazines, which Bolan tucked inside his belt before he dragged the bodies under the cover of some ferns and kept on moving toward the house.

It was the young man dawdling on his solitary beat to take a bladder break who nearly ruined everything. One moment Bolan was in motion, gliding toward the house; the next, he was confronted with a sentry just emerging from some bushes, fumbling with his zipper.

The shooter stared at Bolan for a heartbeat, knowing something had to give.

The AK-47 stuttered, three or four quick rounds at something close to point-blank range. The heavy slugs ripped through the sentry's rib cage, kept on going in the darkness and slammed him over on his back.

The burst of fire would tell the warrior's enemies that he was coming, even if they couldn't get a solid fix on his position from the sound. He took advantage of the shadows and the momentary lag time for reactions, sprinting toward the house.

And got there just as three of Fong's defenders stepped out on the porch with guns in hand. He let the AK-47 rip with a sweeping burst from left to right and back again. Their bodies twitched like marionettes in the hands of a spastic puppeteer before they fell.

He was still firing as he hit the doorway, plunging through. Another shooter on the staircase tracked the warrior with an Ingram submachine gun when the 7.62 mm bullets cut his legs from under him. His body tumbled down the stairs like so much laundry, sprawling in a heap at the bottom.

Around him, angry voices shouted questions, barked orders. Some of them were coming from the porch—the yard men doubling back—and Bolan spun to meet them, palming a frag grenade and yanking the pin for an easy underhand pitch. It touched down just across the threshold, wobbling to the left and out of sight before it blew.

The broad front windows shattered, spraying glass across the lushly furnished parlor. Screams and gagging noises issued from the porch, but there were fewer voices than before.

He heard footsteps at his back in time to pivot, holding down the AK-47's trigger. He caught two more gunners in the middle of a corridor that served the south wing of the house. One went down instantly; the other stopped a bullet in his shoulder but had strength enough to trigger three wild rounds before a second burst slammed home and silenced him.

Moving on, the Executioner ditched the Kalashnikov's depleted magazine and snapped a fresh one into the receiver, moving past the bodies of his latest kills, along the southern corridor.

Two options were readily apparent to his mind—he could have caught the soldiers napping, which appeared unlikely, or they'd been guarding something special in this portion of the house.

A special room of some sort?

Or their master, Chou Sin Fong.

There were two doors on Bolan's left, two on his right, all closed, with nothing in the way of signs or markings that would help him choose.

All four, then, with as little wasted time as he could manage.

Gliding to his left, he hit the first door with a kick beside the knob and entered in a rush, already crouching to avoid defensive fire. The room was dark, and when he found the light switch, Bolan saw it was unoccupied.

He crossed the hall and burst through the second door. Lights were on this time, and the warrior found himself in a library of sorts. A large globe stood in the middle of the room, as if Chou Fong drew pleasure from examining his empire in relation to the world at large.

More soldiers would have entered the house by now, and Bolan knew that he was running out of time. Ramming through the third door and encountering another empty room, he wondered if he might have misinterpreted the presence of the two sentries. Maybe they were on some kind of coffee break when he began his strike, or on routine patrol inside the house.

One door remained, and he took it in a rush, aware of movement on the far side of a massive desk before he cleared the threshold and plunged forward in a diving shoulder roll. The hot wind of a pistol bullet brushed his scalp, and Bolan came up firing with the AK-47, hosing down the desk and the man behind it, knocking photographs and paintings off the wall.

Chou Fong was dead before he fell back in his swivel chair, blood soaking through the vest and jacket of his custom-tailored three-piece suit. His eyes were open, staring into space, but there was nothing like a spark of life behind them as the Executioner advanced across the room.

He would have liked a chance to grill the Triad incense master first, before it came to this, but circumstances didn't permit a leisurely interrogation. He was out of time and then some, conscious of the angry, frightened voices in the corridor outside.

His option was the window, which faced on a garden, and he took the chance without a second thought. Once outside he sprinted through the darkness toward the nearest line of trees and shrubbery.

Floodlights blazed to life around him. He swiveled at the sound of gunfire, aiming at the nearest lights because he couldn't see the muzzle-flashes. One flood-light burst in a trail of sparks as Bolan fired, and a second went dark immediately after.

Better.

Bolan could make out running figures now. He caught one runner with a rising burst and dumped him on his backside, tracking on to catch another as he hesitated and glanced toward his prostrate friend. It was a fatal error, as the AK-47 stuttered briefly, sending death his way.

It was time to move before the other troops got organized enough to start a real sweep of the grounds. He had no way of estimating Chou Fong's total force on-site, and it wasn't his mission to annihilate the Triad rank and file in any case.

He took advantage of the momentary lull, retreating into darkness, homing on the wrought-iron fence at the perimeter. Once there, he veered in the direction of the point where he'd entered and went over in a flash.

They'd be after him in time, but first his adversaries had to check each tree and hedgerow's shadow on the way. They would be under pressure, waiting for the sound of sirens, and the word of Chou Fong's death would damage their resolve as it began to spread among the troops.

All things considered, Bolan reckoned that he had five minutes, give or take.

It was enough.

At the car the warrior dropped his webbing and his weapons in the trunk, slipped on his shirt and slacks and settled in the driver's seat. The engine came to life at once, and Bolan aimed his car in the direction of the airport.

His business was complete in Bangkok—or, at least, as nearly so as it would ever be. He had no word of Michael Lee, but he couldn't afford to linger in the city, chasing shadows.

There were ghosts enough already in the City of the Angels, and he still had other enemies to meet on different battlefields.

The Executioner was blitzing on.

# CHAPTER TWELVE

The military camp was situated in the rugged wilderness of southern Yunnan Province, near the Mekong River. It was approachable by water, air or land, but any choice was perilous to uninvited visitors.

Along the river, southward toward the Burmese border, spotters kept in touch with sleek patrol boats via two-way radio, reporting all unexpected movement. Fishing boats and other craft were searched routinely, sunk with gunfire and their small crews slaughtered if they tried to flee. The local peasants drew small comfort from the fact that river pirates had been almost totally suppressed within the past three years. And smuggling along the Mekong waterway was down, except for periodic river convoys bearing drugs, which got a military escort all the way.

The mountainous terrain and verdant jungle ruled out fixed-wing aircraft, but the camp was well equipped with antiaircraft batteries and ground-to-air rockets just in case. There was a fair-sized helipad in place, but any flight not scheduled and approved at least four hours in advance would be shot down without a warning.

The ground approach was longer and more arduous, with danger lurking every step along the way. The camp lay approximately fifty miles from the nearest point in Burma, more than double that from northern Laos. It was rough country all the way, with thickly wooded mountain slopes and valleys choked with streaming undergrowth. The several trails employed by Chinese troops and local residents were little more than game tracks, and they turned to muddy, rushing torrents in the rainy season. Vipers, kraits and cobras swarmed year-round, and it wasn't unheard-of for a tiger, straying off his range, to chow down on a villager from time to time.

If the terrain and lethal fauna weren't barrier enough, approaching travelers on any of the six or seven ready trails would have to pass by mountain villages whose occupants depended on the sale of opium and morphine base to feed their families from day to day. Each village headman had a radio in good repair, along with standing orders to report the presence of a stranger in the area without delay.

Beyond that first line of defense, there were patrols that swept the game trails more or less at random, carefully avoiding any pattern to their movements, armed and trained to shoot on sight. Sometimes they clashed with bandits from the Burmese Shan states or deserters from the Pathet Lao, stone killers who had set up shop around Yunnan and eked a living out by robbing travelers or stealing opium from mountain caravans. The sudden bark of gunfire was a too-familiar sound in the vicinity, and no one mourned the fallen dead before the jungle claimed their last remains.

The camp itself was reasonably comfortable, as such things go. The quarters housing General Li Zhao Gan were spacious, clean and airy. When the general went to bed at night, he slept on a box spring mattress, with mosquito netting overhead, and he ate breakfast on a small veranda with a dazzling mountain view.

The rest was fairly standard for an outpost of the People's Revolutionary Army in the hinterlands. A large parade ground occupied the center of the compound, and was ringed with barracks and latrines for some two hundred fifty men, the mess hall, generator and communications hut, a combination barn-garage to house and service ten or fifteen Chinese knockoffs on the jeep design. No larger vehicle was able to negotiate the mountain trails around the camp, but there were heavy trucks down-country at a second, smaller camp. For extra transportation there were mules and horses, which necessitated stables on the north end of the camp.

That afternoon three men were seated on the small veranda of the general's quarters, shaded by a tarp in camouflage design and sipping tall, iced drinks. It made a civilized, almost idyllic picture, but their mood was quite the opposite.

"If I may summarize," General Li Zhao Gan said, his tone admitting no objection from the others, "you have now lost some three dozen men in Bangkok and Australia. One of them, you say, is Chou Sin Fong. Two massive loads of heroin have been destroyed, along with other monetary losses that are minor by comparison. Am I correct in my appraisal of the situation, gentlemen?"

The younger of his guests sat stiff and silent, finally reaching for his drink as if he wore some kind of body cast beneath his clothes. The other, crafty Sun Jiang Lao, responded with a frown.

"As ever, General, you are most concise."

"And through it all, you still have no idea of who your enemy may be, no inkling of his whereabouts or what he hopes to gain from these attacks?"

"So far, the vital information has eluded us."

"Who stands to profit by your loss?" the general asked.

"It could be any one of several groups," Sun Lao replied.

"If you were forced to pick out one?"

"The problem needs more thought."

Li cracked his knuckles, staring off across the wooded mountain peaks, where mist wove in and out among the trees like tattered spiderwebs.

"You may not have that luxury," he said at last.

"We are secure for now."

"And what about your markets in Australia? Bangkok?"

"The damage will be mended, General."

"I hope so," Li replied. "It strikes me that our deal may have to be revised if you have no means of distributing the product I supply."

Across the glass-topped table, Michael Lee appeared as if he meant to speak, but Sun Jiang Lao restrained him with a glance. When Sun replied, his voice was as soft as velvet, with a hint of steel beneath.

"We have sustained some unexpected damage, I admit," he said, "but injury and death are not the same. One does not follow from the other automatically."

"Unless the wounds are left untreated and allowed to fester."

"I am taking steps to minimize our losses, even as we speak. The Yi Kwah Tao is strong, well armed, and we have ways of tracking down our enemies."

"So far, your methods have not yielded any great result."

"Our bargain has not changed," the Triad master answered, changing tack. "You will be paid on time, and if our distribution of the product is delayed...well, that has no effect on you, in any case.''

"Indeed, I have no interest whatsoever in the speed with which an addict in New York or San Francisco gets his 'fix,'" the general said, his clipped tone taking on a certain chill.

"What is it, then?"

"Your unknown enemy seems well informed about the operations of the Yi Kwah Tao. He knows your representatives abroad and where to find them when he has the need. In Bangkok he wreaks havoc with your property, then stalks and kills your first lieutenant at his home."

"Our information indicates a local traitor was involved with the affair in Thailand."

"Have you questioned him?"

"He died—a suicide, perhaps—before we had the chance."

"Unfortunate. And now we have no way of telling how much more your enemy may know...perhaps about Yunnan."

"My problems are not yours," Sun Jiang Lao stated.

"I wish that was true," General Li said. "Unfortunately, while you buy your heroin from me, I am compelled to take an interest in your enemies. Especially those who seem intent on closing down the pipeline we have managed to construct."

"That day will never come," Sun vowed.

"How can you be so sure?"

"The methods used thus far are not the methods of police. Men killed and property destroyed without the filing of a legal charge or any order from the courts. The law does not behave this way in Bangkok, much less in Australia."

"So?"

"Competitors," the aging Triad chieftan said. "Their motives are transparent even now, before we learn their number and their names. Whatever else they do, they will not kill the golden goose, as the Americans would say. Your portion of our partnership is not in jeopardy."

"An easy statement," General Li responded, "but I hope you are correct. It is a serious mistake for *anyone* to think that I would stand for interference at the present time."

Sun Lao showed no reaction to the general's threat as he replied, "I say again, your interest is secure."

"And if your enemy is looking for you even now?"

"Where should he go from Bangkok? I have troops on the alert in Burma, Hong Kong, Singapore, Malaysia and the Philippines. One territory is as likely as the next, and all have been prepared for an attack."

"As Chou Sin Fong prepared himself?" the general asked.

"It is a fact that we may never know how Fong was killed, what lapse in personal security allowed the enemy to reach him in his home. I can assure you that my other incense masters will not make the same mistake."

"You spoke of traitors earlier. Suppose one such has given you away? Your nameless enemy may be en route to Yunnan even now."

"If so, he will be forced to pass through territory where my eyes and ears are sharp and on alert. We shall be warned, and every measure taken to eliminate the threat. In the event that any of our foes should actually reach Yunnan... well, General, I need not comment on your own defenses, surely."

Li could smell the bait, but he was not about to take it. He was proud of his defenses at the mountain camp, but he wouldn't allow Sun Lao to make him boast.

"Your last reports make note of an American in Bangkok seemingly involved with one of the attacks upon Chou Fong."

"That is correct. He may have been a mercenary, or his presence may suggest a problem with the Mafia in the United States."

"I understood that the Sicilians were your customers," Li said.

"But they are not well organized of late, and some of them are greedy. It would please them, I imagine, to obtain their heroin from you directly and eliminate the middleman."

Li kept his face impassive, brushing off the tacit question from Sun Lao. Considering the circumstances, it was natural for Sun to look on everyone around him with suspicion. If the general had agreed to strike a bargain with the Mafia, eliminating transport fees and charges from the Yi Kwah Tao, it would have been a major blow—perhaps a fatal one—against the Triad's treasury.

And Li decided that it wouldn't hurt to let Sun sweat awhile, considering the consternation that his own ineptitude had caused in recent days.

"Are you prepared for war with the Sicilians?" he inquired.

"Our troops outnumber them worldwide," Sun answered.

"But only if the other Triad families fight beside you."

"There should be no question of assistance from our brothers to repel a foreign threat."

"And if the Mafia is not to blame?"

He let the implication hang between them, trusting Sun to know exactly what he meant.

"I have no reason to believe that any of my brothers wish me ill."

"But it is best to be on guard."

"Of course."

"And weigh the facts without unnecessary sentiment."

"One thing the Yi Kwah Tao and your political philosophy may have in common, General, is the lack of childish sentiment."

Li changed directions, making every effort to be unpredictable.

"How long shall we be honored with the company of your esteemed associate from Sydney?"

Instant, angry color tinged Lee's cheeks, but he allowed his mater to respond.

"A few more days, I think. Until the situation in Australia has been analyzed. Unfortunately bodies and some traces of Bangkok shipment were discovered on his property. It will require some time for the police to satisfy themselves that Mr. Lee was not at fault."

"A wise decision you will help them reach, no doubt."

A thin smile graced Sun's lips. "It seems the least that I can do."

"And what of the police in Bangkok, Master Sun?"

"A different problem altogether. In the absence of a visible connection, Chou Sin Fong may not be linked with any sales of heroin. Police are free to entertain suspicions as they like, but proving it in court is something else. The members of his staff will not be charged, beyond some trivia concerning weapons in the city proper. As it happens, they killed no one in the final clash. They are the victims.''

''One small benefit of careless aim,'' the general sneered.

''There are some final preparations I must make,'' Sun said. ''If I might use your radio...''

''Of course. And I shall see you both at supper in the mess.''

Li watched them go, the so-called Elder Brother and his stooge. He wondered whether Sun Jiang Lao was past the age of making clear decisions under pressure, whether he would fold soon in the face of new attacks from his elusive enemy.

It never crossed the general's mind that there would be no more attacks. Someone somewhere had taken too much time at planning, laid out too much cash and energy so far, to simply let the matter drop.

For just a moment Li imagined what it would have been like, dealing with America direct, without the Triad albatross around his neck. A whole new world of profit, no doubt, once the grasping middlemen were crushed or shoved aside.

It might be worth a try, at that.

RETURNING TO their quarters on the far side of the camp's parade ground, Sun Jiang Lao and Michael Lee conversed in whispers, well aware that Li's troops were his own and the camp an echo chamber for reports and rumors. It wouldn't do for the general to suspect ingratitude when he had offered them his open hospitality.

''He thinks the other Triads are to blame, Master.''

''It is a natural assumption,'' Sun replied. ''You must not let your anger blind your eyes to logic.''

"No, Master."

"You think our brothers will not move against us, as the act would fall in obvious defiance of their oath?"

"If they are loyal—"

"There are degrees of loyalty. You understand that I do not suspect another member of the Yi Kwah Tao."

"Of course."

"From time to time, however, greed becomes too much for members of our brother clans. You recall White Powder Ma?"

"By reputation only," Lee replied.

"He was the Chiu Chou incense master in Macao, some fifteen years ago. Of course, his name derived from his participation in the drug trade. It was said that none could match his contacts, his ferocity, the skill with which he opened brand-new markets...but he was not satisfied."

Lee walked beside his master, silent, knowing that the story would proceed when it was time.

"At last White Powder Ma conspired to steal the territory of his Hong Kong brothers. They were all Chiu Chou, but he forgot his oath of loyalty and listened to his stomach growling. Japanese assassins were employed, but they were unsuccessful. One of them was captured still alive and made to talk. White Powder Ma was charged with treason and convicted by his family."

"The penalty?"

"As specified by Ma's own oath."

"The myriad of swords," Lee said.

"Correct. It took three days for him to die, and then his brothers made the body disappear."

"I feel that I have failed you by abandoning my post," Lee said.

"And how would you have served me from the grave? The greatest part of wisdom is discretion. You are not a coward and must not regard yourself as such. Self-sacrifice is merely wasteful if the family receives no benefit."

"I should go back and help identify our enemy."

"Too late. He has moved on."

"But if they seek to claim our territory, soldiers will be left behind. They can be found and questioned."

"No possibility will be ignored," Sun Lao replied, "but you should be prepared for other explanations in the meantime."

"Sir?"

"It is not clear, by any means, that these attacks were carried out by members of the competition, as we understand the term."

"Why else?"

"Do you recall the marksman's medal?"

"It was found in Sydney," Lee replied. "I never saw it for myself."

"At first the news meant nothing to me," Sun went on. "An ancient memory, perhaps, but lost beyond recall. It may be true, as some suggest outside my hearing that the march of time leaves mortal men behind to struggle in the dust. The echo of a memory disturbed me. Inquiries were made."

"With what result?"

"Do you recall the name Mack Bolan?"

"No, Master."

"In other days the Western press sometimes described him as the Executioner."

The nickname conjured images of gangsters from Chicago, bringing on a frown. "Was he a friend of the Sicilians?" Lee inquired.

"Quite the reverse. As I recall, he blamed the Mafia for certain deaths among his family and set out to repay the loss in kind. It should have been a suicidal gesture, but he managed to survive against all odds. Alone—or, some say, with the silent backing of his government—he slaughtered hundreds, maybe thousands, of his enemies."

"I do not understand."

"From time to time this Bolan left a calling card behind. A military marksman's medal, from his Army days."

Lee stiffened, stopping short and swiveling to face Sun Lao.

"What happened to this man?"

"It is impossible to say with any certainty. At one point, years ago, the press reported he was dead and buried in America. New York, I think it was. A few months later came the news that he was still alive, his death a ruse. Since then we have reports that he is dead, retired, disabled . . . or alive and well. Still hunting."

"Master, please forgive me, but I do not understand how this affects the Yi Kwah Tao. If we assume this Bolan is alive today, his war is still with the Sicilians. I don't see—"

The Elder Brother raised a hand for silence.

"No. He was not satisfied to punish the Sicilians in America or even in their native land. He hates the powder trade and anyone associated with it. We have verified reports of clashes with the Corsicans, the Yakuza, the Arabs and Colombians. All over drugs."

"And still he lives?"

"Perhaps. I have a theory, but I stress that it is nothing more."

"I would be proud to hear it, sir."

"Are you familiar with your history?"

Lee blushed. "My formal education was irregular at best."

"Of course. In old America, around the time that I was born, the church and government joined forces to forbid all trade in alcohol."

"The Prohibition," Lee replied. "I know of this."

"One group that organized to undermine the law consisted of a few young Jews. They called themselves the Purple Gang, for reasons which are still disputed by historians. Within a few short years they held considerable power, terrorizing their competitors and killing those who would not run away."

Again Lee knew that it was time to wait and listen, keeping both ears open for the moral of the story.

"Over time the Purple Gang grew careless, and Sicilians stole their territory, killing most of them and forcing the survivors to withdraw in shame. It should have been the end, but newsmen and police began to call the new Sicilian family the Purple Gang, and some still use the name today. It was too colorful to die."

"And Bolan?"

"Who can say? I never met the man, and obviously do not know if he is still alive or where his path has taken him, if so. But it occurs to me that, even dead, he might be valuable to others. As a name, an image. Something they could work with."

"A disguise?"

"Perhaps."

"But who?"

At that, the Triad master shrugged. "Whoever hates the powder traffic—or our family—enough to risk his life and everything he owns. Perhaps, if we can find a place where both lists overlap..."

"One man?"

"It is a possibility, though Bolan is reported to have worked with others in the past. We may assume that an impostor might do likewise."

"He will not be waiting for me in Australia, then."

"But there are still police and all their questions to be dealt with," Sun reminded him. "You have no value to the family in a prison cell."

"How long, Master?"

"Consider this a lesson in the art of waiting patiently. You will be told when it is time, if you cannot decide the proper moment for yourself."

"And what of General Li?"

"What of him?"

"Will you share your theory with him?"

"No. At least not yet. He has a military mind, which does not grasp abstractions . . . and, in any case, what preparations could he make that have not been already made?"

"I understand."

"Our troops are on alert and searching for the enemy at every point where he is likely to appear. Whichever way he turns, he will be met."

"And if he finds us here?"

The head of the Yi Kwah Tao was smiling, studying the rugged mountain peaks and forest all around the camp.

"What better place," he asked, "for such a legend to be laid to rest?"

# CHAPTER THIRTEEN

After Thailand, Burma was a different world. The countryside and climate were distinctly similar, but otherwise a Western visitor might be forgiven for believing he had traveled back in time some fifty years instead of simply flying north and west three hundred miles.

Where Thailand generally, and Bangkok most especially, doted on tourists, the authorities in Burma actively discouraged Western visitors, limiting visas and travel permits to a one-week duration. If tourists tired of temples, there was little left to see, and nothing of the nightlife that made Bangkok, Manila and Hong Kong notorious in modern times. Restaurants and taverns closed predictably by 9:30 p.m.

Burmese customs agents prided themselves on picking over baggage, finding things to confiscate and wasting as much time as possible on each new visitor in turn. Since introducing weapons through the airport was a virtual impossibility without arranging complicated bribes, the Executioner had made arrangements for an alternate mode of transport before leaving Thailand.

Bolan's flight to Phuket, in the south, had been the easy part. His pilot was a veteran smuggler who didn't believe in asking questions, and he had connections in the coastal town who didn't mind conveying someone into Burma through the back door, if the price was right. It was nine hundred miles across the Andaman Sea to the mouth of the Irrawaddy River, and Bolan took advantage of the time to rest, reviewing strategies and picking over the mistakes that he had made so far.

The death of Prem Bangsaen weighed heavily on his mind, but there was no way that he could have saved the little Thai, short of refusing the contact and tackling Bangkok on his own. At least Mai Lin Lakhon was safe for now...as far as he could tell.

The marksman's medal back in Sydney could have been another error, Bolan realized. He'd left it on a whim, before he thought of turning one Triad against another, and it might come back to haunt him soon.

So be it.

If his adversaries realized who they were up against, it simply gave them something else to think about. It wouldn't bring them any closer to a tag when they couldn't predict his movements or the next place he would strike.

The worst mistake, to Bolan's mind, was missing Michael Lee. He still had no way of determining where Lee had gone, but he didn't believe an incense master of the Yi Kwah Tao was simply hiding somewhere, sitting on his hands and making no attempt to win his territory back.

There would be work to do in Sydney yet, when he was through with Sun Jiang Lao and General Li.

Assuming he survived.

The lull gave Bolan time to think about alternatives, and he was very conscious of the fact that no man lived forever, least of all a soldier who insisted on front-line duty time and time again. His luck had been phenomenal, assisted by a martial expert's skill and instinct, but the Executioner had taken hits along the way, seen friends and loved ones laid to rest. The minor wounds he'd suffered from the Australian clash no longer troubled Bolan, but he knew they could as easily have cost his life.

The morbid thoughts depressed him, and he shrugged them off, preferring to concentrate on the job at hand. Ahead of him lay Burma, where the opium and morphine from Yunnan was processed into heroin, then packed off for sale in Bangkok to the highest foreign bidder. He was still one buffer layer away from Yunnan Province and the dragon's head, but he was getting there.

If only he didn't let down his guard and lose his own head on the way.

Off shore a smaller craft was waiting for the short run to Rangoon. The river pilot had received half of his payment in advance, enough for him to buy official-looking travel papers in the name of Mike Belasko, circumventing customs with a forgery that should withstand a cursory inspection. He didn't bat an eye at Bolan's heavy duffel bags, nor did he offer to assist in moving them from one boat to another.

"You are booked into the Strand Hotel," the boatman said once they were under way. "You have begun your visit with a day tour of the Irrawaddy villages. Okay?"

"Sounds good to me."

It stood to reason that the Triads would be watching for him in Rangoon, along with every other port of any size in Southeast Asia. Even so, the heat would still be focused back in Bangkok for a while, and Bolan meant to take advantage of the lag time while he could.

THE STRAND WAS a first-class hotel, which meant that Bolan's room was air-conditioned, relatively clean and reasonably priced at slightly under thirty dollars per night. He tipped the porter and was left alone.

The shower in his room was functional, though the water was barely warm, and Bolan remembered to keep his mouth shut tight against the germs and parasites that thrived in Burmese plumbing. Toweling off, he chose the lightest suit he had and slipped his shoulder holster on above a shirt that would be wilted in his first half hour on the street.

Another change from Bangkok was the different mode of dress, men and women alike wearing sarong-type skirts, with women favoring bright colors, the men restricting themselves to plain fabric or modest check patterns in more somber tones. He saw few business suits and fewer blue jeans as he walked from his hotel toward Chinatown on Anawrahta Road.

The names of shops and restaurants were all in Chinese characters, but Bolan's river pilot had advised him what to look for, and he recognized the chemist's shop by its display of patent remedies, as well as by the small red dragon stenciled in a corner of the plate-glass window. Opening the door, he was announced to the proprietor by jangling bells.

The wizened man behind the counter might have been sixty-five or a hundred years old; it was impossible to guess with any certainty. His thinning hair was combed straight back, and ancient wire-rimmed glasses magnified his eyes.

"American?"

"That's right." A glance around the cluttered shop told Bolan they were probably alone. "A friend directed me to you."

"What thing you need?"

"I'm looking for a man."

The druggist frowned and shook his head. "Sell medicine, not men."

"His name is Ne Tin Kyat."

"And your name is ... ?"

"Belasko."

"If I meet this man, how may he find you?"

"I'll be staying at the Strand Hotel for the next three nights."

"No promise, understand?"

"I'll take what I can get."

He spent another twenty minutes touring China-town, confirming that he wasn't being tailed before he started back to the hotel.

To wait.

THE HARDEST PART of working for the CIA in Burma, Jason Stark decided, was the boredom. Days and weeks of monitoring rumors, jotting notes on this or that guerrilla leader who was seen—or was he?—somewhere in the trackless countryside. From time to time the Rangoon government would launch a drive against insurgent forces, briefly driving them across the border into Laos or Thailand, but it never lasted long.

In theory Burma was a bastion of democracy in Southeast Asia, but reality was something else again. The military junta of the 1960s had degenerated into a form of state socialism, with nationalization of industry and agriculture driving thousands of foreign investors from the country. The end result was rampant poverty, economic stagnation and the birth of a thriving black market that made Burma a smuggler's paradise.

Opium ranked first among the wide range of illicit commodities in Burma, with poppies cultivated chiefly in the Shan and Kachin states, adjoining China's Yunnan Province. Mountain tribes produced a staple crop of opium base each season, but Burma's chief contribution to the narcotics trade, since the early 1970s, was its role as Asia's chief refinery for heroin, along with transportation routes from Yunnan south to Bangkok.

The heroin refineries—all highly mobile, all concealed—were financed by the Chinese Triad families, operated and protected by paramilitary forces ranging from the far left to the neofascist right. In Burma private armies needed cash for food and weapons, medicine and uniforms, no matter what the source. If Communist guerrillas earned their daily bread from drugs, why should their Christian enemies be left out in the cold?

Narcotics had become the Burmese equalizer . . . but some dealers would always be more equal than others.

It had taken Jason Stark a month to realize that he wasn't supposed to notice drugs in Burma or submit reports about the nation's role in shipping heroin worldwide. His predecessor destroyed two or three such documents before he finally took Stark aside one day and laid it on the line.

"Look, kid," the grizzled veteran of a thousand cover battles had said, "we've got one job out here, and that's to keep the Communists from gaining any ground. We're not the goddamn DEA or Customs, and we don't have any brief to interfere with commerce to or from a friendly state. Remember that, and you should do all right. Who knows, you might pick up a little something on the side."

The message came through loud and clear. When Stark's CO retired from office eight months later, he'd gone to live in the Bahamas, near his numbered, untaxed bank account. Stark got a boost in salary, a larger office, and he'd been picking up "a little something on the side" from Triad smugglers ever since.

Of course, the Burmese drug trade being what it was, his sponsors generally expected something more for their investment than a silent partner who was also deaf and blind. With Stark's resources, he was tapped for information now and then, commissioned to report on any special plans the DEA might hatch and generally discourage any Western dealers who might feel an urge to trespass on the Triad's territory.

Altogether, Stark considered that he earned his extra paycheck from the smugglers, and he gave good value for the money he received. So far, he hadn't been required to compromise his duty as a guardian against the creeping tide of communism—well, not much, at any rate—and he'd managed to avoid direct involvement in the bloody internecine wars that followed the narcotics traffic everywhere around the world.

Until today.

The news from Bangkok had been grim, to say the least. Somebody had been chewing up the Triads, and there were ugly rumors of involvement by at least one unidentified American. Worse yet, Stark's sources were suggesting that the Bangkok blowout might be linked with similar events in Australia days earlier.

Stark had no patience with coincidence. His twelve years with the Company had taught him that fortuitous events—for either side—were nearly always guided by some unseen hand. The question now was *whose* hand.

Who would stand to profit from disruption of the Triad pipeline? Off the top, he thought of various competitors—the Mafia and Yakuza, to start—but none of them possessed the necessary strength to stage a coup in Bangkok, let alone Australia. Looking closer, he decided that it could have been a war between the families... except that Stark had never heard of any Triad hiring an American to do its dirty work.

But he was on the alert for new arrivals in Rangoon, and when his lookouts noted the appearance of a Yank named Mike Belasko at the Strand Hotel, it was a simple thing to learn that he had also been in Bangkok, as of yesterday.

The geographic link meant nothing by itself, except that Stark had someone he could shadow for a few days, making sure the Triads realized that he was earning every penny he received. If this Belasko was a tourist or an ordinary businessman, no sweat. But if he started playing games...

It would be Stark's call, whether he should try to warn the bastard off or feed him to the Triads, maybe pick up something extra in the nature of a finder's fee. He didn't like the taste of selling an American to the Chinese, but it was all a matter of degree.

If this Belasko was a smuggler or a contract killer, you could hardly call him any kind of bona fide American, no matter how you stretched your definitions. There was more to being a productive citizen than cashing in on accidents of birth, and the United States wouldn't miss one more gangster, either way.

So far the guy had done a day tour of the Irrawaddy, so they said, and he strolled around in Chinatown awhile. It wasn't much, but you could never tell about a man when he was feeling out new territory, settling in. He might be waiting for a contact in the city, maybe lining up his targets for another strike.

If so, Stark meant to have his eyes and ears alert. One accusation that would never stick was that of sleeping on the job.

The telephone distracted him from plotting strategy.

"Hello?"

He recognized the voice and listened for a moment, soaking in the words, while new anxiety began to churn inside his stomach like a nest of worms.

"You're sure? Okay. Yeah, thanks."

A fucking marksman's medal in Australia. Shit! The Sydney office wasn't saying anything for sure, but Stark could read between the lines.

And suddenly he didn't have to wonder who would profit from the downfall of the Triads. All he had to do was close his eyes, and he could smell the gunsmoke, hear the sounds of urban warfare echo in his ears.

He didn't need a crystal ball to tell him that the Executioner was in Rangoon. And Stark would be ass deep in alligators if he didn't keep the lid on, which required decisive action going in.

Beginning now.


THE CALL CAME THROUGH at half-past seven, catching Bolan at the door. He'd decided there was no point in sitting in his room—the hotel operator would have sense enough to page him in the restaurant—but here it was.

"Belasko."

"I believe we have a friend in common," said the unfamiliar voice. "His name is Prem—"

"Bangsaen," the soldier finished for him, "and it's past tense. He's been killed."

There was a heartbeat's hesitation on the other end, then, "What happened?"

"I don't think we should discuss it on the telephone."

"Of course. There is a restaurant across the street from where you asked for help this afternoon."

"What time?"

"You have a car?"

"Not yet."

"Start walking now."

The line went dead, and Bolan cradled the receiver. He had time to think about the prospect of an ambush, finally dismissing it. The ancient pharmacist could easily have fingered Bolan for his enemies, but plucking Prem's name from the grab bag would require some kind of psychic power—or a plot that would include the men who ferried him from Thailand to Rangoon. And if the Triads were aware that he was coming, if they sought his death, it would have been a relatively simple thing to dump him in the Irrawaddy River or the sea.

Hedging his bets, he took a taxi to the nearby railway station, where he left his duffel bags of cash and hardware stashed in separate lockers. Walking back to Chinatown, he had no greater distance to traverse than if he had begun the trek from his hotel.

No more than half the tables inside the restaurant were occupied. The hostess saw him coming, obviously having been alerted to expect a tall American, and led him to a booth in back. The man who waited for him there was stocky, somewhere in his early thirties, with a crescent scar above one eye.

"Mr. Belasko, please sit down."

"Am I addressing Ne Tin Kyat?"

"You are. Let's order before our discussion."

A skinny teenage waiter took their order, disappeared, then returned with pots of tea before he left the two of them alone.

"You have disturbing news from Bangkok," Bolan's contact began. "Please explain."

"It was arranged for Prem Bangsaen to give me certain information on the Triads, more specifically the Yi Kwah Tao. I can't be certain how they learned of the connection. When they came for him, he ran . . . and died."

"They did not question him?"

"I'm told there wasn't time."

"How fortunate for all concerned."

"Except the Yi Kwah Tao."

"Reports of their misfortune reach my ears. You are responsible?"

"I'm doing what I can."

"For their competitors?"

"I don't believe Prem played that game. If you do, I apologize for taking up your time."

He was about to leave the booth when Ne Tin Kyat reached out and caught him by the sleeve.

"Please sit. We cannot be too cautious in the circumstances."

"No."

"What is it that you want from me?"

"I'm going north. I need a guide."

"The Shan states?"

"Farther."

"Ah."

"Is that a problem?"

"You must understand, the trip that you propose is fraught with many perils."

"Anything worth doing has some risk involved."

"If I agree—"

His words were cut off by a spat of Chinese at Bolan's back. He turned in time to see four men push through the door, one of them lashing out to deck the startled hostess with a hard right hand. Before she hit the floor, the new arrivals were producing automatic weapons from beneath their jackets, scanning nearby tables for a likely target.

Ambush!

Bolan flicked a hasty glance at Ne Tin Kyat and knew his contact had no part in the surprise. A curse was forming on the man's lips as Bolan reached across and dragged him to the floor.

All hell broke loose a heartbeat later as converging streams of automatic fire began to rip their booth apart. Bolan hugged the floorboards, praying for a chance to take a couple of his adversaries with him when he died.

# CHAPTER FOURTEEN

The Executioner palmed his automatic, flicking the selector switch to 3-round bursts, and was about to return fire when something near the front door of the restaurant drew his attention. A young Burmese who had been dining on his own, ignored by the invaders, suddenly produced a pistol from the shopping bag that stood beside his chair and triggered two quick rounds into the nearest gunman's spine.

Another member of the fire team swiveled to confront the unexpected threat, his submachine gun laying down a steady stream around the room. He caught the young Burmese waist high and blew him backward through a plate-glass window.

Two other gunners caught a glimpse of Bolan and his contact and loosed another, more determined stream of fire in their direction, riddling the walls and furniture. A large, framed watercolor slithered down the wall and crashed into the floor near Bolan's head.

He had a worm's-eye view of one advancing gunner and squeezed off a burst that ripped his target's knee and thigh to bloody shreds. The Triad gunner screamed and went down in a heap, his submachine gun blasting aimlessly at glassware, ceiling fixtures, hanging lamps. A second burst form the Beretta caught him in the face and pitched him over on his back, unmoving in a pool of blood.

And that left two that Bolan knew about, both firing for effect. He heard them overturning tables, seeking cover as they realized their prey was armed and capable of fighting back. They started shouting back and forth between sporadic bursts of fire, and Bolan had to wonder whether they had reinforcements waiting on the street outside.

"This way!" Ne Tin Kyat snapped, already digging with his knees and elbows, crawling toward the nearby kitchen.

There was no time to argue, as another Chinese gunman charged across the threshold, carrying a sawed-off shotgun in his hands. The burst from Bolan's 93-R stitched a lethal pattern on his chest and blew him backward through the open door before his comrades could return the fire.

The warrior knew his time was running out. It wasn't good enough just holding ground when he was pinned down by his enemies and the police would soon be on their way. He thumbed the fire-selector switch to semiauto, braced himself and waited for a momentary lull when his assailants paused to get their bearings or reload.

Behind him Ne Tin Kyat slid through the kitchen door, a crawling target, there and gone. The Executioner was on his feet an instant later, squeezing off in rapid fire as he propelled himself in the direction of the swing door. He saw one Triad member jerking, slumping sideways, while the other swung around to bring him under fire, and then the door was slapping shut behind him.

"This way."

Again the call came from Ne Tin Kyat, and Bolan followed through the claustrophobic kitchen, pots still boiling on a greasy stove, though all the staff had disappeared. There was an exit at the rear, and his contact was nearly there when Bolan caught an arm and pulled him back.

"It may be covered."

"We have nowhere else to go. My car is there."

"Let's check it all the same."

The 93-R's magazine was close to one-third full, but he replaced it with a fresh one, dropping the depleted clip into a pocket of his sport coat. A rubber thirty-gallon trash can stood near the door, half-empty, and he picked it up.

"This ought to do the job."

Stepping forward, Bolan pitched it through the door, a spinning target in the darkness of the alley just outside. At least two weapons opened up immediately— one of them a shotgun and the other semiauto— pumping rounds into the trash can as it spun and rolled.

The warrior followed it, his keen eyes picking out the muzzle-flashes of his enemies. The nearer of the two, crouched beside a garbage bin and firing a vintage M-1 carbine, was startled by the second target charging into view. He tried to swing his piece around and nearly made it, but choked on a parabellum mangler as the warrior's first shot dumped him on his butt.

The shotgun belched a hasty spray of buckshot, missing Bolan by at least a yard and peppering the wall behind him. He veered away from the Toyota parked there, preferring open space to any move that sacrificed their wheels. His target was a shadow, moving in a crouch and lining up another shot as Bolan hit a flying shoulder roll.

He came up firing, three rounds on the money at twenty feet. His adversary seemed to stumble, falling facedown on his stubby weapon, and a dying finger clenched around the trigger as he fell. The final shotgun blast was muffled by his body, but it caused the corpse to jump and ripple from the impact of a buckshot charge at skin-touch range.

Ne Kyat was in the alley and breaking for the car. He threw himself behind the wheel, and Bolan took the shotgun seat, the engine snarling into life as headlights blazed behind them, bearing down. As they peeled out of there, a Triad gunner cleared the back door of the restaurant and started firing at the car, a couple of his bullets slapping hard against the trunk.

In front of them two man-shapes blocked the alley's mouth, both swinging weapons up and into line. Ne Kyat switched on the headlights, high beams, blinding them for just an instant, giving Bolan time to poke his automatic out of the window and fire four quick rounds.

The opposition melted, one man spinning out of frame, the other dropping where he stood. The Toyota jolted over him as if his body were a speed bump in the pavement, then swung wide into the street beyond.

The chase car was behind them all the way. A gunner aimed from the sun roof, firing as they leveled off and headed east. Pedestrians fell back and scattered for their lives as Ne Kyat tried to clear a path around the traffic, toppling some pushcarts in his wake.

The second burst of hostile fire was right on target, gouging divots in the trunk and taking out the wide back window in a spray of pebbled safety glass. The Executioner squeezed off two rounds in answer, trying for the chase car's grille, but he could tell that neither shot was on the mark.

Their path along Bogyoke Street ran parallel to railroad tracks, and Bolan saw a single headlight glaring at them up ahead. He gauged the distance to the crossing, knew it would be close, and told Ne Kyat exactly what he had in mind.

"It will be dangerous," the driver cautioned.

"This isn't?"

"I will do it."

"Slow down just before you cross. We'll take some hits, but it's the only way to keep them on our tail."

"All right."

At thirty yards Ne Kyat began to brake, the chase car running up behind them with its gunner firing measured bursts. The bodywork took most of it, and Bolan fired several rounds to spoil the shooter's aim but without discouraging the enemy from closing in.

It was a gamble, but as long as they were quick enough, they couldn't lose. One outcome gave them time to run for cover, get themselves a lead and ditch their enemies. As for the other...

"Now!"

Ne Kyat cranked the wheel and the Toyota swung hard left across the railroad tracks, its headlights dancing crazily. The train was close enough that they could smell its diesel breath and feel vibrations through the tracks.

Behind them, sticking close, the chase car made a screeching turn—and met the train head-on. There was a grinding crash, a screech of dragging metal, and the train began decelerating through a cloud of smoke and flying sparks.

They didn't stop to watch.

"We need to go somewhere we can talk," Bolan said, staring at the driver's profile in the soft light from the dash.

"I know a place."

"I UNDERSTAND THAT," Jason Stark informed the caller, scowling at the telephone. "You may recall that I provided an address, which proved to be correct. The rest of it was your men, all the way."

"Unfortunately true," the soft voice on the other end replied, "but they have paid the price for their mistakes. We need to remedy the situation now without delay."

The use of "we" was troubling. Stark worried any time that Chiang Fan Baht, the incense master of the Yi Kwah Tao in Burma, felt inclined to share.

"There's nothing more that I can do unless he shows himself."

"I disagree. You have your sources in the city, just as I have mine. Between us, we can certainly discover who this stranger met and why."

"Your action at the restaurant has the police involved," Stark said. "If you had tagged Belasko, I could send somebody from the embassy with hearts and flowers, ask some questions for appearances and close the book. The way things stand, I start to interfere with the police, and all it does is raise more questions that we can't afford to answer."

"The police are my affair," Chiang replied. "I pay enough of them to help decide the course of their investigation and how far it goes. Your job is to uncover the American."

Stark felt an urge to blurt out his suspicions, give Chiang something he could *really* sweat about, but he restrained himself. If this Belasko was Mack Bolan, there was nothing to be gained by spreading it around. The Triads had no pictures of the guy on file, and they could kill him just as well by any other name.

The flip side was that any leak at all about a Bolan strike meant network cameras in Rangoon for damn sure, and the kind of scrutiny that Stark could ill afford. If Langley thought that he had Bolan anywhere within five hundred miles, they would be breathing down his neck and sending spotters out to supervise his handling of the case. If there was any truth at all behind the rumors, Stark might even be commanded to assist the Executioner and that would simply be the living end.

Chiang Baht would never understand a switch like that, much less forgive it. He'd find a way to fuck Stark over good and proper, even if he let the chief of station live. A simple phone call, more or less, and by the time they wrapped up the investigation, Stark would be retired to Leavenworth for fifty years or so.

"I'll see what I can do," he told Chiang at last.

"Don't fail me, Jason. It would be a shame to see our partnership dissolved."

The line went dead, and Stark replaced the telephone receiver in its cradle, fighting down a sudden urge to run and wash his hands.

Regret was an emotion Stark had flushed out of his system years ago, around the time his marriage fell apart. He sometimes did things on and off the job that raised a momentary doubt about his sanity, but doubts were swiftly overcome by dollar signs. He had his eye on Ireland, someplace he could slip away to, simply disappear when it was time and forget about the Company and all the bullshit he'd waded through to earn himself some breathing room.

Chiang Baht was right, of course: Stark did have contacts in the city who were skilled at poking under rocks and finding out what lived there in the musty dark. He would have tried the restaurant for starters, but it would be crawling with police, and any questions off the record would be asked by Chiang Baht's men. They had a lock on Chinatown, and if the secret of Belasko's contact lay within the neighborhood, it would be hours at most before they dug it out.

And if it wasn't quite that simple, then perhaps Stark just might earn a bonus for himself.

He thought about his options and the way it could evolve from this point on. Chiang Baht was out to kill Belasko and his contacts, plain and simple. There had been no word about a capture and interrogation in the wake of the disaster at the restaurant. A simple hit, provided Baht could find his man and pull it off.

If Stark could find Belasko first, the bastard would be just as dead, but with a difference. Stark could claim the credit for himself next time he spoke to Baht and pick up any bonus the incense master thought was fair. Along the way, if it turned out that Mike Belasko *was* Mack Bolan, Stark would simultaneously mount a major trophy on his wall. No way for Langley to object when it was done, the subject dead and gone before Stark filed his report. If smoking Bolan pissed them off, it was their own damn fault for keeping field commanders in the dark.

So much for need-to-know.

He reached out for the telephone again and started putting wheels in motion, leaving them to mesh and grind until they chewed Belasko up and spit him out again.

The bastard might or might not be Mack Bolan, but there was one fact that he couldn't escape: within a few short hours—days, at most—he would be sorry that he ever brought his road show to Rangoon and crossed the path of Jason Stark.

"IT WILL NOT be an easy thing to leave Rangoon."

"I don't need easy," Bolan answered, "just results."

"How did the Triads know that we were meeting, would you say?"

The warrior shrugged. "I checked for tails before I reached the restaurant. And since I don't have any other contacts in the city..."

"You believe I have—what do you say?—a leak?"

"It's possible. You had some backup at the restaurant. Somebody else most likely knew where you were going, even if they didn't have a fix on why."

Ne Kyat was thinking fast. "Your phone at the hotel."

"Another possibility, except we didn't mention an address."

"If they were watching you this afternoon..."

"Or if the old man sold me out," Bolan said, watching Ne Kyat's face. "Too many 'ifs.'"

"You must forget about Yunnan."

"Not likely, after this."

"Because of this," his contact answered, sipping from his glass of Scotch, "the best that you can hope for is to leave the city with your life."

Their momentary hideout was a building Ne Kyat assured him was secure. At Bolan's stern insistence, there had been no phone calls to alert Ne Kyat's associates or let them know that he was safe. The only way to stop an unseen leak was to eliminate the flow of information at its source.

"Yunnan is still the reason why I'm here," Bolan said, waving off the proffered bottle. "If I turn back now—assuming that I could—it's all just been a waste."

"You would prefer to die?"

"I'm not dead yet. The Triads count on opposition caving in the first time they move in and flex some muscle. So far, what I've seen, I'm not impressed."

"They murdered Prem Bangsaen."

"I'm not forgetting that," he told Ne Kyat. "If you want out, just tell me now. I'll find myself another guide or make it on my own."

"Impossible."

"I guess we'll see."

Ne Kyat sat staring at him for another moment, mixed emotions mirrored on his face.

"The journey you suggest may take a week or more. Eight hundred miles by river to the Chinese border, and from there on foot to General Li's encampment in the mountains of Yunnan."

"You know the camp's location?"

"More or less. Beyond the border, nothing can be guaranteed with any certainty."

"I take it that you haven't been there?"

Ne Kyat shook his head. "As you can see, I'm still alive. The uninvited visitors do not return."

"First time for everything."

"Why are you committed to this plan?"

"The heroin produced by General Li is killing thousands every day."

"And has been for at least a dozen years. Why now? Why you?"

"The first part's easy," Bolan said. "I never heard the general's name before last week. Some news takes time to get around. I took the job because I saw a chance to make it work."

"You look for a crusade."

"Not quite," the Executioner replied. "Crusaders try to change the world. I've given up on that. I see a problem and I try to fix it if I can. That's all."

"And if you kill the general, then what? Do you think his army will dissolve and blow away like dust?"

"I'd be a fool if I believed that," Bolan replied. "I can't wipe out the poppy crop or help ten million addicts change their lives. I *can* disrupt the traffic for a while, take out some heavy players while I'm at it. If it gives the cops back home a breather, maybe keeps some shit from landing on the streets, that's good enough for me."

"And if you die in the attempt?"

"My problem."

"Shared by anyone who joins you on your trek."

"So let's forget about it. Point me toward a river pilot who can keep his mouth shut, and we'll wrap this up right now."

"Americans are so impetuous."

"I don't have any time to dick around. You're either coming or you're not. Make up your mind."

"How long did you know Prem Bangsaen?"

"A day or so."

"We met in jail," Ne Tin Kyat said. "Bangkok. The charges were not serious, and we were innocent, of course."

"I'm sure."

"He helped me then, and later. I will not presume to bore you with the details. Let us simply say that we were more than friends. He was my brother."

"I'm not asking you to help me out because the Triads killed him."

"No. It would be wrong of you to ask ... but I am offering. Tonight they tried to kill me, too. It is a double insult I may not ignore."

"They won't quit trying if we head out for Yunnan."

"Nor if I let you go alone," Ne Kyat responded. "By tomorrow or the next day, they will know that I was with you at the restaurant. My punishment will be the same no matter what I do."

"You could relocate."

"Burma is my home. It is not such an easy thing to start, as you would say, from scratch."

"I understand."

"Perhaps, but I do not require your understanding. Rather, I require your pledge."

"For what?"

"To make the Triads pay for Prem Bangsaen ... and for my death if it should come to that."

"I'll do my best."

"Equipment will be needed for the journey. Weapons."

"I already have some gear close by."

Ne Kyat dismissed the statement with an airy motion of his head. "I have reserves, black-market items meant for Shan guerrillas in the north."

"About that boat ..."

"I know a man. He hates the Triads."

"Bad enough to risk his life?"

"Some years ago they sold his sister into prostitution, where she died. He bides his time to seek revenge. I know of half a dozen Triad soldiers he has killed so far."

"Sounds good, if he's available."

"Leave that to me." Ne Kyat refilled his glass and took another sip of whiskey. His hands were steady now. "We cannot leave tonight. Too risky, with police and Triads searching for us everywhere. Plus I need time to organize supplies."

"How long?"

"Tomorrow night. Our enemies will still be searching Chinatown, and we must make the river journey after dark, in any case. There will be enemy patrols we must avoid."

"Tomorrow night, then," Bolan said. "And in the meantime?"

"In the meantime," Ne Tin Kyat replied, "we hide."

# CHAPTER FIFTEEN

"I understand."

The incense master of Rangoon sat stiffly in his chair and listened to his orders on the whispery long-distance line. It sounded like the airy voices of a hundred ghosts, but Chiang Fan Baht could not make out their words.

"Of course, Master. At once."

More orders, each delivered in the same familiar tone, so calm and reasonable in the face of crisis that it made Chiang wish he could pick up the telephone and hurl it through the nearest window.

It was easy to be calm about a crisis in Rangoon when you were sitting in Yunnan, surrounded by an army.

"Yes, Master. It shall be done, as you suggest."

He wouldn't let the anger or frustration surface in his tone, of course. The Elder Brother of the Yi Kwah Tao wasn't a man to trifle with, despite his years. Chiang Baht had seen the pitiful remains of those who set themselves against the will of Sun Jiang Lao, and he wasn't prepared to join their company.

Not while he had a madman running loose around Rangoon.

"Goodbye, Master."

He cradled the receiver with a great sense of relief, his mind already sorting through the various instructions from Yunnan. Sun Lao had ordered him to track down the wild man and capture him, if possible; as an alternative, his swift death would suffice. While taking care of that, Chiang was supposed to learn the name of the American's confederates throughout Rangoon and find out who they worked for. If there was a broader threat of war within the families or from an outside source, he was to brief Sun Lao without delay.

It didn't faze Sun Lao that seven of Chiang's men were dead, five shot and two more mangled by a train in what should otherwise have been the simple execution of a contract. The tall American who called himself Belasko had escaped, along with Ne Tin Kyat, and every effort to uncover him had so far failed.

He would be found, of course...but not because Sun Lao had ordered it from his seclusion in Yunnan. The round-eyed bastard had Chiang Baht to deal with now, and he would rue the day that he had ever set foot in Rangoon.

Chiang knew about the Bangkok massacre and Chou Fong's death, but he wasn't afraid. The Thai branch of the Yi Kwah Tao had long been fat and lazy, resting on its laurels as the source of heroin for dealers and their customers around the world. It was an article of faith that Chou Fong was invincible, a pipe dream of his ego that had now been proved false.

Chiang Baht didn't intend to make the same mistake.

His tenure as the Burmese incense master had been marked by nearly constant struggle with guerrillas of the left and right, hill bandits, independent smugglers, hijackers and renegades. The caravans of opium and heroin that wound their way through Burma seemed an easy mark for outlaws in the trade, and Chiang Baht had been forced to prove himself a hundred times in brushfire wars. The smaller independents scarcely rated mention; they were killed and cast off in the jungle at a rate of five or six per week.

Chou Fong had been too soft, his territory insulated from the harsh realities of fighting to protect the pipeline day by day. When trouble came, his troops were unprepared, and they had let him down.

Chiang Baht was ready now—but would it help?

The raid in Chinatown should logically have been a simple operation, in and out. The CIA, through Jason Stark, had tipped Chiang off to the American who'd traveled by himself from Bangkok, and a faithless friend of Ne Tin Kyat had tipped them to a scheduled meeting in the restaurant. It wasn't certain that Belasko was their man, but he'd come from Thailand, he was meeting with a mountain guide and it would do no harm to kill him just in case.

A simple thing, until it blew up in Chiang's face.

He had no doubts about Belasko now—the fact that he was armed and capable of killing seven men erased all doubt—but they'd lost him on Bogyoke Street, and he was nowhere to be found. Rangoon was barely half the size of Bangkok, population-wise, but it was possible for men to disappear within its bounds if they were so inclined. And there was still a chance Belasko and his guide had fled the city, heading . . . where?

If Chiang could figure out their goal, he would be waiting for them with a nice surprise to finish off their quest. But where would someone like Belasko go in Burma, after killing Chou Sin Fong and several dozen of his men in Bangkok?

It would be sheer insanity for one or two men to attack the caravans, assuming Ne Tin Kyat knew when and where they moved. If this Belasko tried recruiting soldiers in Rangoon or its environs, Chiang would know before the day was out, and he'd have a target he could deal with swiftly and effectively.

And if the caravans weren't Belasko's target—then what?

Why would an American assassin, fresh from victory in Bangkok, need a mountain guide in Burma? What could his plan be?

Chiang Baht was reaching for the telephone before he caught himself. Not yet. A false alarm would only make him look more foolish then he did already, with his soldiers dead and nothing in his hand to show for it. Alerting Sun Jiang Lao without hard evidence would hurt his case if it turned out that he was wrong.

But Chiang was certain in his own mind that he knew the answer now.

The American was heading toward Yunnan.

The raids in Bangkok and Australia had been warm-ups for the main event, in which he meant to find and kill Sun Lao.

At the moment the wild man's motives were irrelevant to Chiang Baht. Later, after he was dead, there would be time enough to figure out who paid his salary and pulled his strings. Swift retribution would be called for, but they had to stop the front man first.

Or... did they?

Chiang considered what would happen to the Yi Kwah Tao without its Elder Brother. Sun Lao would certainly be missed by some, but could the family survive? Would his connections cut and run without the old man they had dealt with for so many years?

And who would be selected to replace Sun, if and when he fell?

The post of Second Elder Brother had been vacant for the past six months, since Yuan Li Ma had died of cancer in a Hong Kong hospital. Sun Lao had stalled about selecting a replacement for his second in command, and now the empty post might work to Chiang Baht's benefit.

Who else was fit to take Sun's place if he should suddenly expire? Chou Fong was dead, and there could be no question of promotion for the half-breed, Lee, when he had just been driven from his territory in disgrace. Wo Ming, in Hong Kong, would be sixty-seven when his birthday rolled around in March, and he would have no territory left come 1997, when the Communists absorbed the colony.

Chiang Baht appeared to be the logical—in fact, the *only*—choice to take Sun's place, and he'd have to give some thought to this Belasko business, if discovering the hunter meant delaying his ascension to the throne.

Of course, it wouldn't do to leave a wild man on the loose if he was bent upon destruction of the Yi Kwah Tao at large. The family structure must survive, if Chiang was to preside over its coming glory days.

His guards were waiting when he left the office. Two men flanked him, two more were in front and a fifth gun brought up the rear. His pointmen checked the sidewalk east and west before he left the building. His car door was open, waiting for him. It was purest chance—or fate—that Chiang glanced up when he did and saw Death staring at him from a roof across the street.

He didn't recognize the weapon from a distance, but he saw its muzzle-flash. Recoiling with the instinct of a born street fighter, he ran into guards who formed a tight ring at his back. They wouldn't let him through, and there was no time to explain.

The limousine erupted into flame and hot shrapnel, and the shock wave scattered Chiang Baht and his assembled troops like broken toys. The incense master of Rangoon knew he was dying from the taste of blood inside his mouth and the numbness in his legs, and all he felt was anger.

Chiang marshaled all the strength he had for one last scream of rage before the darkness carried him away.

"CHIANG BAHT has stumbled over the American," Sun Jiang Lao said, "but it will take some time to run him down."

"If Chiang can manage it at all."

The open scorn expressed by Michael Lee produced a frown on Sun Lao's face. "It has not been so long since you were beaten by this man."

"A fluke, Master. He took me by surprise."

"And that was your mistake. Do you expect your enemies to cordially announce themselves before they strike?"

"No, Master."

The color in Lee's cheeks denoted anger and embarrassment, but Sun Jiang Lao cared nothing for the young man's feelings. Lee had managed to survive one critical mistake already; he couldn't expect to be so fortunate a second time unless he learned from that mistake and took steps to improve himself.

"At least," the Elder Brother of the Yi Kwah Tao announced, "we know where he is going now."

"We do?"

"Of course. Our enemy is coming here, to me."

Lee frowned. They had reviewed the possibility, of course, but it had all been hypothetical.

"How can you be so sure, Master?"

"If he were merely striking at our outposts, trying to disrupt the powder trade, he would have gone from Bangkok to Macao or Hong Kong. Rangoon has less importance than New York or Amsterdam...unless he seeks a gateway to Yunnan."

"We must alert the general."

"I will suggest the possibility," Sun Lao replied. "It would not do for us to raise alarms when there is still a chance that I may be mistaken."

"You are never wrong."

If Lee intended irony in the remark, it didn't show. Sun Lao allowed himself a narrow smile, remembering the virtue of humility.

"All men are capable of error," he replied. "If I appear less apt in that regard than some, it is because I take my time and analyze the movements of my enemies. A man who rushes into battle will inevitably find himself surprised, and thus defeated, by the very foe he underestimates."

"As I was," Lee replied, a trace of bitterness remaining in his voice.

"You followed the correct procedure," Sun declared, allowing Lee some vestige of his dignity, "but you were not confronted with an ordinary man. Our enemy has done this sort of thing before."

"You know him, then?"

"I do not know his name," the Elder Brother replied, "but I have seen his type before. A man committed to his mission past the point of no return. He may agree to fight for money, but the goal becomes its

own reward. The Japanese would call this man a sam-
urai.''

"And you, Master?"

"I call him dangerous."

"More reason to rely on General Li."

"If he should get this far. Chiang Baht has dealt with
such men in the past, and we have days before our enemy can reach Yunnan."

"He may be on his way right now."

"Perhaps," Sun said. "But Chiang has soldiers
watching for him all along the way. And we have other
friends, as well. This time there will be no surprise."

He saw no point in telling Lee about the CIA connection in Rangoon, but Sun Jiang Lao had hopes that
the Americans would prove adept at hunting down
their own. If not...

Eight hundred miles were between Yunnan and
Chiang Baht's bastion in Rangoon. Assuming that
their enemy escaped, he would most likely use the
Irrawaddy River as a highway to the north. The air
approach was too restricted, and a trek the length of
Burma could take weeks, assuming he wasn't picked
off by soldiers, bandits or guerrillas on the way.

If he was coming—Sun Lao felt sure that he was—
then it would have to be the Irrawaddy. Somewhere
south of Myitkyina, he would leave the river and begin the trek through rugged mountains, homing on
Yunnan. Before he reached the border, there were Kachin rebels to be dealt with, most of them involved in
cultivating opium and dealing with the Yi Kwah Tao.

It wouldn't hurt to spread the word among their villages, Sun thought. More eyes to scan the forest for his
enemy. More guns prepared to bring him down.

The border crossing into China would be no over-whelming obstacle. The People's Army theoretically patrolled the vast perimeter of the republic mile by mile, but if the truth were told, no army in the world was large enough for such a task. Yunnan was bounded on the south by "friendly" neighbors—Laos and Vietnam—which left the troops of General Li to con-centrate on Burma to the west. In practice they made periodic overflights in helicopters, launched patrols from time to time and scrutinized the Mekong River where it snaked along the Burmese and Laotian bor-ders to the south.

But mostly General Li's men were concerned with guarding opium consignments, shepherding the cara-vans and convoys on their way to make deliveries to refineries just across the border in the Burmese Shan preserves. Li's actual assignment from Beijing re-quired him to perform the tasks of a policeman in Yunnan, enforcing rules that ranged from prosecuting local peasant homicides to overseeing mandatory birth-control campaigns, but Li Zhao San was not a man to let himself be limited by his superiors, their lack of vi-sion.

Sun Jiang Lao couldn't be sure which officers and politicians in the Chinese capital were sharing in the bribes he paid to Li. In truth he didn't care as long as everything ran smoothly in Yunnan, the Yi Kwah Tao receiving what it paid for in the end.

Without Yunnan and the opium that peasants culti-vated under General Li's protection, Sun Lao's family would still be pimping teenage girls in Bangkok as a major source of income, watching while the other families grew fat and sleek on heroin. Sun's people still sold girls, and always would, but drugs were certainly the mainstay of the Triad's revenue.

He thought about the tall man he had never seen, perhaps already moving north to kill him—and for what?

To crush his family, perhaps, and interrupt the flow of heroin to the United States. It was a futile hope—Sun could have told him that—but there was no negotiation with a zealot. Men who honestly confessed their greed could come to terms, but a crusader closed his mind to reason, willing to forsake his life itself if called upon to do so. He wouldn't be stopped except in death.

And that was coming, soon.

Chiang Baht would have another opportunity to prove himself, assisted by the CIA, and if they failed a second time, there would be General Li. His troops were numerous, well-armed and trained for fighting in the jungle. They had defeated Shan invaders in the past, and bloodied prowling forces of the Koumintang who strayed outside the Golden Triangle in search of peasant villages to terrorize. One man, against such troops, would never stand a chance.

He felt Lee watching him, but took his time. The Elder Brother wasn't obliged to pamper his subordinates or hold their hands when they were frightened. It was Lee's job to defend the family, and not the other way around. Another week at most, and he'd have to send the young man back to prove himself in the Australian territory he had nearly lost.

He could almost feel the enemy, a hostile concentration focused on the sanctuary in Yunnan. Could he be certain where Sun Lao was hiding? Would he need more time to pinpoint General Li's encampment?

No.

This man had come prepared, from Sydney on through Bangkok and Rangoon. He knew where he was going, and he didn't intend to stop until he had accomplished everything that he set out to do.

Or died in the attempt.

If Sun Jiang Lao had anything to say about it, there would be no mystery about the outcome of their final confrontation. Only one man could emerge from such a clash, and Sun had spent his whole life learning to survive.

It was a trait that wouldn't fail him now.

FOR GENERAL LI ZHAO GAN, the worst part of his dealing with the Triads was that they were all civilians and lacked the rudiments of military discipline. He understood their oaths and code of honor, having been inducted to the 14K himself when he was just a boy, but they could never match the nerve and discipline of seasoned troops.

Li didn't care how many men the Triads killed in Hong Kong restaurants or in the teaming alleyways of Bangkok. It would never be the same as lining up for battle with the Kuomintang or the Vietnamese. Li's uncle was a major in the spearhead force that crossed the Yalu River to repulse American Marines from North Korea in the winter months of 1950, and the general kept a photograph that showed his uncle, all smiles, standing on a heap of Yankee dead.

Today, of course, the round-eyes were supposed to be great friends of the People's Republic…or they had been until recently. A show of force with snotty students in Beijing, and all the smiling words came down to nothing, as the general had warned his closest comrades from the start.

Beijing wasn't Li's problem now, and he wasn't concerned with the Americans per se. One of them troubled him, but he'd have to bide his time and see if there was anything he could do about the problem, if and when it came his way.

The Triads in Rangoon were catching hell, so he was told, and only one day after the storm had blown into Bangkok. Sun Jiang Lao didn't appear to be concerned, but you could never tell about the old man's inner thoughts and feelings. Sometimes General Li believed that Sun would rather die in agony than ask his best friend for an aspirin to relieve the pain.

Li had been thinking more and more about the prospect of a clean break with the Yi Kwah Tao, of making contact with a Western outlet on his own. He had facilities for reaching out to those who used his product, making the connections, even if he had to make a trip or two himself. His contacts in Beijing might not approve at first, but Li believed that he could sell them the idea if he applied himself and took the time.

How would the Yi Kwah Tao react in such a case?

Li smiled and pictured the reactions of assorted incense masters when their Elder Brother was severed like melon off the vine. One down already, if you counted Chou Sin Fong, and Michael Lee would be another easy target if and when the general made his move on Sun Jiang Lao. As for the rest, they would complain, let accusations fly, but who could they rely on to redress their grievance?

The police?

Perhaps, if they were truly furious, they might submit their case to Interpol.

The notion brought a smile to General Li, but it seemed out of character, more like a grimace of distaste. The Triads were a law unto themselves, but they weren't prepared to wage extended war against the People's Army. If and when they found the nerve, they'd be massacred, and General Li would find himself proclaimed a hero for suppressing desperate criminals.

It was a fanciful idea, but there were other means of gaining the desired result. Sun's enemy, for instance, might elude the Triad forces in Rangoon and travel north. Or, he might not elude Chiang Baht, and travel north in any case.

Appearances were everything in business, as in politics, and if the Yi Kwah Tao couldn't produce a corpse in Burma, who could say their enemy hadn't survived to reach Yunnan and execute Sun Lao? The fact that he was never seen or heard from in the world again would merely verify his great efficiency as an assassin.

It was perfect, Li thought, if only he could guarantee that there would be no body in Rangoon to cause embarrassment. A simple message should suffice, to put his Burmese agents on the job—and he would brief the White Flag rebels, too, in case they happened to encounter an American who needed help to find his way.

The fates were set to smile on General Li Zhao Gan, and all he had to do was wait for it to happen, either way. It made no difference in the end whose finger curled around the trigger... just as long as they took time to aim.

He thought about Sun Lao and knew he owed the old man nothing. If the Yi Kwah Tao hadn't approached him first, it would have been the Chiu Chou or the 14K, and he'd still be richer than a dedicated Communist could ever dream of being. One day soon, when he was rich enough to run, the general would be trying out his wings.

There was a whole wide world awaiting him beyond the rugged mountains of Yunnan, and Li had hopes of seeing more before old age crept up behind him like a thief and stole the final hours of his life away.

He'd become a gentleman of leisure with the riches he'd socked away. A member of the jet set, as it were, respected by great men and lusted after by their women. It was written in the stars.

But first he had to put the wheels in motion for a change that he considered overdue.

His time was coming. And all things come to those who wait.

# CHAPTER SIXTEEN

The boat was waiting at the dock when Ne Tin Kyat and Bolan arrived shortly after dark. The skipper was a slim Burmese named Mon, who wore a camouflage fatigue cap on his shaven head. A Browning automatic pistol protruded from underneath his shirttail, cocked and locked. He obviously knew Ne Kyat, and solemnly shook hands with Bolan after they were introduced.

Their baggage for the trip included Bolan's duffel bags and several that Ne Kyat had packed himself. The Executioner knew three of them were filled with weapons, ammunition and explosives, but he didn't feel inclined to ask about the fourth. It took them ten or fifteen minutes to get squared away before Mon cast off his mooring lines. The engines grumbled to life and laid down a murky wake as they got under way.

The boat was twenty feet from bow to stern and roughly eight across. Low-profile all the way, with claustrophobic space below decks if the passengers were disinclined to sit or sleep beneath an open sky. The engines were an asset, powerful enough to give them decent speed in an emergency, but Mon wasn't intent on showing off before they left the capital behind.

Reclining in the hold and safely out of sight while Ne Tin Kyat consulted Mon about their travel plans, the Executioner reflected on his busy afternoon. Ne Kyat had taken care of the arrangements, happy to accept a gift of cash from Bolan to defer expenses for the trip. He didn't say where he acquired the arms, and Bolan didn't ask, but they included M-16s, an M-40 grenade launcher, a Heckler & Koch MP-5 submachine gun and various explosives.

At the outset they'd planned to hide all day and make the necessary stop to pick up Bolan's cash and hardware after dark before they met the boat. Bolan changed his mind when he began to inventory Ne Kyat's hardware. He borrowed a car to make the trip downtown, the squat M-40 and a belt of high-explosive rounds in a shopping bag beside him in the passenger seat.

Ne Kyat had given him the office address in return for Bolan's promise to forget the mission if he missed his quarry there. Chiang Baht maintained tight security at home, and it was more important for the Executioner to reach Yunnan than to score a hit on one more Triad leader in Rangoon.

Still, if he had a shot at both . . .

It went down smoothly in the end. He was across the street at closing time, already primed and ready when the scouts emerged to check the street. It was a cursory examination, and it missed the tall man lying in wait.

Chiang Baht had emerged a moment later, moving toward the limousine behind a human shield, and Bolan ditched his shopping bag, the ''bloop gun'' heavy in his hands as he'd lined up the shot. A couple of the bodyguards were digging for their hardware when he'd fired, the HE round impacting dead on target, making Chiang's own car a lethal weapon as it blew up in the incense master's face.

Retreating from the hit had been simple, with the palace guard wounded, dead or stunned. He didn't know if Chiang Fan Baht was still alive, nor did he care. The gesture had been enough to let them know an ambush in a Chinese restaurant wasn't the end of anything.

By night the river was a different place, with less traffic than the daylight hours. Many of the small craft were docked and showed signs of occupancy once the sun went down. It was a common trait of Asian river towns that numbers of their people lived on boats or rafts, sometimes conducting business from the decks that ranged from sale of fruits and vegetables to prostitution.

Bolan saw no working whores as they departed Rangoon, but he wouldn't have been surprised to learn that they were being watched. The Yi Kwah Tao had sharp eyes everywhere, and they would be especially alert tonight, with what appeared to be a war in progress in the streets. Police patrols would be another risk until they cleared the capital, but Mon showed no concern for his illicit cargo, holding to a steady course and speed.

At their current rate of progress it would be three hours, give or take, before they reached the Irrawaddy River and began the journey north. From that point on they'd be facing somewhat different perils, but the price of failure would remain unchanged.

If they were jumped at any point along the way, the choice came down to fight or flight. Swift death was the alternative to victory.

It troubled Bolan, putting other lives besides his own at risk, but Mon and Ne Tin Kyat had axes of their own to grind. Ne Kyat was marked already—from the ambush in the restaurant—and Mon would be out hunting Triads even if he wasn't playing skipper on the long trip north. The hunger for revenge was powerful incentive, as the Executioner himself could testify, and both of his companions on the boat were volunteers.

But how many times had allies in his private war been sacrificed? The names and faces crowded in upon him any time he let his guard down, dating back to Bolan's first campaign against the California Mafia. Some of the friendly dead were lawmen. Some were predators who offered up their lives in the attempt to make a change. Some died without completely understanding how or why.

So many ghosts, and he could add the names of Prem Bangsaen and several aborigines within the past two weeks. The roster would grow until the Executioner himself lay down and died.

But not tonight. Not yet.

He had a mission to accomplish, and the end result was more important than his own life or the lives of his companions on the boat. He cherished no illusions of his own ability to win the worldwide war on drugs, but he could make the traffic more expensive for the savages who profited from human misery and death.

Within the next few days, if he survived, he'd be calling in some markers on the Yi Kwah Tao and General Li Zhao Gan. The strike, if carried off as planned, would teach his enemies that there could be no hiding place, no sanctuary from the judgment they had brought upon themselves. No river, mountain range or artificial boundary exempted them from punishment for their accumulated sins.

The Executioner had never viewed himself as a religious man, but he believed in retribution and a strict accounting for the choices people made from day to day. There might not be an afterlife—none of his absent friends or enemies had ever found a way to pass the word along—but the accounting could be found on earth, as well.

He didn't judge his enemies; they did that for themselves with every word and action as they looted nations and disrupted decent lives. The penalty, once handed down, could never be rescinded or revised.

Mack Bolan wouldn't be the judge or jury for his adversaries.

He would be their Executioner.

And when his own accounting rolled around, he was prepared to stand or fall upon the record of his choices, life-or-death decisions he had made along the way. It was the only way he knew to play the game and keep it clean.

Yunnan was waiting.

THEY SPENT THE FIRST DAY holed up in a reed-choked tributary of the Irrawaddy south of Prome. Well back from the main waterway, concealed by overhanging fronds and branches, they were free to watch the passing river traffic, dozing off in shifts and eating out of cans Mon heated on a compact butane stove.

The first night's passage had been uneventful, but the risk increased with every mile they traveled toward the Chinese border and their adversaries in Yunnan. Outside Rangoon, Ne Kyat didn't require the tall American to hide himself below the decks by night, but he was still alert to prying eyes on every darkened boat they passed.

Most of the river traffic after nightfall would be smugglers, some of them undoubtedly involved in the narcotics trade, but they weren't Ne Kyat's concern. The Triads rarely undertook such errands on their own, and by the time a scout reported any sighting to Rangoon, they'd have slipped away once more.

It was the armed patrols they had to watch for now, and most of them were mounted during daylight hours. The army and police disliked patrols at night, when they were twice as vulnerable to attack by rebel forces hidden on the riverbanks. The interdiction of narcotics traffic was a flexible priority in Burma, where security was paramount and the authorities were more concerned with politics than profitable crime.

Especially when the watchdogs had been paid to close their eyes.

Ne Kyat had drawn the second watch, from 10:00 a.m. to 2:00 p.m. He counted three patrol boats on the Irrawaddy, one of which passed by their hideout twice, first running north, then doubling back in the direction of Rangoon. The others, separated by approximately ninety minutes, traveled north at speed and didn't reappear.

Which meant that they were somewhere up ahead.

Above Myingyan the river's course divided, with the Irrawaddy bearing to the east and rolling on past Mandalay, near Bhamo, snaking closer to the Chinese border near the twenty-fifth parallel. The Chindwin formed the west arm of the Y, past Monywa, along the eastern border of Assam. There was an outside chance that one or both of the patrol boats would proceed that way.

By this time soldiers of the Yi Kwah Tao couldn't have failed to grill their contacts in Rangoon. A search would still be underway, of course, but it was logical that someone would suggest the river course as an escape route. There would be patrols in both directions, north and south, but Ne Tin Kyat didn't concern himself with wasted efforts in the Irrawaddy Delta.

When the danger came, it might be thrown across their path from ambush, or come bearing down upon them from behind. A combination of the two would probably be fatal, especially if the military was involved. Their river boats were armor plated, with machine guns mounted fore and aft to battle river pirates and guerrillas, even though the crews traditionally preferred inactive tours with nothing to report. Mon's boat was swift enough, but it couldn't stand up to concentrated armor-piercing fire for any length of time.

Evasion was the key, and it was fortunate that they'd found a decent hiding place their first day out. Mon knew the river well—the inlets used most commonly by smugglers—but they'd still need luck, as well as skill, to cover eight hundred miles without encountering their enemies.

Less now, Ne Kyat thought. One night of traveling was well behind them, and they hadn't been discovered yet.

How many nights to go?

A sound of movement on the deck behind him brought his head around, the muzzle of his automatic rifle following the movement easily. Belasko wore a set of camouflage fatigues, the sleeves rolled up above his elbows, with the Uzi submachine gun from his duffel slung across one shoulder, muzzle down. He crossed the open deck and sat beside Ne Kyat, back braced against the low-slung cabin's face.

"How's traffic?"

"Normal," The Burmese told him. "Three patrol boats. I expected more."

"You think the Triads will rely on the police and military?"

"Not exclusively, but it would be unwise to underestimate their contacts in Rangoon."

Bolan nodded, frowning. "Is there some way you can save your piece of this when it's all over?"

"I am not sure that I still have anything to save. By now the Yi Kwah Tao is certainly aware of my connection to their enemy. They may not know your name, but mine is readily available. It will be difficult—perhaps impossible—to coexist with enemies like these."

"I'm sorry," the warrior replied.

"The fault is not entirely yours. I chose my life, as any man must do. One of the choices was my friendship with a dead man."

He didn't refer to Prem Bangsaen by name. It wasn't necessary in the circumstances, and it would have indicated certain disrespect.

"You know another sacrifice won't bring him back."

"But, on the other hand, he may rest easier because he is avenged."

"We may not even get there."

"It is the thought that counts."

Bolan smiled. "If you want some rest, I'll take the watch from here. I'm slept out, anyway."

"It will be time for eating soon."

"More rice and pork?"

"What else?"

"We'll have to talk about that menu when we have some time."

"Another day, perhaps."

"Another day."

BY MIDNIGHT, they were north of Yenangyaung and running smoothly through the darkness, with a sliver of the waning moon to help Mon guide his boat. It seemed to Bolan that their pilot could have made the journey blind, but it was comforting to know that he was keeping both eyes open ... and his free hand near a loaded M-16.

The greatest risk of running dark would be collision with another craft, most likely smugglers, but they managed to avoid a pileup, logging one near-miss for two nights on the open water. Based upon his memories of Mekong Delta forays, Bolan thought that they were doing reasonably well.

Until they met the two patrol boats coming south.

They weren't military craft, as Ne Kyat had described, but something on the scale of fishing boats, their Chinese crewmen in civilian dress. If there was any doubt that they were Triads, the display of automatic weapons put it instantly to rest.

The enemy was running dark as they approached, but Mon had picked them out by moonlight, whispering a warning to his passengers before the floodlights blazed as bright as noon. By that time Bolan had his gear zipped up inside a duffel bag and he was in the water, drawing one last breath before he started swimming hard against the current, stroking on a hard collision course.

It was a gamble, but he had no other way to go. The Triads wouldn't open fire at once unless they recognized their enemy on sight. A search was called for, and without a tall American on board, Ne Kyat and Mon could probably explain the weapons with a hasty lie. It wouldn't have to keep the Triads guessing very long.

The underwater swim was risky. If Bolan lost his bearings in the darkness, came up short or missed the boat entirely, he'd have to surface in the open for a breath of air. The spotters might not see him—it was fifty-fifty, with the bulk of their attention focused on the boat—but he could ill afford time wasted on correction of his course and a new approach.

Each second counted now if he was going to prevent the slaughter of his allies and himself.

Mon had a fair idea of what he had in mind, from watching Bolan load his bag, but Ne Kyat would be playing it by ear. The Executioner could only hope his guide was still in fighting trim and thought as clearly in a river boat as in a Chinese restaurant.

His lungs were burning now, and he ignored the brush of something long and sinewy against his leg. An eel or water snake, perhaps, and neither one was any major threat to Bolan at the moment. His important enemies were somewhere overhead and drawing closer by the stroke.

His outstretched fingers brushed a solid surface, and he recognized the keel. A few more seconds, if his air could last that long.

He surfaced on the starboard side, beyond the floodlights. Reaching up, he grazed the railing with his fingertips, slid back and took another breath before he tried again. An unexpected sound would doom him.

The sound of angry voices asking questions reached his ears. Ne Kyat and Mon took turns answering, providing evasive comments that fell short of satisfying their inquisitors. While Bolan couldn't translate the exchange, he understood the different tones employed and knew the Triad soldiers would be running out of patience very soon.

He threw one leg across the starboard railing, set his duffel on the deck and dropped beside it in a crouch. The zipper sounded like machine-gun fire in Bolan's ears, but no one else on board the fishing craft appeared to notice.

Keeping both eyes on the enemy, he counted one man in the cockpit, three more on the deck, the latter group with weapons and a floodlight aimed in the direction of his comrades. Farther off, the second boat had pulled in close to Mon's, preparing for the search. Five men stood on that one, four of them with guns in view.

He had less time than he'd banked on. Working swiftly and by touch, he emptied out the dripping duffel bag.

The Uzi first. It might be damp, but it would function on command, as would the hand grenades that he'd brought along for ballast. It would be his call, unless the Triad hardmen started firing first within the next few seconds, and he knew that they were past the point of no return.

He circled toward the pilothouse, the Uzi in his left hand and an eight-inch Ka-bar fighting knife in his right. The Triad skipper missed him somehow, concentrating on the show at center stage. The first he knew of Bolan's presence on the boat was when the knife's blade sliced through his windpipe, releasing plumes of crimson.

The dying river pilot fell toward Bolan, one hand snagging on the wheel before it slipped away and out of reach. The boat swung hard to port, with force enough to pitch the floodlight off its target, lancing toward the velvet sky.

On deck the gunners shouted angrily and turned toward the wheelhouse to discover what was going on. They saw a man-sized shadow rising from the cockpit and might have recognized a glinting weapon, then the choppy muzzle-flash removed all doubt. A stream of parabellum manglers swept them from left to right and back again.

The first thug took a tight burst in the chest and vaulted backward, across the rail and into the water. The next in line was swinging up his automatic rifle when the bullets found him, spinning him around and teaching him a jerky little dance before they dropped him on the deck.

Number three was blinded by the swinging floodlight for an instant, hearing shots before he realized that he was now a target. Bolan's stream of automatic fire came in around chest level, putting out the light and riddling its keeper in a single move. The dead man slumped across the nearby rail and hung there like a seasick traveler intent on giving up his last meal to the waves.

As soon as Bolan started firing, gunshots had erupted from the other boats, as well. Mon found his M-16 and played a stream of fire across the second gunboat's deck, one Triad gunner screaming as he fell facedown and wallowed in a pool of blood. The others were retreating, blasting at the smaller craft, and Ne Kyat opened up to pin them down while Mon began negotiating a retreat.

The distance wasn't great in concrete terms, but Bolan had to take the rolling deck into account before he made his pitch. The first grenade was more or less on target, but it struck the cabin's roof and bounced away, exploding on the far side of the Triad craft before it touched the water.

Number two was better, rolling on the deck and going off with smoky thunder near the cabin, windows shattering under the fierce concussion of the blast. He saw a couple of bodies airborne, splashing down along the starboard side, while Ne Kyat kept on firing at the gunboat from a distance with his M-16.

The Triad skipper had his engines in reverse now, trying for a back-away and turn, but Bolan couldn't let him go. In any clash like this, the only victory was death for one's opponents, sparing none who would be able to report your whereabouts and call in reinforcements.

So be it.

Number three was an incendiary, and he dropped it in the cockpit, narrowing his eyes against the thermite glare when it exploded. Bolan saw the human torch flung topside, screaming through a futile bid to quell the hungry flames with slapping hands. A leap across the rail, and even that was useless, since thermite burned underwater just as well as in fresh air.

With any luck at all, the man would drown before the white-hot coals ate though his flesh and out the other side.

The second Triad boat was going down as a sole survivor dashed for the rail but stopped short, exploding in a hail of 5.56 mm tumblers from the M-16s.

The stench of burning flesh in Bolan's nostrils brought back memories of other jungle nights, when he was still a young man learning what the everlasting war was all about. He shrugged the images away and waited on the gunboat's deck while Mon came back to pick him up.

"It would be wise to sink the other boat, as well," Ne Tin Kyat stated.

"I guess."

They used C-4, a strip the size of Bolan's index finger laid along the waterline and detonated with a simple timer. By the time it blew, they were a quarter mile upstream and running fast against the current, making up lost time.

The damage to their own craft had been minimal, a few stray bullet holes, a scratch on Ne Hyat's thigh, and Bolan knew they'd been lucky.

This time.

He wouldn't lay any odds against the next.

# CHAPTER SEVENTEEN

Beyond the river it was a different game, familiar in a different way from Bolan's time in Vietnam. The Asian jungle felt like home, though years had passed since Bolan had walked those narrow, snake-infested trails and laid in wait for human targets.

And yet each jungle is its own. The Burmese highlands weren't Vietnam; a subtly different climate nurtured varieties of plants and wildlife than were found eight hundred miles to the southeast along the lower Mekong. It was slightly cooler here than he remembered from the months in Nam, despite humidity that hovered in the ninety-five percentile range year-round. There was less swampy ground and tangled undergrowth than would be normally expected in the lowlands, but the cobras were as deadly here as anyplace on earth.

And being hunted helped to make it feel the same.

Somewhere behind them the enemy would still be searching for their tracks. The numbers were impossible to guess, but even if they never found the trail, it mattered little, for the major opposition waited up ahead, directly in the warrior's chosen path.

Mon had delivered them to a secluded landing point some sixty miles below Myitkyina, offering to join them for the mountain trek if they required an extra gun. Their solitary clash with Triad hardmen along the Irrawaddy hadn't satisfied Mon's appetite for ven-

geance by any means, but Bolan and Ne Kyat released
him with their thanks and the remainder of the liberated cash in Bolan's duffel bag.

They'd been lucky, Bolan realized, to live through
five nights on the river and encounter only one patrol.
On two occasions military boats had come within an
easy pistol shot of finding them by daylight. Both times
luck or circumstance had saved them, with the searchers moving on before they scored. Each time the Executioner had asked himself what he would do if they
were faced with death or capture at the hands of Burmese regulars.

If it was Fate that spared him from a choice, then
Bolan owed a debt of gratitude to unseen forces in the
universe. If it was pure, dumb luck...well, that was
fine, as well.

Ne Kyat wasn't a native of the Burmese mountains,
but his years of trading contraband and information
with the north had given him a native's knowledge of
the countryside. He knew the rivers, trails and villages—including which were likely to be hostile or in-
dentured to the Triads through their yearly trade in
opium. He obviously couldn't guarantee safe passage
through the mountains to Yunnan, much less beyond
the Chinese border, but without his help the Executioner might not have come this far.

Together they divided up the gear as best they could:
an M-16 for each, with extra magazines in bandoliers;
Bolan packing the M-40 and grenades, while Ne Kyat
carried the Heckler & Koch with its spare clips of 9 mm
parabellum hollowpoints. The Uzi and some hand
grenades were left with Mon for his protection on the
trip back to Rangoon, replaced by food and water for

a week, provided Bolan and Kyat ate sparingly along the way.

With less exposure in the forest, they traveled during the daylight hours, long hours spent on winding trails and fording mountain streams. A break for rest and lunch near noon still gave them close to sixteen hours travel time.

When they had a chance to talk along the way, Ne Kyat regaled him with the history of Burma's land and people, dating from the British-Burmese war in 1885, through palace massacres and military coups, to the endemic civil strife of modern times. He seemed to understand and sympathize with every faction in the strife that had consumed three decades of his nation's recent history, admitting no definable perspective of his own.

They were in Kachin territory at the moment, well above a "secret" base where outcast soldiers of the Chinese Kuomintang supervised the flow of Burmese opium into neighboring Thailand. The Kachin Independent Army—or KIA—had been waging war against the Rangoon government for thirty years, and close affiliations with the Burmese Communist Party had been documented since 1968. As a result, the Red Chinese delivered arms to Kachin allies for a price, which the insurgents raised by cultivating opium and selling off their crop to Triad brokers farther south.

The mountain strip along the border with Yunnan was Burma's leading source of opium, bar none. Avoiding hostile villagers or independent outlaw bands required finesse, and Ne Tin Kyat was constantly alert to any sign of recent passage on the jungle trails they utilized.

From time to time Ne Kyat would take off on his own to speak with villagers he knew from prior excursions in the area. On those occasions he'd take a pistol with him, leaving his other gear with Bolan in a place they had selected for defensibility. When he returned with current information on the movements of endemic bandits or the KIA, they would continue on their way, sometimes correcting to avoid collision with a hostile column somewhere up ahead.

He trusted Ne Tin Kyat, because the Burmese guide had everything to lose and nothing visible to gain by helping Bolan with his quest. Whatever profit Ne Kyat made from their excursion—if he even managed to survive—it would be logged in terms of private satisfaction at a job well done, a debt of friendship paid in blood.

The mountain forests felt like home, but Bolan never lost sight of the fact that most men die within a mile or two of home, from illness, accident or violence in the family. Statistics weren't necessarily a comfort on the battlefield.

But home lies where the heart is, and the Executioner's heart had been invested in his private war.

Despite the noted author's claim, you *can* go home again.

But you might not like what you see when you arrive.

IT WOULD HAVE BEEN a sweet relief, thought Sun Jiang Lao, to hear some good news for a change. If nothing else, it would provide an old man with the seeds of hope.

But so far all the news that he received from outside sources had been bad.

Chiang Baht was murdered in Rangoon, for starters, and there seemed to be no doubt the crime was carried out by the American who called himself Belasko. It was shocking that an incense master of the Triads could be executed in the middle of a city like Rangoon, worse yet that his assailant had the power to simply disappear like smoke once he'd done the evil deed.

If there was any doubt concerning the American's objective, it had been removed by more bad news, collected from patrols along the Irrawaddy River. Two boats and nine good men had disappeared on night patrol, mere hours before Chiang Baht was laid to rest.

Two men, at last, were moving toward Yunnan, and they'd managed to elude police, the military and the Yi Kwah Tao these past five nights. It was discouraging, to say the least, but Sun Jiang Lao had learned to live with disappointment in his lifetime.

Success was relative, in any case. A military officer who counted on winning every battle often found that he'd lost the war by failing to consider larger issues, greater issues than the petty movements of a few platoons. Grand strategy required broad vision, and the Elder Brother of the Yi Kwah Tao had confidence in his ability to look beyond the moment, planning for the future on a scale his enemies could never realize.

Five days would bring Belasko and his guide to a position for the launching of their long trek overland. They couldn't reach Yunnan by water, and the Triad chieftain's spotters were alert to any sign of aircraft in the area.

How long would it take for them to make their way across the mountains, if they weren't physically opposed by rebels, villagers or bandits on the way? It was impossible to guess with any certainty, but Sun Lao estimated that a week or ten days ought to put Belasko within striking distance of the general's camp.

They had a week, then, during which to find two strangers in a territory of some twenty thousand square miles, most of it mountainous, covered with forest.

No easy task, but neither was it totally impossible. The worst scenario—with Ne Kyat and Belasko slipping through to reach the camp—would scarcely be a victory for Sun Lao's enemies. If the American and his pet jackal got that far, they'd be hunted down and ruthlessly exterminated by the general's troops.

The ultimate result wasn't in doubt, but it would still look bad for Sun Jiang Lao if he couldn't eliminate two men with all the guns at his command. Some might suggest that he was past his prime, incapable of standing fast against the family's opposition short of seeking help from General Li Zhao Gan.

But who would challenge him?

With Chou Sin Fong and Chiang Fan Baht effectively removed, his leadership in Hong Kong riddled with dissension and the younger Michael Lee discredited, it seemed unlikely that a challenge would originate within the Yi Kwah Tao itself. The other Triad families were a different matter, each propelled by greed that matched Sun's own, commanded by men who were sharks in human form, capable of smelling blood—or human weakness—miles away.

They wouldn't hesitate to move against Sun Lao if he appeared to be dysfunctional as leader of the Yi Kwah Tao. Regardless of their Triad oaths commanding brotherhood and loyalty, survival of the fittest was the only rule they recognized outside of their respective clans. If any other Triad chief believed his troops could overrun the Yi Kwah Tao, Sun's days were numbered.

Sipping whiskey from a tall, thin glass, Sun Lao considered his options and decided there was nothing he could do about his problem, personally, at the moment. He couldn't have helped the hunters run his enemies to earth; if anything the presence of an old man in their midst would only hamper things and slow them down.

But he could supervise the manhunt from a distance, skillfully applying pressure when and where he thought it necessary, nudging those who seemed to drag their feet, reminding them of what they stood to lose in the event of a disaster for the Yi Kwah Tao.

And what of General Li Zhao Gan?

Although a member of a Triad in his youth, the general wasn't a loyal adherent at the present time. His first consideration was supposed to be the ruling party in Beijing, but Sun Lao recognized an opportunist when he saw one. The officer assigned to rule Yunnan had all the signs. Of course, he had approved the basic sale of opium with his superiors, who shared the profits in direct and striking contradiction of the Communist ideals, but General Li was also prone to making judgments on his own, without consulting any higher-ups.

In time, Sun thought, the general would be ready to forsake his uniform and relatively Spartan life-style for the creature comforts of the outside world. Already Li evinced dissatisfaction with the people's government, its vacillation toward the West and back again, to hard-line orthodoxy in the face of civil strife. He was a soldier who had long ago run out of decent wars to fight, and he was clearly sick to death of watching over peasants in the hinterlands, policing idle thoughts, invading hovels to insure that proper means of birth control were used, as ordered by the government.

If there had only been a serious external threat, Li could have felt that there was still some purpose to his life in uniform. But as it was, his ego and the ticking clock inside his head demanded action to preserve his own identity and self-respect.

How long before the general bolted? Sun Jiang Lao had monitored Li's bank accounts. In another year, perhaps, the general would be able to support himself in style for the remainder of his days.

The key was making friends and keeping them, in spite of General Li Zhao Gan and his self-serving schemes. It might be necessary, somewhere down the road for Sun to sacrifice the general, leak his plans to private contacts in Beijing and let the chips fall where they would. All things considered, it would be far easier for Sun's political associates to frame the general on some unrelated charge and put him up against a wall than to explain their own involvement in the drug trade to a revolutionary people's hearing in the capital.

Sun kept his options open, knowing that a premature attack on General Li would be disastrous for them both. The Triad master's most immediate concern lay with the enemies who were approaching now, intent on grinding him to dust beneath their heels. It was an egoistic pipe dream, granted, but the tall American's success so far produced a chill of apprehension that reminded Sun Jiang Lao of fear.

It had been decades since the Elder Brother of the Yi Kwah Tao had experienced real fear, and he didn't appreciate the new reminder of exactly how it felt. His enemies would have to pay for the discomfort they had caused, and Sun Lao's only true regret was that he probably wouldn't be present when they died.

It would have been a treat to squeeze the trigger himself.

MIDAFTERNOON, their second day of hiking through the mountains, Ne Tin Kyat announced that they were closing on the border of Yunnan. There would be nothing in the way of signs or boundary markers, no established checkpoints on the borderline, but compass headings and familiar landmarks told the guide that they were nearly there.

Beyond that invisible line their danger would increase, if only for the presence of the People's Revolutionary Army. Chinese regulars were more efficient in their duties than the rebel bands that staked out part of northern Burma as their private game preserves, committed to the preservation of their country's borders from incursion by the outside world.

It wouldn't mean patrols through the area—no nation had an army large enough for that—but Bolan couldn't rule out aircraft, even infrared devices tuned to seek out body heat, which hadn't been a problem on the first leg of their trek.

They were within a half mile of the Chinese border, give or take, when they encountered trouble and it almost went to hell.

Ne Kyat was leading, as he had since they began their long walk from the Irrawaddy, following a narrow game trail that resembled every other they'd seen so far. Some thirty yards ahead the trail appeared to widen slightly, and the gap was closing when a solitary figure stepped into the middle of the trail.

Behind him two more bodies partially obscured by shadow closed ranks. All were armed.

"Kachin," the guide told Bolan in a whisper, stopping short.

Bolan unslung the M-16, flicking off the safety with his thumb. There was a live round in the firing chamber, primed to rock and roll.

The leader of the trio spoke in a language Bolan didn't recognize, but Ne Kyat responded fluently. There was a cold smile on the stranger's face that didn't touch his eyes, and Bolan knew his words were a formality before the strike.

More to the point, a conversation covered sounds of movement in the forest to their left and right, more bodies shifting into place.

"We're not alone," he told Ne Kyat, remembering to keep his voice pitched low.

"I hear them."

"Left or right?"

"The right, I think."

A few more words were exchanged, the Kachin rebel leader sounding anxious now, as if he might be running out of patience with the dialogue. Some threats would follow, if the script ran true to form, and then a blast of gunfire from the trees to finish it before the looting could begin.

Ne Kyat was smooth—you had to give him that. Still talking as he made his move, he was all smiles as he swung up the M-16 from his hip and fired a burst that blew the rebel mouthpiece backward, startling the men behind him, who hesitated for a crucial second and a half.

Too long.

Ne Kyat took out one of them, already dodging for the cover on his right and Bolan hit the other with a burst that knocked him over backward into the middle of the narrow trail.

Hostile fire erupted immediately from the trees on both sides, a swarm of bullets drilling through the empty space where Bolan and Ne Kyat had been standing heartbeats earlier. The fact that both of them survived the opening barrage was a resounding tribute to their speed, agility and nerve.

The worst part of a jungle ambush, Bolan knew, was that your enemies had time to plot their fields of fire, while you were forced to scramble for your life and try to sort out the action by echoes, muzzle-flashes or the evidence of falling twigs and leaves. He estimated four guns on the left side of the trail, another three or four on Ne Kyat's side, but he could easily be off by one or two.

And any error in the next few minutes would be fatal.

Wriggling on his stomach under ferns and creepers, Bolan put some space between the open game trail and himself. His enemies were firing blindly at the moment, hoping for a lucky hit, and he had no intention of obliging them.

The nearest gunner had an AK-47, recognizable by its distinctive sound. As Bolan circled wide around his mark, the sounds of gunfire helped to cover his advance, eliminating any need for extraordinary caution that would slow him down.

Approaching on the shooter's flank, a gliding shadow in the forest, Bolan drew his 93-R and thumbed back the hammer. At twenty feet he had the sniper spotted, but he moved in closer, wanting no mistakes.

Ten feet, a range that qualified as point-blank for the finely tuned Beretta, and he knew he had his man.

The head shot struck his target behind one ear like a hammer blow and slammed him forward onto his face. If any of the rebel's comrades noticed that his gun had fallen silent, they were too caught up in blasting at the enemy to give it any thought.

The high-pitched stutter of an M-16 had joined the other sounds of combat as Ne Kyat weighed in with everything he had. It might not be enough, but there was nothing that the Executioner could do to help him at the moment, when he had his own hands full.

He came on the second gunner in much the same way as he'd taken number one, a silenced parabellum round from ambush and the job was done. He left the body where it fell and closed with numbers three and four.

The last two were positioned close together, crouched behind a fallen log. Instead of using up the time that it would take to flank them, Bolan laid his M-16 aside and raised the 40 mm launcher to his shoulder, making an adjustment to the sights for range and elevation, aiming through a gap between two trees.

The high-explosive impact round went in on target, the concussion rocking Bolan where he crouched some twenty yards away. A dying scream, the sound of shrapnel smacking tree trunks, and then ringing stillness fell across the jungle trail.

The sound of the explosion heralded a whole new ballgame for the rebels who were still alive. One AK-47 and a lightweight submachine gun were against Ne Kyat and his efficient M-16. The guide had dealt with one or two already, from appearances, but there could still be more troops up the trail, already closing on the sounds of battle.

No time to waste, then, as he crossed the trail behind his enemies and came in from the flank. Somewhere in front of them, the M-16 was laying down short bursts of fire, attracting swift responses that appeared to have no great effect.

He reached the gunners as they made a desperation move, both charging out of cover, rushing toward the spot where Ne Kyat had himself entrenched. They weren't expecting Bolan on their flank, and that mistake cost them both their lives.

The two Kachin were up and running when he shot them, stitching left to right as Ne Kyat responded with a long burst from the front that kept them on their feet a moment longer, twitching in a macabre dance of death. Their lifeless bodies hit the ground together, the forest echoing gunfire for a moment.

He was prepared for anything at this point, but the Executioner picked up no indications of a fresh assault. The rebel squad had done its level best and died in the attempt, no backup close enough to give them any help.

"I'm coming out," Ne Kyat told Bolan, calling from a pocket in the trees.

"All clear."

"How many did you kill?"

"I counted four, besides the one you left me on the trail."

"A small patrol. We must not linger here."

The warrior reloaded as he spoke. "I'm ready anytime."

"Then let's go."

# CHAPTER EIGHTEEN

Relaxing in the shade of his veranda, General Li Zhao Gan reflected on the grief that traveled on the heels of most entanglements with other human beings. Friendship, love and business were the same in that respect: all led inevitably to a parting of the ways, and there was always pain involved, regardless of the cause.

Li's wife had left him years earlier, complaining that the People's Army was his mistress, one with whom she couldn't actively compete. It was the truth in some respects, but General Li had missed her all the same. The other members of his family were long dead—more pain—and he'd seen friends die in combat on the Russian border when he was a younger man.

These days Li had no friends of any consequence, but there were still acquaintances, associates in business, and they were about to bring him grief, as well.

It never crossed the general's mind to think of Sun Jiang Lao as any kind of friend. Their common bond was opium, together with a grudging mutual respect, but even that would never cross the line to friendship. It would have startled General Li to learn that Sun had any friends, although the members of his family and other Triad clans professed to view him with the utmost "brotherly respect."

Sun Lao wasn't a figure to inspire affection, nor was he an easy man to trust. In all their business dealings, General Li had watched him closely, sometimes using agents of the people's revolution in Rangoon and Bangkok to make certain that his cash and merchandise didn't go far astray. Thus far, the operation had been relatively smooth—some minor inconvenience from the law on rare occasions, but the odd loss was anticipated in a business of this sort.

The new threat posed by Sun Jiang Lao was something else, however, and it couldn't be ignored.

According to his scouts, eleven Kachin rebels had been killed the day before, while trespassing across the border in Yunnan. Unfortunately they'd hadn't been slain by soldiers under General Li's command, nor even by the villagers who cultivated opium throughout the border range. In fact, their killers were unknown, but military weapons had been used—including some explosives—in what seemed to be a brief pitched battle on a nameless jungle trail.

Li sipped his glass of wine and thought about his options, trying to explain the massacre. The Kachins were pro-Communist, at least in theory, and they might have clashed with right-wing rebels in a running fight that carried them across the unmarked border to Yunnan. Of course, the rebels would have helped themselves to weapons, ammunition and supplies before they left the dead to rot, a circumstance not noted by his scouts.

No caravans were moving at the moment, which eliminated the possibility of bungled hijacking attempts. Besides which, General Li would certainly have been informed at once of any move to steal the opium that he protected in Yunnan. If the Kachins had tried to pressure local villagers for money or supplies, he likewise would have been advised and called upon to mete out fitting punishment.

The solitary option that remained wasn't attractive, but he had to face the facts. The enemies of Sun Jiang Lao had reached Yunnan against all odds, and they were drawing closer by the moment.

It was the worst scenario, but he could still contain the damage if he moved in time to head them off. Beijing wouldn't concern itself with an incursion if the news got lost somewhere along the way. And if Sun Lao was right in his contention that the enemy consisted solely of a two- or three-man team, their trespass hardly constituted an invasion of the motherland.

Once they were safely dead and buried, it would be as if they had never lived, much less set foot on Chinese soil.

Eliminating the intruders, though, was only one of General Li's concerns. He'd begun to view Sun Lao as an increasing liability, and the general was becoming more and more attached to the idea of moving heroin himself, without the Triad's help. It would be simple to dispatch an emissary from Macao or Hong Kong to negotiate firsthand with dealers in America. The general had been watching Sun Lao long enough to know how it was done.

He saw it now, unfolding like a play before his eyes. An "accident" would take care of Sun Jiang Lao and Michael Lee, blame falling on the tall American and his companions from Rangoon. Once they, in turn, were dead, there would be no one to dispute Li's version of events. The Yi Kwah Tao might doubt his word, but they were helpless to oppose him in Yunnan.

He almost wished the strangers luck, aware that they'd need much more to last the final fifty miles. Li's troops were on alert, together with civilian scouts and peasants who derived their daily bread—or rice—from trading opium.

Yet the mountains hid their share of secrets, even from the leader of an occupying army. General Li lost men from time to time, and never learned if they were cowardly deserters, food for jungle predators or victims of some ambush that was skillfully concealed. Some villagers among the Yunnanese still loathed the Beijing government and prayed for a return to power of the right-wing Kuomintang. In many ways the frontier province that he occupied was still a riddle to the general after all this time.

He watched Sun Lao emerging from his quarters on the far side of the compound, trailed by Michael Lee. The younger man was hanging on his master's every word, as if the wisdom of the ages might emerge between Sun's lips at any moment. Lee did everything but run ahead and sweep his Elder Brother's path to clear the dust away.

Observing them, Li wondered how much of the young man's visible respect for Sun was real, and how much was a sham to keep the Triad master happy. Lee had suffered a traumatic loss of face when he was driven from Australia by his enemies, and Sun Jiang Lao would be within his rights as leader of the Triad clan to name another incense master in Lee's place. Avoiding the demotion would require diplomacy, and Michael Lee was clearly doing everything he could to save himself.

It was unfortunate, Li thought, that all the young man's efforts were to be in vain. By catering instinctively to Sun Jiang Lao, Lee had unwittingly cast his lot with the losing side.

No matter what became of the American and his companions from Rangoon within the next few days, Sun's days were numbered. And when his time ran out, there would be no point whatsoever in preserving Michael Lee.

The general felt his pulse quicken slightly, as it always did when he anticipated action. Soon he'd have a chance to test his men—and himself—against an unknown enemy. More exercise than test, perhaps, but Li would take what he could get.

And afterward, when he was done with the intruders, he'd burn his bridges with the Yi Kwah Tao.

A brand-new day was coming, bright and warm. The general closed his eyes and saw himself reclining on a beach, waves creaming on the sand, an adoring woman at his side. Perhaps she was Caucasian, though it scarcely made a difference to his fantasy. The world was filled with infinite varieties of women—colors, shapes and sizes—eager for the company of one who had the wealth and instinct to command.

Li scanned the dream beach left and right in search of a familiar face, and was relieved when none appeared. He would feel more at home with strangers, after all.

Above all else, no trace of Sun Jiang Lao.

It was an omen, Li decided. He was looking at the future through a window in his mind, and he appreciated what he saw.

The trick, he realized, was making dreams come true.

THE WORLD WAS CLOSING IN on Jason Stark, and it was little consolation that he represented the United States. Whenever there were crises in the past, he'd drawn comfort from his diplomatic status—he was listed as a cultural attaché at the embassy—and rested easy in the knowledge that the combination of his CIA connection and his business dealings with the Yi Kwah Tao would keep him safe.

Today he'd begun to think all bets were off.

The death of Chiang Fan Baht had shocked Rangoon. While bought-and-paid-for journalists bemoaned the heartless murder of a great philanthropist and businessman, Burmese authorities were waiting for the other shoe to drop. They still believed there was a gang war in the making, and for Stark's sake he couldn't afford to disillusion them. The news of Chiang's assassination by a lone American—if that, in fact, was what had happened—would have raised more questions than it answered, none of which Stark felt the inclination to resolve.

He was exposed now, working the trapeze alone and without a safety net. His ranking contact with the Triads had been liquidated, and to Stark that meant a great deal more than interruption of his supplemental monthly paycheck. He relied upon the Yi Kwah Tao for hard Intelligence about the Communists, guerrilla movements in the north and countless lesser items that a native source could turn up so much easier than any round-eye from the West.

Without that contact, he'd have to start from scratch, rebuild his information network with a brand-new cast of players. It would be expensive, time-consuming, and the obvious delay in information bound for Langley could be most embarrassing.

More questions, right. And Stark knew he couldn't avoid them all.

He wondered if it might be time for him to simply disappear. It would require a day or two to stage his death effectively, but Stark knew how to pull it off. If all the proper clues were found, there wouldn't be a search, and he had money stashed away to see him through the first few months. A year or two, perhaps, if he was frugal.

The various alternatives were grim. It wouldn't bother Langley to discover he was dealing with the Triads—"patriotic" gangsters had been helping out the Company since World War II—but if it came down to an audit, an examination of his numbered bank accounts, Stark's ass was grass.

The local Yi Kwah Tao was shaken, scrambling to recover from the blow that had stripped it of its leader, but it might be possible for Stark to take advantage of the chaos, open new lines of communication with the family while the members were picking up the pieces.

Chiang Fan Baht had known there were advantages to working with the CIA, and his lieutenants—those who survived—should have a working knowledge of the incense master's deal with Jason Stark. If he could do a favor for them now, perhaps they would repay his generosity in kind.

But what had Stark to offer at the moment?

What, indeed.

The smile felt out of place, but he enjoyed it all the same. The answer, when it struck him, was simplicity itself.

He could provide the Triads with the name of Chiang's assassin to facilitate their hunt. Mack Bolan was the sacrificial offering and Stark's salvation, all rolled up in one.

It served the bastard right.

So what if Bolan's family had been murdered by a bunch of stateside mobsters years ago? He had reportedly avenged their deaths a thousand times or more, from coast to coast. The goddamn lunatic was out of line, invading Burma and upsetting all the progress Stark had made through years of work, negotiation, compromise.

The tough part would be knowing whom to tell and how much information he should share.

There wasn't that much to begin with, nothing in the way of photographs or current whereabouts, though Stark could guess the latter just by following the trail of bodies from Rangoon. He heard things through the covert grapevine, even with his main connection broken down. There had been fighting on the Irrawaddy some days earlier, and the latest rumor spoke of an encounter to the north along the Chinese border. Kachin rebels up that way had failed to stop the Bolan juggernaut.

So far.

The madman's days were numbered, any way you sliced it, once he tried his luck against the Chinese regulars. If Stark was going to cash in on what he knew, there was no time to waste. His information would be useless once Mack Bolan was dead.

But where to start?

He skipped the Rolodex file and turned directly to his private address book. The entries were in code, a system he had worked out on his own.

Stark didn't plan on calling from his office at the embassy. The lines weren't routinely tapped, as far as he could tell, but he wasn't about to take the chance. A public telephone would do just fine, and he made certain that he had a pocketful of coins before he locked the office door behind him, moving briskly toward the stairs and out past uniformed Marines.

He could have drawn a driver from the pool, but that was one more witness Stark could do without. The fewer people who were privy to his errand, the better he'd feel.

Stark drove to the shopping district near the Shwe Dagon pagoda, where he paid to park his car and started walking, stopping twice from force of habit, glancing back along the sidewalk long enough to satisfy himself that he hadn't acquired a tail.

The crowds were out in force, more Burmese faces on the street than tourists, bartering for clothing, jewelry, handicrafts, utensils for the home. Stark moved among them in his lightweight suit, a stranger, feeling somewhat lost and out of place.

It never failed to irk him, after all the time that he'd spent in Burma, that he never quite fit in. His pale skin and his Occidental features made him stand out in the crowd, an alien imagining that natives watched him from the corners of their eyes in passing, instantly suspicious of the white man in their midst.

An argument erupted on the street in front of him. Two Chinese youths were shoving, shouting angrily at each other, while a third stepped in to mediate. Stark hesitated, veering left to give them room, and froze when one of the belligerents glanced furtively in his direction, blinking once.

He smelled the trap, and suddenly his mind was racing, looking for an exit. Never mind why the Chinese would have him marked or how they'd tracked him there without Stark noticing. There would be time to sort the details later, after he was safely back inside the embassy.

He swung around to make a swift retreat and met the blade that was intended for his kidney, slicing in and up beneath the rib cage, penetrating vital organs with a pain of perfect, crystal clarity. The round face of Stark's killer hovered inches from his own, and Stark could smell the garlic pork the man had had for lunch.

A final twist, the blade withdrawn, and he was falling, groping blindly to support himself. He caught the near edge of a market stall and hung there for a moment, finally surrendering to gravity as several dozen of the curious surrounded him. Stark scanned their out-of-focus faces, noting that the four Chinese were gone.

A setup, and it had to mean that someone in the Triads had erroneously linked him to the hit on Chiang Fan Baht. A little payback, and it wouldn't cost the Yi Kwah Tao a moment's sleep when they found out that they were wrong.

Tough.

AT LUNCH with General Li that afternoon, they got the latest news. A group of rebels had been ambushed in the forest—or had tried to ambush someone else—but the result was just the same. Eleven dead, and General Li appeared convinced that the American, Belasko, was responsible.

Sun Lao didn't dispute the general's claim, nor did he seem upset by Li's prediction that their nemesis was drawing closer day by day. To Michael Lee, the reason for his master's peace of mind was plainly obvious.

Sun Lao had never seen the tall American at work.

So far the Elder Brother of the Yi Kwah Tao had listened to reports, including Lee's, and tried to regulate the action from afar. He hadn't dodged the bullets, listened to the screams of dying men or smelled their burning flesh.

How long, in fact, had it been since Sun Jiang Lao had stepped outside of his protective shell and moved among his brothers in the real world, living day to day?

The Elder Brother of the Yi Kwah Tao was insulated from reality by many levels of subordinates—the incense masters, red poles, all the rest who carried out his bidding far and wide. As long as there were telephones and messengers, he never had to leave the house he lived in...or, in Sun Lao's case, the camp where he had come to rest with General Li as one more strong line of defense.

"How long until they reach us?" Michael Lee inquired, half startled by the sound of his own voice.

"Assuming that they do," the general answered, "time is difficult to estimate. They may encounter other difficulties on the way. My own patrols have recently been doubled in the territory they must cross, and there are other obstacles."

"None great enough to slow them down, so far."

"Are we discussing failure, Mr. Lee? Perhaps you could enlighten us, with reference to your own example in Australia."

Lee could feel the angry color rising in his cheeks, but he restrained himself from lashing out. Humility was best for these occasions.

"You are correct, sir. I was unprepared for the attack and failed to stop this man—Belasko, is it?—when I had the opportunity. It now appears that others, though forewarned and with a larger force of troops behind them, fared no better in the same regard."

The general's smile remained in place.

"We are about to change all that," Li said, pausing to sip his wine. "With all respect to your blood brothers in the Yi Kwah Tao, they do not have the training or equipment of the People's Revolutionary Army. Two or three intruders from Rangoon—or from America—are no more than a minor inconvenience in Yunnan."

"You have not seen their handiwork."

At last the words were out. Lee sat back in his chair, relieved, aware of Sun Lao's disapproving gaze.

"Perhaps I still may have the chance."

"And what news of the merchandise?" Sun Lao inquired, distracting them before the civilized discussion could degenerate.

"We have collected thirty tons of opium," the Chinese officer replied, "approximately half of what we should expect within the next four weeks. Tomorrow or the next day, the refineries shall go to work."

"It will be easier, I think," Sun Lao explained, "transporting heroin instead of opium or morphine base."

"More profit on the other end, as well," General Lee stated.

"A valuable consideration in itself."

"As for your own refineries, in Burma..."

"At the very least, their service will be interrupted while I search for someone to replace Chiang Baht. By that time we may find it much more economical to go on as we are."

"And will the members of your clan in Burma not feel cheated, Master Sun?"

"They follow orders, General Li."

"Good soldiers, then."

"Perhaps the best outside your own command."

It came to Michael Lee at once what they were doing, cutting back the Burmese operation to a shadow of its former self, reduced to transportation chores between Yunnan and Bangkok. It would mean a whopping loss of revenue, but Sun Jiang Lao didn't appear concerned about complaints. With Chiang Baht gone...

Incredible!

Could it be possible?

Lee thought about the recent violence in Rangoon, all blamed on the American. There had been no reason to suspect that he *wasn't* involved, but even if he was... who pulled the strings and paid his bills along the way?

Sun Lao, perhaps?

It felt like paranoia running wild, but hadn't the American's attack in Bangkok cleared the way for what was happening before Lee's very eyes? A relegation of the Burmese family to scaled-down status as a band of couriers and river pirates.

If he looked deep enough, Lee thought he might discover Sun Lao's twisted, egocentric logic in the Bangkok massacre. It made no sense initially, but he'd learned enough to realize that Sun Lao often viewed the world in ways apart from those of other men.

And if he could have used the tall American in Bangkok, what about Australia?

Why?

Lee felt his grip on rationality escaping, and he let the anger bring him back to earth. If he was being targeted by either of the two men at this table, he wouldn't go down without a fight.

Disgraced and dispossessed, he might surprise them yet.

He might surprise them all.

# CHAPTER NINETEEN

To Bolan's eye, the mountains of Yunnan were indistinguishable from the wooded slopes of northern Burma. There was no sudden change in flora, climate or topography to indicate that they'd crossed the border between a "free" republic and a Communist dictatorship, no warning crack of thunder from the cloudless sky. Except for the direction of the sun as it traversed the crystal blue from east to west, they might well have been trudging in a giant circle, going nowhere fast.

Ne Kyat was certain of his bearings, all the same. As he explained to Bolan, he'd made the Yunnan crossing twice before to meet with private businessmen who dealt in ancient Chinese artifacts. It was a story Bolan could accept or spurn as he saw fit, and he decided that it made no difference either way... as long as Ne Kyat knew where they were going, and he got them there on time.

The numbers had begun to worry Bolan. He had no certain schedule for the strike inside Yunnan, but every day's delay allowed his enemies more time to strengthen their defenses, even flee the area if they were frightened off. He hoped that Sun Jiang Lao would feel secure enough to stand his ground, but you could never tell where human nature was concerned.

And what of the elusive Michael Lee? He hadn't surfaced in the raids on Bangkok or Rangoon, but that didn't mean he was hiding in Yunnan. Lee could as easily have run to Hong Kong, Singapore, the Philippines or any of a thousand other hiding places he'd laid out in advance against the prospect of emergencies. By now he might have made his way back to Australia, lying low and waiting for the heat to dissipate before he started to rebuild what he'd lost in Bolan's blitz.

No matter.

Lee was small-fry in comparison with General Li Zhao Gan and Sun Jiang Lao. If necessary, Bolan could retrace his steps to the Australian continent another time and finish what he'd started with the dealer. Odds and ends could wait until he finished off the main play of the game.

And he was getting there. The soldier felt it in his gut.

The end was coming, one way or another, and he never doubted for a moment that the trip was worth his time and effort. If his brief campaign had slowed the Triads down a little, wiped out any portion of the China white earmarked for addicts in Australia or the States, he'd have done his job.

The hard part now was getting out alive.

Ironically it was another Asian jungle that had helped a younger Bolan come to terms with death the first time, in a rather different war against the savages. He'd been taking orders from the U.S. Army then, and modifying some of them when he could find a better, quicker way to do the job at hand. But the experience of watching friends and enemies cut down on every side had been instructive to a young man, teaching him the vital lesson of his own mortality.

Before his first full week in Vietnam was out, he'd realized that death could come for anyone at any time.

Preparedness was something that you lived with day to day, instead of waiting for a doctor in some plush, oak-paneled office to inform you that your time was drawing near. When you were living on the edge, one slip away from darkness and the void, you learned to make each heartbeat count. You did a job with the materials at hand the best you could, and gave no quarter to the enemy.

Some men of Bolan's age, confronted with their own mortality in Vietnam or other wars, had panicked, turned their backs and run away. Some others found the prospect of annihilation so exhilarating that they let it all hang out, gave in to every brutal, violent fantasy their shell-shocked minds could vomit forth. And somewhere in between the cowards and the homicidal maniacs stood Bolan and the countless others like himself, who recognized their duty and pursued it with the utmost zeal.

It was a different ball game in Yunnan, of course, but *every* game was different from the last. You had to take the long view, scoping out the broader similarities, to understand that Bolan's war transcended politics, religion, even what society defines as crime from one year to the next.

His war was based on good and evil, recognizing that the two extremes of human conduct were immutable and unaffected by the changing times. He didn't punish violations of the printed law, but rather violations of the human spirit, savages who trampled on the rights and basic dignity reserved for every man.

The Executioner didn't concern himself with legislative acts or constitutional amendments when he set out to attack narcotics traffickers. He had no interest in politics or the religious views of terrorists who slaughtered random targets in an airport, shopping mall or restaurant. The psychiatric diagnosis of a rapist-killer who dismembered teenage girls was Greek to Bolan, and he was content to let it stay that way.

Some men—and women—in the modern world were cunning, brutal savages who preyed on others for the profit, pleasure or prestige that they derived from victimizing others. They were evil any way you sliced it, all the arguments from civil libertarians and psychoanalysts aside. It might be true that some of them were products of bizarre, abusive homes or victims of peculiar mental quirks that drove them to commit sadistic crimes.

So what?

The simple fact remained that while such predators survived, no woman, man or child on earth was truly safe. When psychiatric hospitals and penal systems failed to stem the tide of violence threatening to swamp a civilized society, there could be only one response.

Extermination of the savages.

No single man could reach them all, but he could do the best with what he had. And if the effort cost his life... well, any worthwhile effort had a price attached.

Ahead of Bolan, Ne Tin Kyat was crouching in the middle of the game trail, checking tracks or other signs of recent human passage. Afternoon was slipping into evening now, with shadows falling long and dark among the trees. Below them, in the valleys, it would be full dark within an hour, and they'd need a place to spend the night.

"There is a village two miles ahead," the guide informed him. "We can rest there for the night."

"You think that's wise?"

"Some residents of Yunnan Province do not cultivate the poppy or salute the 'People's' flag," Ne Kyat replied. "I have friends here, but I must speak to them alone before you join us."

Bolan felt a momentary ripple of suspicion, but he buried it and nodded to his guide.

"Do what you have to do."

"When we are closer to the village, I will find a place for you to wait. The introductions should not take much time."

"Let's do it."

Moving east along the narrow, winding trail, their shadows stretched in front of them like giants scouting out the hostile ground.

CAPTAIN YUAN LIN CHOU was playing cards with three of his lieutenants when the order came from General Li. The captain was to organize his troops for yet another jungle sweep, beginning at the crack of dawn. They would be ferried out by helicopter and deposited a two-day march from camp, returning on their own and capturing or killing any strangers they encountered on the way.

So much for resting up between patrols.

It was a job that one of Chou's lieutenants could have done as easily, but General Li was testing him, or so the captain thought. Yuan Chou had heard the stories of an enemy in transit from the Burmese mountains to Yunnan—a lone American, some said, perhaps accompanied by a guide or two—but he couldn't make out the urgency of sending out patrols in force.

Assuming the American was CIA—and what else could he be?—there were no military secrets in Yunnan that justified the effort of a four- or five-day hike across the mountains. Everyone of any consequence in Burma, Laos and Thailand knew where General Li Zhao Gan was stationed, his assignment in the district and a rough approximation of the occupying army's strength. The Laotian Communists were friendly, more or less, while leaders of the Thai and Burmese governments were neither strong enough nor fool enough to risk their lives with any kind of thrust across the border into China.

In the old days, prior to Nixon, it would certainly have been a propaganda coup to catch a U.S. spy on Chinese soil. More recently, as international relations warmed between Beijing and Washington, embarrassment was something both sides struggled to avoid.

And yet the rift that had developed after 1989, with the Tiananmen disaster, set the stage for a resumption of the Cold War in the East. If the Americans were found to have an agent in Yunnan, he could be taken prisoner and used against the White House when the time was ripe.

The captain frowned and shook his head, still unconvinced. The CIA dreamed up some harebrained schemes from time to time, but it was smart enough to cultivate its foreign spies among the native dissidents and traitors of a country it desired to penetrate. It made no sense for any white man, fluent in Chinese or not, to risk his life in territory where his face and skin were all the evidence a firing squad would ever need.

Assuming that the American existed, then, and ruling out the CIA or other Western agencies, what could his mission be?

A grimace crossed the captain's face. The obvious conclusion left a rancid taste inside his mouth, and the vehemence of his reaction told him that he was probably correct.

It had to be the old man, Sun Jiang Lao, or his companion, Michael Lee. Yuan Chou knew who and what they were, and he despised them for it, much as he had come to look on General Li Zhao with thinly veiled contempt.

Yuan Chou had joined the People's Revolutionary Army in his teens because he thought his country needed smart young men to guard its borders and defend the strides in government and cultural development that had been made since 1949. He was a true believer in the Communist ideal, but he was also wise enough to understand the way things worked in politics and daily military life.

There might be ways of speaking out against the general and reporting Li's involvement with the Triads, but Yuan Chou had reasoned through the situation, realizing Li Zhao Gan wouldn't have risked such compromises in the first place if his actions hadn't been approved by someone in Beijing. The network of corruption might be relatively small, but Yuan Chou couldn't risk delivering his evidence to one of Li's accomplices.

A wise man knew when it was best to keep his mouth shut and his eyes wide open, gathering the ammunition he might need to help himself another day.

Preparing for the dawn patrol was busy work. He had to supervise his soldiers stripping weapons, loading extra magazines and priming hand grenades, collecting two days' worth of rations and the other field gear they'd need. The captain listened to complaints and shrugged them off, responding that the order wasn't his, and any man who disagreed could take his case directly to the general for review.

That shut them up and sent them scurrying about their final chores, as he'd known it would.

The general might be lax in revolutionary zeal, corrupted by his contact with the Triad running dogs of Western decadence, but he was legendary for his discipline. Deserters from the Yunnan regiment were hunted down and shot on sight on command of General Li. Some three months previously, two of Chou's young corporals had been charged with raping a civilian woman in a nearby village, leaving her alive because they were convinced their uniforms assured them of immunity. The afternoon Li personally shot them both in front of his assembled troops, the violated woman and her family were brought to camp and given front-row seats.

When Yuan Chou went to bed late that night, he found that sleep eluded him. He wasn't frightened of the dawn patrol, but he experienced a certain apprehension based on his own suspicion that he wasn't being fully briefed by his superior.

How many men had the American enlisted for his raids in Bangkok and Rangoon? Could it be true that only one or two accompanied him on his penetration of Yunnan? A smaller group would stand a better chance of passing unobserved through hostile territory, but evidence suggested that this small team had recently destroyed a hostile force four or five times its size.

The captain would be taking thirty soldiers with him on his jungle sweep, but would it be enough? His men were young, well-trained, experienced at tracking bandits in the hills, but they'd never clashed with hard-core opposition up to now. A skirmish here and there, with peasant thieves or hijackers, wouldn't prepare them for a pitched engagement with determined mercenaries.

The good news was that they'd probably spend two days in the mountains, scouting trails, inspecting caves, and never see their enemies at all. A waste of time, but it would put the general's mind at ease, and if they managed to destroy their enemies, so much the better.

It would mean prestige for Captain Yuan Lin Chou, perhaps promotion if the general was suitably impressed. He'd been elevated to the captain's rank three years ago, and he wouldn't object to moving up the ladder of command.

He liked the sound of "major" in conjunction with his name. It had a certain ring that generated feelings of respect and pride.

One more inducement, then, to do his job with more enthusiasm than he felt initially. Impressing General Li was all he had to think about. With his promotion there might come a transfer to some other post, where he could serve the People's Revolutionary Army with distinction, casting off the link between Yunnan, the Yi Kwah Tao and opium.

At last, near midnight, Yuan Chou fell asleep. All night he chased a hulking, faceless enemy through brooding shadows in his dark, disturbing dreams.

THE MOUNTAIN VILLAGE was small, with fewer than two dozen huts collected in a forest clearing and set back from the nearest trail by fifty yards. The occupants regarded Bolan silently as Ne Kyat led him in and made the introductions.

"These people are not Communists," his guide had offered on the short hike back from Bolan's hiding place. "They still remember the Americans as allies from the last world war, against the Japanese. Most of them have lost friends or family members in the government 'reeducation' camps. They live this way because it is the farthest they can travel from Beijing and still remain on their native soil."

"You trust them all?"

"I place my life in their hands, along with yours."

The Executioner accepted his sincerity and hoped his judgment wasn't flawed.

"Who do they think I am?"

"An enemy of General Li Zhao Gan. It is enough."

Bolan noted that a number of the villagers were armed with rifles dating back to World War II, along with several newer weapons. Since the very act of keeping weapons was a serious offense, he knew the villagers must either have permission from the local commandant, or else they simply didn't give a damn. The latter explanation seemed more likely, granting Ne Kyat's personal interpretation of their politics, but Bolan kept his own arms handy, just in case.

A cook fire had been kindled in the center of the village, underneath a blackened pot of something that resembled stew. At Ne Kyat's urging, Bolan joined him in a group of what appeared to be the village leaders seated on the ground. The best part of an hour passed while Ne Kyat fielded questions from the elders, now and then soliciting innocuous remarks from Bolan that he paraphrased before translating into Mandarin.

The mountain village was his temporary haven in a hostile world, no more, no less. The warrior wasn't in the market for recruits, scouts, bodyguards or spies. A hot meal underneath his belt and some place he could sleep the night away were more than he had counted on between the Irrawaddy and their final date with General Li Zhao Gan.

The general's name was mentioned several times in passing, members of the tribe apparently describing airborne searches as they gestured with their hands to indicate a plane or helicopter skimming treetops. Ne Kyan told him that patrols had been stepped up the past few days, but members of the tribe weren't afraid. If necessary, they'd relocate their village for the fifth time in the past two years.

"Why don't they leave?" Bolan asked, knowing in his heart what Ne Kyat's answer had to be.

"Because they are Chinese."

"It's over forty years," Bolan said. "Most of them weren't even born when Mao moved in. They can't believe the government's about to fall."

"You think of time in Western terms," Ne Kyat replied. "Your homeland is a child among the nations of the world, two-hundred-some years old. The Chinese trace their ancestry back seven thousand years. What do a few short generations mean to people such as these?"

"But they resist."

"They are not rebels in the common sense. The weapons you observe are kept for hunting food and self-protection, mainly from the bandits who are plentiful throughout Yunnan. The drug trade lures all the worst men here, as in the Golden Triangle."

"And if the general's troops stop by?"

"They will be warned by scouts and the guns will disappear. If one or two are found, they pay a fine in rice or someone goes to jail. It is the way things are for now."

"I hope they don't imagine anything I do in the next few days will change the way they live."

"I have explained your mission, more or less," Ne Kyat replied. "They hate the drug trade, even though participation in the traffic could provide security for all their families."

"There could be repercussions if the general traces us back here."

"I tell them you are one man who cannot be forced to talk. As for myself..."

Ne Kyat put on a smile and spread his hands to indicate that he was trusted here.

"Okay."

A couple of the older men around the fire cracked smiles at that, repeating Bolan's final word.

"Okay."

The stew was served in wooden bowls, with Bolan and Ne Kyat receiving theirs before the other men. The women formed a separate group, as if for privacy, when everyone was served. When Bolan tried the stew, he was surprised to find it flavorful—indeed, quite spicy—and more pleasing to the palate than it looked.

At length Ne Kyat began another animated conversation with the village men, responding to their questions with elaborate answers. The warrior was content to sit and watch—it would have been too much to say that he was listening—while Ne Kyat played the role of raconteur. From time to time he picked out names, specifically the general's and Sun Jiang Lao's, which let him know the general direction of their talk.

Without an active role to play in the discussion, Bolan let his mind drift free, imagining the life these peasants had with small thatched huts and tiny garden plots they carved out of the forest, moving on the average of twice a year to keep one step ahead of General Li's patrols. They could have knuckled under, mouthed the party line and cultivated opium for sale to Sun Lao's family, but they refused to profit from the auction of their dignity.

How many others like them were there in Yunnan? In all of China? Were they even conscious of the changing tides in Eastern Europe, Africa, the Middle East? How insulated were these people from the world at large?

How well in tune with life was any man?

He thought about the scattered souls of the Arunta tribe, so different in their rituals and level of development that they would seem like cavemen even to the humble Yunnanese. And yet the widely separated tribes had more in common than was readily apparent on the surface.

Both were clinging to a way of life that had been left behind by changing times. Both had been victimized, in somewhat different ways, by agents of the same common conspiracy—a clique of men whose lust for wealth and power was bottomless, whose callous disregard for life and human rights was legendary.

It was said that politics created strange bedfellows, and the same could easily be said of greed. When diehard Communists and right-wing Triads came together in pursuit of narco dollars, it could only be described as an unholy marriage made in hell.

The Executioner might not be able to arrange for a divorce, but he could raise a little hell himself before they rang the curtain down.

And he was looking forward to the opportunity.

## CHAPTER TWENTY

The villagers were up before the crack of dawn, and Bolan with them. Ne Tin Kyat dissuaded him from helping with the cook fire, as it would have been an insult to their hosts. He counted heads and noted two men missing, posted east and west along the nearby trail to serve as guards.

Their breakfast was a bowl of rice, dried fruit and stringy meat that Bolan didn't recognize by sight or taste. He swallowed it, along with the desire to ask, and found it good enough to have a second helping for the trail.

Ne Kyat was in no hurry to depart, discussing something with the village leaders, nodding now and then toward Bolan as he spoke. The Yunnanese were nodding slowly, thoughtfully, and it wasn't entirely clear if they agreed with what Ne Kyat was saying or if they were merely urging him along.

The women had collected between two huts, and watched the men with evident concern. Whatever Ne Kyat was saying, it had struck a nerve, and they appeared concerned.

The morning sun was barely visible above the treetops, far from burning off the ground mist, when the conversation started losing steam. Ne Kyat was making grateful noises, bowing to his hosts, and some of them were bowing in return. One of the women ventured forward, passed the guide a lumpy leather pouch and hastily retreated to her place.

"Some extra food," Ne Kyat explained, tucking the pouch inside his belt as he rejoined the Executioner. "All ready now."

"You took awhile to say goodbye."

"I wanted to confirm directions to the general's camp. We did not get around to it last night. Also, there was the question of patrols."

"Learn something new?"

"In fact—"

Before he could impart the information, they were both distracted by a throbbing, chopping sound that Bolan recognized as helicopter rotors. There were three or four birds by the sound of it, and they were swiftly drawing closer to the clearing where the village stood.

The Yunnanese retreated toward the tree line in a body, one young woman hanging back to kick dirt on the cook fire, smothering its flame. They couldn't hide in the huts, but with some luck the overhanging trees and early-morning shadows might conspire to camouflage the clearing at a glance.

It all depended on the searchers, whether they were hunting earnestly or merely passing through.

Concealed by ferns and undergrowth, with Ne Kyat crouching at his side, the Executioner couldn't obtain a clear view of the choppers passing overhead. They didn't hesitate or hover, which was good, but neither were they running at the limit of their flying speed. A spotter could have seen the village, made a note and sent the helicopters west to find a better landing zone.

"We must go now," the guide informed him. "There is no more time."

"The others?"

"They have dealt with General Li's patrols before. Once they conceal their weapons, they should be all right."

It was a toss-up whether to stand or run, but Bolan knew his presence in the village was a danger to the people who had sheltered him the previous night. They had experience in dealing with the local occupying troops, and they'd cover any evidence of strangers in the village once he cleared the scene and gave them half a chance.

"All right, let's go."

A couple of the Yunnanese were visible, and Bolan and Ne Kyat struck off in the direction of the trail. One raised his hand, and Bolan answered with a wave, aware that he'd never see the man again or have a chance to thank him for his help.

It felt like running, and he swallowed the emotion, knowing that withdrawal from a pointless fight was part of solid strategy. An army that engaged the enemy each time he showed his face was soon exhausted, at the very least. The rule applied in spades to any one- or two-man unit operating deep in hostile territory, where they lived by stealth or not at all.

THE FLIGHT FROM CAMP had taken better than an hour, leaving Captain Yuan Lin Chou with stiff legs as he disembarked from the lead helicopter, waving his men toward the trees so that one ship could take off from the jungle clearing and another could disgorge its human cargo.

Landing zones were hard to come by in the mountains of Yunnan, but they'd found one. Five or six miles due east, there was a peasant village they'd sighted from the air. It wasn't much, but it would serve the hunters as a starting point, and at the moment it was all they had.

The pilots had their orders. One more helicopter settled in the clearing and unloaded swiftly, giving Captain Chou a force of twenty men. The third ship would be doubling back a few miles beyond the village, searching for another landing zone in which to drop the last ten soldiers. That force would proceed due west and meet Chou's spearhead, closing off the main escape route as they came.

The captain had no reason to suspect his targets would be sheltered in the village, but his troops were primed for action, and the peasants were not part of General Li's established network in the western fringe of the province. It was possible that they had noted strangers passing by without reporting them, and Yuan Lin Chou couldn't afford to leave potential enemies unquestioned when he made his sweep.

The trail that served the village was a narrow, winding track, worn smooth by animals and human feet through years of travel. Chou sent two scouts ahead to feel out any opposition on the trail, then led the other eighteen troopers in their wake. His men had taped their gear to keep canteens, grenades and extra magazines from rattling along the way, and Chou didn't remind them to refrain from talking on the trail. It was unnecessary in the circumstances, with his briefing on the mission fresh in mind.

He'd informed his men that they were searching for guerrillas, known to be responsible for killing several dozen persons in the past two weeks. It may have been a small exaggeration, and he didn't tell them that the bulk of victims had been killed in Bangkok and Rangoon. The captain knew his men were bored with spot patrols and aimless jungle sweeps along the border of Yunnan, arresting independent smugglers from time to time, more often wasting days and nights that could be better spent in camp, perhaps with whores imported from Simao.

If he kept his men on edge, they'd be more alert, less anxious to forget their training and embarrass Chou with some ridiculous mistake. A warm-up in the peasant village would be good for morning exercise . . . and better still if they uncovered any useful information in the process.

Chou didn't believe that they'd find the men that they were looking for, but he was bound to try. His orders from the general were explicit, and they left no room for argument. Whatever happened, they were looking at a two-day mountain trek, and it would be a smoother journey if his troops were actively involved, instead of merely going through the motions.

The trail was steep in places, but they found it relatively clear. In less than forty minutes, they'd reached the village, where his scouts had driven in a sentry and corralled the others in a group, surrounded by their small thatched huts. The captain counted seventeen in all, and hoped that he wouldn't be forced to question each and every one.

Their leader first.

Chou asked the question twice before an older man stepped forward to acknowledge his position as the chief, of sorts. The others showed blank faces, nothing in the way of deference or respect, and Chou couldn't be certain if the man was who he claimed to be.

No matter.

He had volunteered, and he would do.

Preliminary questions started the process, drawing vague denials from the chief. There were no strangers in or near his village. He hadn't encountered any unknown persons in the forest for at least a month. His people wanted only to be left alone.

The last response, at least, was probably the truth. Yuan Chou was counting on it as he drew his automatic pistol, flicking off its safety with his thumb.

He didn't aim the gun at first. Its very presence in his hand was threat enough, his soldiers standing with their rifles at the ready. Captain Chou enjoyed the surge of power that he felt, with every villager immobile, silent, staring at his face.

He had their full attention, and they weren't smirking at him now.

"I ask again, old man." His voice was soft and low, not quite respectful. "Where are the strangers that you sheltered here?"

One of the women caught her breath, and the old man flicked eyes like flint in her direction, just enough to silence her. It was the first time Yuan Lin Chou had reason to believe his enemies had passed this way.

"I have not seen the men you seek," the village chief replied.

If one man knew, they all knew. Yuan Chou felt a surge of anger mingled with excitement as he thumbed the automatic's hammer back.

"As you prefer."

He swept the pistol up and fired in one smooth motion, smiling as the bullet struck his human target just above one eye. The old man toppled backward, blood and flecks of mangled tissue spattering the nearest of his followers. A fragment of the mutilated bullet struck a young man in the cheek and dropped him to his knees.

The captain felt his soldiers watching, trembling on the edge of an explosion. They had tasted blood, but he wouldn't unleash them yet. He still had information to collect before he passed his final judgment on the band of traitors they had found.

"You next."

He pointed with the pistol to another man of middle years. One of the soldiers grabbed his chosen subject by the sleeve and dragged him closer, two short paces from the captain.

Chou's sudden anger at the villagers had nothing to do with their avoidance of the trade in opium which he himself despised. It had still less to do with any plot they might have joined to overthrow the rule of General Li.

These peasants had betrayed the People's Revolution, helping foreigners to leave their filthy tracks on Chinese soil. If left unpunished, they would spread the virulent contagion of their counterrevolutionary attitude throughout Yunnan, like plague germs passed from one infected victim to the next.

Chou had discovered a malignancy, and he would root it out...but first the information he required.

"The strangers," he repeated in a level, easy voice. "When were they here?"

The man glanced down at his fallen leader, frowned and shook his head.

A heart shot this time, the sudden impact lifting Yuan Chou's target off his feet before he fell and lay unmoving on the ground. One of the women gasped; another two or three were weeping softly, standing with their eyes closed, offering their prayers to nonexistent gods.

The captain chose another gray-haired candidate, and soldiers ran the short man forward into striking range.

"Which way did the intruders go?"

The man didn't answer him for several seconds, waiting until the automatic pistol had been leveled at his face. At last, reluctantly, he pointed east, in the direction of the trail . . . and, ultimately, toward the general's camp.

Behind him someone cursed, the fierce words terminated with a whimper and the impact of a rifle butt.

"How long?"

"Perhaps an hour."

"Sir."

"Perhaps an hour, *sir*."

"How many?"

"Two," the old man said, remembering the "sir" a heartbeat later. Anger and humiliation drained the color from his withered cheeks.

"You have done well," the captain said, all smiles.

And shot him in the face.

Yuan Lin Chou retreated several paces, turning to his men. He raised his voice so all of them could hear him, even with the women sobbing as they were.

"These peasants have betrayed their country and the People's Revolution," he declared. "The penalty for treason shall be death. Prepare to execute the sentence on command."

Rifles aimed and ready, the assembled troops were careful not to catch one another in a crossfire. Standing in a loose half circle, not a man among them hesitated when their captain gave the order.

"Fire!"

The roar of twenty rifles left Chou with a ringing in his ears. Most of the soldiers had their weapons set on semiautomatic, but a few sprayed long, uneven bursts around the clearing, dropping human targets as they turned to flee. Chou was surprised to note that most of the assembled traitors stood their ground and died with no attempt to break away.

He took their stoicism as a frank admission of collective guilt. If they were innocent of treason, surely more of them would try to save themselves.

It took some forty seconds to complete the job, his men reloading as the echoes of their gunfire rippled through the forest, dying out in waves. Somewhere beyond the now-deserted village, still within his reach, Chou's enemies were making for the general's camp... but they'd find his own advance guard waiting in their path.

It was the anvil and the hammer, a maneuver taught to every fledgling officer in military school. His plug team was the anvil; Yuan Chou held the deadly hammer in his own right hand.

He started shouting orders, watching as his soldiers formed their ranks again, some moving sluggishly, like men who have enjoyed a bout of satisfying sex. He chose two scouts and sent them off along the trail, delaying several precious moments more before he led the column off in hot pursuit.

Soon he'd be a hero. General Li couldn't deny him that.

The hammer was about to strike, and Yuan Chou's enemies wouldn't withstand the power of its blow.

"The village," Bolan said, hearing the barrage of gunfire.

"We cannot help them now."

"God*damn* it!"

"We must hurry," Ne Kyat said.

"Hang on. The helicopters."

"What about them?"

"They came back too soon."

The guide was unimpressed. He shrugged, glanced back along the trail in the direction they had come from, finally facing east again.

"They dropped the hunters off," he said, "and then returned to camp."

"Could be. Or maybe they dropped *some*, and doubled back to plant a spike team up ahead."

He couldn't have explained the sudden urgency he felt, the need to change their course before they met another ambush on the trail. It was a burning in his gut, and he'd learned to trust his instincts under fire.

"If you are right . . ."

"They should be working back this way," Bolan said, "or they may stake out the trail and wait for us to come in range. I don't much like our chances either way."

"We cannot simply wait."

"It wasn't what I had in mind."

"Explain, please."

"If they dropped another team, it won't be far ahead. Say two or three miles, at most. We split up now and pick a place to meet, it costs some time but maybe keeps the heavies guessing. Either way it reduces by half our odds of being caught."

"But you are unfamiliar with the country," Ne Kyat said.

"I've got a compass," Bolan told him. "I can manage two or three miles all right. Let's pick coordinates and one alternative position, just in case."

Ne Kyat produced a map with obvious reluctance, pointing with his index finger to a blob of green that was the forest where they stood.

"The trail runs east from here, then south, perhaps a quarter of a mile. It loops back north beyond the river here, and then goes east again until you reach the outskirts of the general's territory."

"How far to make the river?"

"Roughly five miles," Ne Kyat replied.

"So that's our second choice. The first drop should be . . . here." His finger jabbed the map approximately three miles out from where they stood. "Let's say two hours, just to make it on the safe side."

"And how long to wait?"

"I get there first, I'll wait until I see you," Bolan said, "or till it's obvious you won't be coming. If you beat me there, say thirty minutes past the time that we agreed. From that point you'll be on your own."

"I do not like this plan," Ne Kyat declared.

"I'm not thrilled with it myself, but it's the only way to go."

They parted on the trail and went their separate ways, with Bolan striking off due south two hundred yards and Ne Kyat moving north, before they each turned east again and started moving in a parallel direction. If their luck held out, the searchers waiting up ahead of them would stay in closer to the trail and pass them by.

Provided that there *was* a hostile team ahead, and they weren't just wasting time.

# CHAPTER TWENTY-ONE

The first ten minutes on his own, Ne Kyat was nervous. It wasn't the forest that concerned him or the fact that he was suddenly alone. The last time he'd visited Yunnan, the Burmese trader had been traveling by himself, disguised in peasant clothes to minimize the chance of robbery by mountain bandits.

It was the proximity of death that preyed on Ne Kyat's mind this time. More to the point, the fact that he'd seemingly brought death upon his friends.

Behind him there were Chinese soldiers, and he had no reason to suspect Belasko was mistaken in his warning of a likely ambush to the east. It would be typical of military thinking, and the troops of General Li Zhao Gan were known for their efficiency.

Three hundred yards of forest lay between Ne Kyat and the established trail they'd been following short moments earlier. He couldn't see the track from where he stood, but he'd burned its path in his mind. The compass in his hand would be enough to guide him to his river rendezvous with the American, provided that he met no opposition on the way.

He made fair progress for a quarter of an hour, paying more attention to his compass than the woods around him as he navigated unfamiliar ground. He didn't hear the enemy until an anxious pointman fired a hasty shot, the bullet spraying chips of bark and wood pulp into Ne Kyat's face.

He fell back, cursing, rolling into cover in the shadow of a giant fallen tree. Tense voices now, one shouting instructions to the others in excited Mandarin. A burst of automatic fire plowed up the earth before his barricade to keep their target pinned in place.

As if Ne Kyat had anywhere to go.

How many hostile guns?

Three voices he was sure of, and he called it five for caution's sake. It wouldn't take them long to work around his flank and bring him under fire from either side. If he had any hope at all of breaking through the trap, he had to do it soon.

He raised his head, a calculated risk, and marked two separate muzzle-flashes on his right front as the soldiers opened fire. With the locations fixed in mind, he palmed a frag grenade and pulled the safety pin, rehearsing the procedure in his mind before he made the pitch.

It would be too much, hoping for an easy kill, but the grenade might slow them down and give them something to consider, buying him some extra time. Three hand grenades remained after it was gone, but he'd still have ample ammunition for the M-16 and for the German submachine gun slung across his back.

If nothing else, he'd exact a fair price from his enemies.

He made the pitch, high overhand, retreating under cover as another burst of automatic fire ripped pieces from the fallen log. His aim was off—he knew that going in—but there was nothing he could do about it now.

The blast seemed muffled by the forest, but it captured the attention of his enemies. There were more shouts in Mandarin before the man in charge called out for silence, cursing those who raised their voices in surprise.

They would be doubly cautious now as they attempted to encircle his position. He'd have to watch his flanks as they began to creep around behind him and—

The rush was unexpected, as his opposition meant for it to be. Three soldiers broke from cover, firing as they came, with streams of automatic fire converging on the point where Ne Kyat lay. He wriggled swiftly to his left and came up blasting with the M-16, saw one man stagger, dropping to his knees before the others went to ground.

One hit, at least.

The wounded soldier lay in no-man's land and cried out to his comrades in a youthful voice, beseeching them for help, until a pistol shot rang out and he was still.

Ne Kyat was cornered, but he wasn't beaten yet. The plan that came to mind was crude and desperate, but it was all he had. If nothing else, it might confuse his enemies enough for him to score another kill or two before they cut him down.

He worked the submachine gun off its sling and lay back with his shoulders braced against the fallen log, the automatic rifle in his right hand, H&K MP-5 in his left. The hardest part was not to laugh, as Ne Kyat called out in Mandarin, "Watch out for flankers on the left!"

Then he answered himself in a slightly gruffer voice, "They're covered. Pass me some grenades."

It was a clumsy ploy, but when the next rush came—

Again, three soldiers, firing from the hip as they began their charge. Ne Kyat fired back with both his weapons set on automatic, sweeping left and right as if two men were answering hostile fire. It was impossible to aim with any accuracy, but he was rewarded with a squeal of pain from one of his assailants, while the others went to ground.

So far, so good.

The latest casualty was either dead, unconscious or had learned enough from the example of his predecessor to suppress his cries for help. In any case Ne Kyat allowed himself the comfort of believing that the hostile odds had been effectively reduced by two.

Wild firing came from the trees to pin him down, and Ne Kyat wondered if Belasko had encountered any opposition on the south side of the trail. With all the racket close at hand, it would have been impossible for him to pick out distant gunfire, and he'd be helpless to respond in any case.

The hand grenade came out of nowhere, wobbling in the air before it struck the fallen log, bounced once, and landed six or seven feet to Ne Kyat's right. He bolted, swallowing a cry of panic, trying to remember that the main force of explosions on the surface of the ground were channeled upward. If he just kept low enough—

The shock wave struck him like a giant fist and drove the air out of his lungs. White pain erupted in his feet and lower legs as shrapnel ripped the soles of Ne Kyat's hiking boots and burrowed deep. He lost the submachine gun somehow and felt the M-16 beneath him as his consciousness flowed in and out like rough waves breaking on a rocky beach.

He heard the enemy before he felt their hands upon him, rolling Ne Kyat over and disarming him. The muzzle of a gun was pressed against his cheek, still hot enough to mark the skin, but Ne Kyat didn't flinch. He was about to learn exactly what it felt like to die, and he was surprised to find that curiosity outweighed his fear.

A sign of shock, no doubt, but he'd take what he could get.

Instead of bullets, though, more words. A Chinese officer was bending over him and shouting questions, his angry face distorted by the grit and blood in Ne Kyat's eyes. There was a ringing in his ears from the explosion, which worsened when the officer began to slap him, and he couldn't make out the rapid questions.

No matter.

He wouldn't be answering his enemies. They might as well go on and kill him while they had the chance. If he could reach the pistol tucked inside his jacket...

No. They had the pistol now, and it was gone. Rough hands were lifting him and shifting his position. Someone knotted tourniquets around his legs, below the knees.

And, understanding that they meant to let him live awhile, Ne Kyat began to pray for death.

THE SOUNDS OF BATTLE left Mack Bolan with a choice to make. He could attempt to reach Ne Kyat in time, or he could forge ahead and carry on with his appointed mission on his own.

No choice at all.

He navigated by the sounds, uncertain just how far Ne Kyat had traveled since they separated nearly half an hour earlier. The forest alternately amplified or muffled sounds almost at whim, and Bolan had to estimate the general direction as he worked his way northeast, alert for an ambush on the way.

The first explosion told him they were using hand grenades, but he had no way of determining which side had raised the ante in their skirmish. When the sound of automatic fire resumed a moment later, he relaxed a little in the knowledge that Ne Kyat must still be capable of fighting back.

It took him fifteen minutes to regain the trail. There was a second blast, immediately followed by another sputtering of rifle fire, and sudden stillness froze him in his tracks.

He waited for a moment, and another, shoulders sagging when the battle sounds didn't resume. All finished, then, whatever that might mean.

If he was close enough, he could have used the cordite smell of combat to direct himself, but Ne Kyat might have covered half a mile or more between their separation and the time that battle was engaged, depending on his speed. Toss in the fact that Bolan had no way of plotting his precise direction through the woods, and any search would have to cover something like a full square mile.

Too late.

If Ne Kyat had prevailed, he'd be moving toward the river rendezvous with all deliberate speed.

If not, the options weren't encouraging. A kill or capture—either way, his guide was out of it, and Bolan would be risking too much in a blind quest for revenge. If he continued on his way, he stood a chance of reaching General Li and Sun Jiang Lao within a day or two. A major deviation from the plan would sacrifice his mission and, potentially, his life.

Case closed.

He'd proceed to the established rendezvous and wait awhile to see if Ne Kyat showed himself. Beyond that, there was nothing realistically that he could do to help his Burmese guide.

And in the meantime, if he didn't miss his guess, the hunters from the village would be double-timing toward the latest sounds of combat, anxious for another taste of action. He'd been there, in another time and place, pursuing unseen enemies on treacherous terrain. He knew the hunter's rush, excitement tinged with fear, that seemed to make the senses more acute.

It was a feeling that could carry you away if you forgot about the downside of the hunt, the price of human life involved. For some the rush became addictive, and they never truly broke its hold.

For Bolan war had never been an object of desire. He recognized the grim necessity of a response to hostile overtures, swift action to annihilate the savages, but he could never bring himself to relish killing. Even when he pulled the trigger in a spirit of revenge, the Executioner experienced a corresponding sense of loss, as if he sacrificed a portion of himself each time he took the field.

Another mile, approximately to the river rendezvous, and Bolan struck off to the east, alert to any sign of hostile troops within a radius of fifty yards. If there were snipers waiting for him in the trees or booby traps along the way, he would be forced to deal with any threat as it appeared. As far as Ne Kyat was concerned, there seemed to be no likelihood of finding him by scouring the woods.

The best part of an hour had elapsed before he heard the sound of helicopter rotors once again. A single chopper was skimming above the treetops, drawing closer by the heartbeat. Slowing. Circling.

Hunting.

He was almost to the river crossing now, a narrow rope suspension bridge his ready means of access to the other side. The drop-off to the water measured roughly thirty feet, and Bolan knew that he would have a hard time managing the current even if he wasn't under hostile fire.

He crouched between two trees and let the chopper pass directy over him. Its presence in the area might be coincidence, or it could mean Ne Kyat was still alive—and talking under rough interrogation from his captors. Either way, the Executioner was now confronted with a choice: to hide and wait the chopper out, assuming that it carried no sophisticated tracking gear, or make his move and try to bring the warbird down.

The matter was decided for him moments later, when the helicopter circled back toward his position, hovering a few yards to his left. He crouched, immobile, listening as something clattered through the branches overhead, a deadweight falling, growing closer, closer, until—

The explosion made his ears ring, snapping Bolan's teeth together with concussive force. The air burst from a hand grenade was designed to wound or stun him, and he knew the first would soon be followed by another if he gave his enemies the opportunity.

His mind absorbed the fact that they were using infrared detectors, tracking body heat, and he was moving off the mark before the hunters had a chance to drop their second charge. With infrared it made no difference where he ran, unless he found a cave to hide in or a rushing stream to mask his body temperature. And if he tried the river, even granting he could get there, they'd have a perfect chance to strafe him as the current carried him downstream.

No hiding, then. He had to stand and fight before his adversaries in the air touched base with reinforcements on the ground.

He made a beeline through the trees, directly toward the riverbank and the swaying bridge. No cover there, but at the moment the surrounding trees worked equally in favor of his enemies. The overhanging limbs that sheltered Bolan from a rifle bullet likewise blocked his own shot at the helicopter, while providing no protection from grenades.

A second blast behind him, slightly to the left, was intended more to keep him running than to bring him down. The trackers knew where he was going now, and they were glad to help him get there, where they could lay down fire from automatic weapons, cutting him to pieces on the open ground.

He hesitated long enough to sling the M-16 and bring the fat M-40 into play. The bloop gun had a high-explosive round inside the firing chamber, and he raised the folding sights, adjusting them for fifty yards.

It would be close, but Bolan knew he was unlikely to get a second chance.

He hit the open ground and made directly for the rope suspension bridge. The sound of rotors thrashing air was louder now, without the insulation of the trees. He saw the chopper from the corner of his eyes, a dark, insectile shape emerging from beyond the tree line, homing in to pick him off.

He reached the bridge and kept on running, shaky on his feet as each step rocked the creaky structure back and forth. He pictured stepping on a rotten plank and plunging through, the final irony, a burst of bubbles and machine-gun bullets as he disappeared from sight.

Not yet.

The helicopter had begun its strafing run, and a gunner tracked Bolan from the port side, firing for effect. The rotors nearly drowned out sounds of gunfire, but he saw the spurts of water marching toward him, bullets skittering across the surface, leaving spray behind.

He raised the stubby launcher, sighted quickly on the chopper's nose and fired before the pilot could correct or veer away. For something like a heartbeat and a half, he thought that he'd missed his one and only chance, but then the helicopter shuddered, rocked by an explosion in the cockpit, and a ball of flame engulfed the forward fuselage. One of the rotor blades tore loose and hurtled through the treetops, clipping branches like a huge machete blade.

The helicopter went in on its shattered nose, tail jutting from the current like the sting of a defiant, wounded scorpion. The river pushed it steadily along downstream, directly toward the swaying bridge where Bolan stood.

He cursed and started running for the eastern shore, uncertain whether he could close the gap in time. A sudden tremor in the bridge was all the answer he required, and Bolan caught the nearest guide rope with his free hand, clinging to the launcher as the tail blades of the helicopter clipped the bridge in two behind him and the free ends fell away.

He hit the foaming surface with a splash, still clinging to his lifeline and the launcher simultaneously, gritting teeth against the icy chill of water soaking through his camouflage fatigues. The dangling sections of the bridge were borne away downstream, but as the terminus on Bolan's side was anchored firmly to the shore, the motion actually swung him closer to the muddy bank. He rode the current out, dug in with both his feet on contact and in several grueling moments had dragged himself ashore.

Behind him, in the water, there was no trace of the helicopter left. It had submerged or else been swept along downstream, where it would ultimately come to rest as one more jungle artifact and curiosity. If any of the crew survived, they were beyond his reach and posed no threat.

But there were others coming, all right. The airborne chase had gone on long enough for someone in the chopper to relay coordinates, and Bolan had no time to waste. The severed bridge would slow his trackers down, but he was confident that they'd find a way.

The other helicopters, for example.

Any time now, burning up his trail.

The Executioner was far from rested, but he knew that it was time to move. Abandoning the riverbank, he set his face due east and struck off through the trees.

THE DAY HAD GONE from bad to worse for Captain Yuan Lin Chou. At first his breakthrough in the peasant village had been heartening, a bit of information proving he was close behind his quarry. The elimination of a traitor's nest would boost him in the general's estimation, and a speedy capture of the men he sought would further strengthen his position in the regiment.

And then, quite inexplicably, his luck began to turn.

It wasn't obvious at first. The message from his point team to the east had seemed initially encouraging. They'd engaged the enemy and captured a survivor, at the cost of one man dead and one more wounded. Granted, the lieutenant in command of the patrol suspected that another terrorist had slipped away in the confusion—they'd found two guns, and their disabled prisoner wasn't American—but there was every hope that they could make the captive talk.

And so he had.

There was resistance at the outset, as expected, but a man with shattered feet and legs couldn't hold out for long. Yuan Chou was educated in the usages of pain, and it had taken all of fifteen minutes to persuade the Burmese scum that he should share the story of his life in detail if he cherished any thoughts of living through another day.

The track lay east—that much was elementary—but the invaders had prepared a rendezvous beside the river two miles away. Assuming the American had made good time, he would be well across the bridge before Chou's troops could catch him. He might well escape.

The helicopter was a masterstroke, called in by radio and sent directly to the target area, complete with tracking gear. It should have worked...but something had gone terribly wrong.

Instead of bringing down his target, Chou had lost the helicopter and its three-man crew. His first hint of disaster was the loss of contact via radio, with angry static swarming from the walkie-talkie in his hand. After a march through ringing silence to the riverside, with two men carrying their captive in the cradle of their arms, they stood beside the water, staring at the torn and twisted remnants of the bridge.

One of his soldiers found the twisted helicopter rotor blade, bent double in the upper branches of a tree, some thirty feet above the ground. Chou felt the hot blood rushing to his face, a surge of sudden rage that left him dizzy, standing with his fists clenched at his sides.

The general would be furious, of course, and rightly so. He might remind Yuan Chou, with gloating irony, that helicopters didn't grow on trees, and thus should not be wrapped around them. He'd certainly regard the loss of the machine as more significant than four dead soldiers, when recruits were relatively easy to replace.

To balance out the loss, Chou had his prisoner, already fading fast from loss of blood, and the elusive hope that the American might somehow have been killed before the helicopter crashed. He couldn't reconstruct the incident precisely from the meager evidence in hand, but it was possible his quarry could have been on the bridge when it was cut in two. Perhaps the helicopter struck him, coming down, or he was swept away and drowned.

It would take hours to repair the bridge, if they could even manage it with the materials they carried, and the captain didn't feel like wasting any more time. A search on this side of the river would be pointless, even if the American was stranded when the bridge went down, and they would lose their prisoner if much more time was wasted in the forest.

Chou called out to his communications sergeant for the radio, and sent a signal for the other helicopters to return. If nothing else, at least he could return his prisoner to General Li alive.

With any luck it just might be enough to mitigate the overall disaster and preserve some vestige of the captain's dignity.

If nothing else, he hoped that it would save his life.

# CHAPTER TWENTY-TWO

The pain was waiting for Ne Kyat when he returned to consciousness. Forgetting for a moment the extent and nature of his injuries, he tried to move his shattered legs and was rewarded with a lightning bolt of agony that made him cry out.

When he could breathe again, he used a sleeve to wipe the tears out of his eyes and scanned the room as best he could without unnecessary movement. He was lying on a simple army cot, a blanket covering his lower body. Someone had removed his boots and trousers, by the feel of scratchy cotton against his thighs, and they'd done a makeshift job of binding his wounded legs below the knees.

His prison measured roughly eight-by ten, no windows, with the ceiling fixture featuring a solitary naked bulb. A transom just above the door was open to provide some ventilation, but it couldn't compete with the oppressive level of humidity. His face and naked chest were filmed with sweat.

If there were guards outside the door, they had ignored his cry of pain. Of course, there might be no one there at all. A simple padlock would have done as well, and even that was overkill when Ne Kyat couldn't stand, much less escape.

It crossed his mind to wonder why he lived. They should have killed him in the forest, after he'd shot the soldiers, but his captors had been under orders to provide a prisoner for questioning. The officer in charge, when he arrived, had wasted no time getting to the point.

Shame brought a rush of heat to Ne Kyat's cheeks. He had betrayed Belasko in his agony, disclosed the river rendezvous and set the hunters on his track. If the American had managed to survive, it meant the gods were watching over him, for he had no friends left on earth.

Again the question of why Ne Kyat was still alive.

He felt a sudden rush of hope. If the Chinese had killed or caged Belasko, they'd surely have no further need for maimed accomplices. A bullet in the head would settle the account, and Ne Kyat would have wakened in a better place, perhaps another life.

But he hadn't been killed, and that meant General Li had found another use for him, alive.

Suddenly, beyond the shadow of a doubt, he knew Belasko had managed to elude the hunters. He was still on track, still coming for the general and his nest of vipers in Yunnan.

The best part was that Ne Kyat couldn't harm him now. Once General Li's patrol blew their assignment at the river rendezvous, Belasko's guide could tell them nothing of the man's whereabouts. It didn't matter what they tried or how they made him scream.

As if on cue, he heard a sound of muffled voices from beyond the door. It opened seconds later to admit a pair of Chinese officers. The younger one, with captain's bars, was immediately recognized as Ne Kyat's tormentor from the forest. His companion was an older man with graying hair, a riding crop, and the insignia of a commanding general on his collar.

Li Zhao Gan.

"I'm told you speak Chinese," the general said.

"That is correct."

"Your legs are broken. Crushed, in fact. The shrapnel, as you may recall. I doubt that you will walk again."

"I have some doubts myself."

The general smiled without a trace of mirth.

"My men were careless in the forest," he remarked. "They let your comrade slip away and lost a helicopter in the process."

Ne Kyat smiled at the discomfort on the captain's face. At least he knew that he wasn't the only one in trouble here.

"And what is that to me?" he asked.

"You have another chance to save yourself," General Li told him. "You helped us once, and it is not your fault that the American escaped. I need your help again."

"What kind of help?"

"More information," Li replied.

"How should I know where he has gone?"

"The two of you were traveling companions. One might even call you coconspirators. You must have planned for the contingency of separation."

"As I told your men, the river bridge—"

"Beyond that."

"There was nothing else," he answered truthfully. "We knew that if one of us failed to make the rendezvous, it meant that he was dead."

"But both of you are still alive . . . so far."

Ne Kyat pretended to consider his alternatives. "If I had dreamed," he said, "perhaps I could predict your future. As it is . . ."

"My future is secure."

The general drew his blanket back and let it drop beside the cot. The very motion of it, dragged across his legs and feet, made Ne Kyat stiffen, beads of perspiration rising on his cheeks and forehead as he bit his tongue.

"Your future, on the other hand..."

"Has been decided, I expect. If I could save myself with lies, I would oblige you. As it is, I have no story worth the price."

"I'm not convinced."

"In that case, you may fuck yoursel—"

The riding crop descended in a blur and cracked across his swollen ankles. Ne Kyat screamed and tried to roll away, the action serving only to redouble the effect of the initial blow.

"I would prefer to speak like gentlemen," the general told him. "Possibly to let you live."

"A crippled mountain guide," Ne Kyat responded when he found his voice again. "What a promising future I would have."

"You would prefer to die?"

"I would prefer *your* death, but in the meantime—"

There was nothing he could do to brace himself against the rain of blows. Li whipped the riding crop repeatedly across his legs and feet, the captain moving in to pin Ne's shoulders down and stop his thrashing off the cot. It seemed to last forever, but he knew that only seconds had elapsed before the general stepped away to catch his breath.

"I might admire your courage," the general said, panting, "if you were not such a fool."

This time it took Ne Kyat a few beats longer to regain the power of speech. His voice was raw from

screaming, and he didn't recognize the sounds that issued forth.

"I have no information that would help you," he
replied. "That much is simple truth and common
sense. Which one of us ignores the obvious, and
thereby proves himself a fool?"

"I have all afternoon," Li said. "All night, if necessary."

"Do you really?"

Color rose in the general's face before he raised the
crop and brought it slashing down. The jolts of pain
blurred into one another, formed an endless, rising tide
of agony that overwhelmed Ne Kyat and left him
breathless, like a drowning man. And somewhere in the
middle of it came the blessed darkness, echoing with
screams.

EMERGING FROM THE HUT with the captain in tow, the
general slapped his riding crop against one leg. He
didn't seem to notice that it stained his khaki pants with
flecks of blood.

"Do you believe he spoke the truth, sir?" Chou inquired.

"Perhaps. It makes no difference, either way. What
damage can a single mercenary do to all of this?"

Chou didn't answer. General Li was scowling,
thinking of the damage this American had done already. Four men dead, one wounded and a helicopter
lost, with nothing but a twisted rotor blade to show
that it had ever been. Against those losses, Li had captured one intruder who was worthless as a source of
information, and his men had massacred a village full
of peasants who defied the general's rule of law.

He was ahead in terms of bodies, but still Li felt like he was losing.

It made him angry that his troops had missed their chance to bag the American. There would be another chance, of course, but next time it would be on the enemy's initiative, when *he* decided it was time to strike. A garrison this size, and they were placed on the defensive by a single foreigner who couldn't even speak the language.

It was humiliating, and the general had no tolerance for personal embarrassment. Someone would have to pay for the discomfort that he felt.

He had considered blaming Captain Chou, perhaps demoting him or even putting him on trial, but Li Zhao Gan was wise enough to know that laying the blame upon a junior officer would only breed dissatisfaction in the ranks. If Captain Chou had made some special blunder, it would be a different case, but he'd followed recognized procedure all the way.

His enemy was simply more proficient in the field, and that was something that a military trial would only highlight, to the detriment of general morale. Li's time was better used preparing for the blow to come, ensuring that his people weren't taken by surprise a second time.

He'd already doubled the patrols within a mile of his perimeter, with scouts on watch around the clock. Of his four remaining helicopters, one was stationed at Li's secondary camp outside Simao, and he'd placed the other three on red alert, with pilots standing by to take the air on a moment's notice. Likewise, while he had no armored vehicles in camp, a number of his jeeps were fitted with machine guns, and he had them on patrol of the approaching mountain roads that would accommodate machines. Inside the camp he had increased the force of sentries standing watch along the wire, extending duty shifts and issuing each man supplies of ammunition in excess of what they normally would carry to their posts.

The worst that General Li had faced before, in terms of confrontations in Yunnan, had been sporadic skirmishes with independent smugglers, mopping up behind the Yi Kwah Tao or driving Burmese rebels back across the border to their homeland. Hungry peasants had encroached upon his camp a time or two, intent on stealing food, and he'd made examples of the idiots...but this was different.

Even though it seemed preposterous, the general had no doubt that his American opponent meant to breach the wire and murder Sun Jiang Lao. It was a point of honor, now that he'd come so far and risked so much to do the job. Li understood the drive behind a suicidal quest, and there was room for grudging admiration in his mind, despite the fact that he was plotting to exterminate Belasko.

He left the captain with a curt dismissal, moving toward the quarters where Sun Lao and Michael Lee were waiting for the latest word about their nemesis. Sun's door was opened by the younger man almost before Li had a chance to knock. He brushed his way inside, ignoring Michael Lee and concentrating his attention on the leader of the Yi Kwah Tao.

"What have we learned?"

"The peasant has no further information," General Li replied. "I am convinced that he is ignorant of the American's location at the present time."

"Suppose he did not cross the river?" Lee inquired. "Your people said there was a chance the bridge went down before he got across."

The general shrugged, enjoying it. "He has had ample time to find another crossing point. I am expecting him by late tomorrow, possibly the next day."

"And the prisoner?" Sun Jiang Lao asked.

"He lives. We may have other uses for him yet, if they are truly comrades."

"An exchange?"

"Fresh bait, perhaps, to draw the shark's attention from his target."

"You imply some knowledge of this mercenary's goal," the Triad master said. A frown etched shadows on his face.

"I think it safe to say that he has not come all this way to test the People's Revolutionary Army for its own sake, Master Sun. You may recall that he has stopped at several points along the way to punish your lieutenants."

"He has killed your men, as well."

"Because they stood between him and his goal."

"And now?"

There was suspicion in the old man's voice, and General Li responded with a smile to put his guest at ease.

"We understand each other, Master Sun."

"I hope so, General Li."

"My home is yours." Li spread his hands to indicate the camp at large. "You are an honored guest, and it would mean embarrassment to me if harm befell you in my keeping."

An embarrassment that he could live with, Li decided, but he kept it to himself.

"It is encouraging to find such honor in a trusted friend."

"I must be going now," the general said. "I have a meeting shortly with my officers to make sure all of our defenses are in place."

"I would not keep you from your duties, General."

They traded bows in parting. As the door swung shut behind him, Li was smiling as he crossed the compound to his CP hut. His "honored guest" was living on a gift of borrowed time, and in another day or two, at most, Li meant to call for an accounting on the loan.

Meanwhile he meant what he had said about the Burmese prisoner, Ne Kyat. The man—or what was left of him—might still be useful in a showdown with his friend from the United States. No trade would be arranged, but if the captive merely served as a distraction, he could still have value. Anything to throw the round-eye off his stride when he began his final push, allowing General Li the extra edge that he would need.

If all his troops and war machines weren't enough, the general was prepared to use deception, guile and trickery to best his enemy. There were no rules in the survival game, and he'd played it long enough to know that winners walked away because they showed no mercy to the opposition. Grind them into dust, and they won't return to trouble you another day.

The mill of death was primed to roll on a moment's notice.

They only needed soft, white flesh to press between the grinding wheels.

THE FINAL MILES of Bolan's trek were necessarily the hardest, not because of any change in the terrain, but because his enemies were on their guard, prepared for anything. He had to watch his step and move with extra caution, listening for foot patrols and searching helicopters all the way.

He would have to reach the general's camp before he started making any further plans. And once there, he would see what he could see.

The first night, after his encounter with the helicopter, Bolan slept reluctantly. He would have kept on walking through the darkness, but he didn't trust himself or the terrain, especially with the fatigue that crouched upon his shoulder like a buzzard, waiting to be fed. A little rest, however slight, and he'd face the morning with a new resolve and grim determination to complete his job.

The second day he hid from helicopters in the forest, and they passed him by. He encountered no ground patrols as yet, but he was getting closer by the moment. It was only a matter of time.

That night Bolan used the darkness as a screen for his reconnaissance. A cautious half mile past the clearing where he planned to sleep, he smelled the cooking fires and followed that aroma to a point where floodlights smudged the sky, eclipsing stars. He climbed a tree, a creeping shadow thirty feet above the ground, and found a vantage point from which to scan the camp of General Li Zhao Gan.

The camp was more or less what Bolan had expected for the home base of an occupying regiment. It covered several acres, with a fenced perimeter—chain link and razor wire on top—and buildings that were mostly prefab, tailored to their different uses. From his aerie Bolan picked out barracks and a mess hall, the CP, communications and a generator hut, latrines and showers, a fair-sized car barn and several smaller structures he couldn't identify.

The one and only gate that he could see faced south, accommodating what appeared to be a one-lane, unpaved mountain road. Guard towers were positioned at the southeast and the northwest corners of the camp, their searchlights darkened at the moment, lookouts smoking cigarettes and leaning over their machine guns as they scanned the forest. On the ground Li's sentries worked the inside of the wire in pairs, without the benefit of dogs.

It wouldn't be an easy cage to crack. From Bolan's estimate the camp could house one hundred fifty or two hundred men with ease. Three helicopters rested on the concrete pad, until the first gray light of dawn released them to begin a fresh round of patrols. And from the car barn's size, he knew that there were several vehicles to be accounted for. A truck or two, perhaps, and almost certainly a few more jeeps in addition to the one parked inside the structure.

As if on cue, Bolan heard an engine whining as the driver shifted gears. It took a moment for the headlights of the jeep to appear. Three soldiers were returning from night patrol.

As the gate men opened up and waved their comrades through, a notion formed in the warrior's mind.

He left the idea where it was to ferment for a while, and started checking out the weak points of the camp. The long perimeter was fairly well patrolled, but he was thinking past the entry now, imagining himself inside the compound with the doomsday numbers running in his head. A pair of fuel pumps stood between the car barn and the helipad. One was for aircraft and the other for landlocked vehicles, which meant at least two fuel tanks buried underground. If he could get that far, a simple spark—or a grenade—would do the job.

The generator was another weakness, feeding power to the floodlights, lookout towers and communications hut. The problem with remote encampments was the need for absolute reliance on a self-serve power source, and what any generator man could build, some other man could blow away.

The timing would be critical. He couldn't risk a move when too many troops were abroad, but the obvious alert would limit his chances to penetrate the compound at all.

Another jeep rolled in with three more soldiers. Twenty minutes later he was watching as an eight-man foot patrol came back from scouring the nearby jungle, passing through the gates in single file. They had the look of weary men who felt their task was hopeless, but he knew that they'd follow orders to the bitter end.

There was no sign of Ne Tin Kyat inside the compound, but he could have been sequestered in one of at least half a dozen different buildings...if, in fact, he'd survived to reach the camp at all. Would they have any use for Bolan's guide once he had pointed out the river rendezvous and they had failed to bag their man?

It was a long shot, but he couldn't rule out the possibility that Ne Kyat was alive. Yet, on the other hand, it might be better—anyway, more merciful—if they'd simply left him in the jungle with a mercy bullet in his skull.

Retaining him alive would mean more questions, further pain, and how would Bolan extricate him in the end? If Ne Kyat had been wounded during capture, his condition might prohibit travel, leaving Bolan with the choice of whether he should live awhile or die with something close to dignity.

He pushed the morbid thoughts away and scanned the compound once again with compact glasses, looking for the other men he sought. His targets would be waiting for him, but he needed some idea of their location in the compound to prevent a waste of precious time once he began his strike.

Due north, in the direction of the helipad, were what appeared to be the quarters of selected visitors. He kept the glasses focused, waiting, and was soon rewarded by a profile at the nearest window, framed in artificial light.

The face of Michael Lee.

It was enough. If Lee was present, Sun Jiang Lao couldn't be far away. As for the general . . .

He leaned back, resting shoulders on the smooth bark of the tree, his features molded in a thoughtful frown. The players were assembled, and it would soon be time to launch the final game. The odds were with the house, of course—they always were—but it wouldn't prevent the Executioner from giving everything he had to cross the finish line.

It seemed forever since he'd shared a bed with Barbara Price at Stony Man. How long in days? No matter.

He'd either see the Farm again or he wouldn't.

Tomorrow night he'd be moving out against his enemies.

And in the meantime, there was nothing for the Executioner to do but hide. And wait.

# CHAPTER TWENTY-THREE

The sleep that Ne Kyat sought eluded him, and he was still awake when gray dawn crept in through the transom of his cell. There was less pain as time went by, provided that he didn't try to move. His back was stiff from lying in the same position all night long, and he couldn't help crying out when he was forced to shift his weight and use the empty can that was his urinal, but he was holding on.

He'd returned to consciousness sometime within the hour after he was beaten, waves of brutal pain assaulting him and bringing tears to Ne Kyat's eyes. He drew some consolation from the fact that they'd left him, either satisfied that he was being truthful or deciding that it wasn't worth their effort to interrogate him any further.

Either way he drew hope from the fact that he was still alive.

Without new information to reveal, he must have some more basic value to the general, or they would have killed him while he lay unconscious on the cot.

He thought about the questions General Li had asked him in between the slashing blows that made him scream, and knew Belasko was alive. Their ambush at the river bridge had missed him. He was out there somewhere, and the knowledge had his enemies on edge.

A victory of sorts, before he ever fired a shot.

If Li allowed Ne Kyat to live, it meant the general thought that he could somehow use his prisoner when the American arrived. It was a futile hope, Ne Kyat decided, knowing that Belasko wouldn't compromise himself or his mission for a wounded man, but if it helped distract the general and it bought Ne Kyat some time, so much the better.

His swollen legs were bandaged—he could feel the pressure of the dressings now—but he couldn't be sure if anyone had set the broken bones. It hardly mattered, since he couldn't walk in any case, but he was thinking of survival now and what might lie beyond the camp.

He caught himself and pulled up short. It was a brief reprieve, and nothing more. Ne Kyat wasn't in any shape to help himself, regardless of Belasko's plans. It didn't matter when the man came or what he did when he arrived. Ne Kyat wouldn't be leaving with him. He was running out of time, and all that he could do was try to make the final hours count.

Perhaps if he'd given General Li some false directions, he would now feel better toward himself. Instead, his stubborn silence forced the Chinese officer to mount patrols on every side, perhaps preventing the American from getting close enough to strike.

No fear of that, Ne Kyat decided, putting on a smile.

Belasko would be here in time, and General Li would pay the price accordingly.

His stomach growled, reminding Ne Kyat that he had not eaten since his breakfast with the Yunnanese. All dead now, in the village, if he wasn't very much mistaken, and their lives were one more debt Li owed to Fate.

Belasko would be coming to collect, soon.

There was a scuffle on the threshold of his cell, and someone threw the door back. He could see a guard outside, another pushing through to bring his breakfast in a metal plate. It smelled like cabbage, looked like something chewed and then rejected by a pig.

The soldier dropped a metal spoon into the glop and set the plate on Ne Kyat's chest.

The breakfast tasted even worse than it appeared, but it was warm and it was food. He wolfed it down and licked the plate, determined not to let the final vestiges of strength escape.

You never knew when you might need a ready eye or hand, despite the lack of legs. A cripple could sometimes surprise his enemies if they began to take the handicap for granted, underestimating him. Ne Kyat had seen it done in variations countless times before.

He left the spotless plate and spoon beside his cot, decided not to bother with the urine can just now and settled back to wait.

THE JEEPS WENT OUT at eight o'clock, returned at noon, gassed up and left the camp again with different crews by half-past twelve. Bolan logged them in at five for mess, and saw them off again by six-fifteen. If last night's watch was any sampling, they'd shorten their patrols by night, returning to the camp at staggered intervals, between the hours of nine and ten o'clock.

The foot patrols were something else, and Bolan put them on the clock, as well, but he didn't intend to meet them in the forest if a clash could be avoided. Stealth would see him through, with just a dash of luck to help things out, but he'd have to time things perfectly.

A night probe, when the day shift had begun to let their guard down slightly from fatigue, and those assigned to guard through the night were still digesting starchy meals. If he'd planned to penetrate the camp alone on foot, he'd have timed the raid for dawn, but there was too much chance of stumbling over sentries or alerting lookouts in the towers at the corners of the camp.

The best way of obtaining entry, he decided, would be straight in through the gate. And to accomplish that, he needed wheels.

A Chinese jeep, to be exact.

The vehicles were knockoffs, to be strictly accurate. While there'd been cultural exchange and lowering of economic barriers since Nixon had produced new markets in the People's Republic, China still prided herself on home production of her military hardware, by and large. In practice that meant poaching from the Soviets, the Eastern Bloc and the Americans where possible.

If you examined Chinese weapons, you would find that they were ripping off the Russians right and left, attaching homegrown nomenclature to designs they stole from Moscow. Thus, the Soviet Tokarev automatic pistol became the Chinese Type 51, while Beijing's Type 56 assault rifle was a carbon copy of the classic Russian AK-47. North Koreans and Vietnamese played the same kind of name games with their rip-off armament, and the technique extended into vehicles, as well.

Which meant that Bolan would experience no problems with a Chinese jeep if he could only put himself behind the wheel. The problem was that there would be at least three soldiers armed and ready to obstruct him when he made his move.

The choice of ambush points was relatively simple, since there was only one main road that served the camp. A network of surrounding trails were wide enough for infantry to travel one abreast, but motorized patrols were limited to looping circuits of the camp or winding journeys south, in the direction of Simao, where General Li undoubtedly arranged for his supplies.

Again it all came down to timing in the end.

He had to watch the first two shifts, allowing them to pass by unmolested, calculating how much time he had between one scouting party and the next. The jeeps didn't appear to run in tandem; four were assigned to circulate while one remained in camp, perhaps reserved for General Li. The choppers were abroad, meanwhile, but they paid no attention to the open road.

He wondered whether they were using infrared by day, with Li's own soldiers in the woods. If so, it would imply a dedication to routine and patterns that would make the ground search that much easier to duck. A squad compelled to follow certain trails for the convenience of a chopper overhead—or to avoid false readings on the infrared—couldn't afford to deviate by much from their predicted course.

It had to be the last jeep out, and so, the last one back. He counted, watching from his vantage point, before he shimmied down the tree and started winding through the undergrowth to reach his chosen ambush point.

Each vehicle was slightly different, in its own way. One had a rust spot growing where the left-front fender had been bashed and hammered out again. Another boasted slightly crooked headlights, while a third had camouflage paint in place of primer daubed along one side where it had been repaired. The fourth—his choice—was notable because the extra fuel can bolted on behind was painted brown instead of olive drab.

Three men, all armed, and Bolan knew how he'd take them when it came to that. It must be swift and silent, leaving them no opportunity to fire a warning shot and rouse the camp.

Waiting for the other jeeps to pass in turn, he marked the time and dropped his rucksack in the middle of the road. A small thing, but the driver or his scout was sure to spot it in their headlights, wondering how it had come to be there since the last patrol went by. They'd be on alert, and he'd have to make his move exactly right, without a fatal slip.

He heard the jeep before he saw its headlights, and crouched under cover with the customized Beretta 93-R in his fist. In front of him the jeep was slowing down, the driver and his shotgun rider talking back and forth, the rear-deck gunner leaning on his automatic weapon, studying the tree line with suspicious eyes.

They sat, the engine idling, while the front-seat passenger climbed out to check the rucksack, moving slowly, worried that it might be booby-trapped.

Not even close.

It took precision work, but Bolan pulled it off. His first shot took out the rear-deck gunner, opening a hole between his eyes and slamming him away before he had a chance to make the big gun rock and roll. The warrior swung toward the pointman next because he had an automatic rifle in his hands. One silenced shot put him on his knees, the second keeping him there.

The driver fumbled for a pistol, simultaneously looking for reverse and grinding gears. The parabellum round that drilled his left eye socket pitched him over sideways toward the empty seat, and let his foot slip off the clutch. The engine chortled, coughed and died.

He spent a moment with the bodies first, arranging them. He first hauled the pointman off the trail and tucked him under ferns where he wouldn't be noticed in the dark. The driver simply moved next door to occupy the shotgun seat, his own belt looped around his chest and holding him erect. In back, the lifeless gunner took some work, but Bolan finally got him braced in something like a seated posture with his chin slumped on his chest.

It hardly mattered, since his enemies would have the headlights in their eyes, but he couldn't roll into camp alone. Three men had left the camp an hour earlier, and three men were coming back.

He got the engine started on his second try and found first gear, proceeding with the scheduled route of his patrol. In time, he knew the narrow jungle road would take him back to camp.

And when he got there, Bolan had a few surprises for his hosts.

THE CALENDAR was troubling Sun Jiang Lao. He knew that ample time had passed for the American to have reached the camp by now, and there was still no word from General Li's patrols.

Sun wished that he could slip away and find himself another hiding place, but there was nowhere left for him to run. The outposts of his empire had been toppling one by one, and there was nothing he could do, so far, to stop it. Sun felt trapped, but he didn't allow the new, unmanly feeling to assert itself or surface in his public attitude.

A leader must be strong for those who follow him, and that was doubly true of military leaders in a wartime situation. It was easy, in the circumstances, for the Elder Brother of the Yi Kwah Tao to see his family as an army, suddenly besieged by enemies on every side. The years of peace and relative inaction had been swept away, to leave them suddenly exposed and vulnerable in the face of unprovoked attack.

Sun caught himself and doubled back along that line of thought. No violent act was ever unprovoked or motiveless to he who was responsible. The driving motivation might be greed or jealousy, revenge or simple lust, but there were always reasons, and those reasons could be ascertained with time.

The problem was that they were quickly running out of that commodity.

And, if the Elder Brother of Yi Kwah Tao was honest with himself, he had too many enemies from bygone days to sort them out.

Survival was the first priority in any killing situation, and he didn't fully trust in General Li to keep him safe. Unfortunately leaving now would only place Sun Lao at greater risk, and he wasn't prepared to take that chance.

Not yet.

He stood outside his quarters in the dark and scanned the camp with narrowed eyes. It wasn't brightly lit by urban standards, but the general had floodlights where it mattered, covering the gate and sections of the fence where it ran closest to the trees. A number of the buildings were illuminated also, and he stared at the command post for a moment, wondering if General Li was still behind his desk, still puzzling out the riddle of the enemy whom he couldn't pin down.

One man.

It seemed impossible, but Sun Jiang Lao was learning to accept the fact. Of course, it didn't follow that this soldier had conceived the plan himself. Great warriors customarily preferred to follow orders, leaving someone else to say when wars were necessary and decide what happened to the losers after they were won.

Sun Lao wouldn't be truly safe until he found out who had hired this soldier, given him his marching orders and unleashed him on the Yi Kwah Tao. Elimination of the American was the first step toward redemption, but it wouldn't be the last. While the man's employers were alive, Sun knew his own life would remain at risk.

Despite the temperature and the humidity, he felt a sudden chill. It was ridiculous, of course, and he ascribed it to his age, in preference to privately admitting fear. A man of honor and respect, he couldn't lead his troops unless his own performance in the face of danger was above reproach.

Behind him Michael Lee emerged from the adjacent bungalow he occupied and came to stand beside Sun Lao, hands tucked inside the pockets of his slacks.

"You think that he will come, Master?"

"I think that he is here."

Lee scanned the distant tree line nervously. "You mean right now?"

Sun shrugged. "Tonight, tomorrow night. It makes no difference. He will come because he must."

"You sound as if you know this man."

"I know his type. He will not stop until his work is done, unless we kill him first."

"The general will not fail us."

"I sincerely hope that you are right."

"You doubt him?"

"Tonight," he answered, "I doubt everyone."

THE GENERAL WAS behind his desk. He had no papers spread in front of him, but none were necessary. He didn't need maps or field reports to tell him where he stood, the danger he was facing at the moment.

It was now the second night since he'd lost his helicopter and its crew to the American intruder. There'd been no sign of the enemy since then, but Li could almost feel him drawing closer, homing on his target like a guided missile. It would be the general's task to intercept him and eliminate the threat before it struck and caused irreparable damage to his own prestige.

It wouldn't be much longer now. Prolonged delay meant that his enemy would soon be out of food, reduced to hunting if he didn't wish to starve. Li had a feeling the American would be adept at living off the land, but even bare subsistence hunting used up precious time and energy, increasing risk of capture if the subject hung around one area for any length of time. The wiser course would be to strike as soon as possible, inflict whatever damage he was able and retreat to fight another day.

It would be so much simpler, Li decided, if he could remove Sun Lao and Michael Lee for use as human bait. His mind's eye saw the two of them, staked out like goats to draw a hungry tiger, while the hunter waited in his blind to make the perfect killing shot.

Unfortunately Li couldn't afford to take that step... nor would it be effective if he did. The man he hunted would have smelled the trap and fallen back to bide his time. The evidence from Bangkok and Rangoon told Li his foe wouldn't be one to fall for shopworn tricks.

Conversely General Li wasn't afraid of frightening Belasko off with the precautions he'd taken to protect the camp. A soldier would expect no less, and he'd make allowances for the security. It would have been alarming if the general did less to make his base secure against attack. Belasko would be looking for an angle, something he could use to put himself inside the wire, and when he came...

The general reached inside his lower right-hand desk drawer, found the whiskey bottle and poured himself a drink. If any of his officers had done the same, he'd have punished them, but Li was in command. He made the rules for others, and he felt no obligation to explain himself.

He replaced the bottle in its drawer. The liquor warmed him up inside, and he could feel the tightness in his shoulders easing slightly as the warmth began to spread. It wasn't weakness, he decided, but a simple and effective form of therapy.

One final sip.

The sound of automatic weapons jarred him, and he spilled the whiskey down his shirtfront, angrily discarding the glass as he rushed toward the door. Along the way he grabbed his pistol belt from where it hung behind the office door.

Outside, the firing was dramatically intensified. More weapons joining in, by now, and all of them from the direction of the gate. He saw a jeep in motion, hurtling across the compound, muzzle-flashes from the driver's side and others from the sentries who were firing back.

Suddenly he understood. The enemy had come, and he was already inside the camp. Li watched a couple of his soldiers fall, cut down as they were running on a course to intercept the jeep.

No time to waste!

He drew his pistol, threw the belt aside and started running for the bungalow where guards were standing watch over his prisoner.

# CHAPTER TWENTY-FOUR

The sentries on the gate marked Bolan's headlights from a hundred yards, and they were opening the gate before he rolled in close enough for them to notice anything amiss. The M-16 was braced across his lap, both gate men on the driver's side as Bolan leveled into his approach.

The shorter of the two was first to notice something out of place, a shout of warning on his lips as Bolan brought the automatic rifle up and hit him with a burst across the chest. He let momentum carry it, the burst sustained until his second target spun and toppled in the dust, his arms outflung, the AK-47 spinning out of reach.

The fat was in the fire now, and he kept on going, racing toward the car barn and the helicopters on the far side of the compound. Soldiers on the ground were moving toward him, following his progress, and the tower guards were wide-awake, their automatic weapons tracking him as best they could without endangering their own from friendly fire.

Two Chinese soldiers closed on his left, and Bolan caught them with a sweeping burst of 5.56 mm tumblers, blowing them away. The jeep was drawing fire from other angles, taking hits, and he was dampened by a spray of something wet as rifle bullets struck the dead man in the shotgun seat. Another fifty yards to reach the car barn, running through a hail of hostile fire.

At Bolan's speed, he had no eye for faces, little more for numbers, but he knew precisely where he was. The quarters occupied by Sun Jiang Lao and Michael Lee were on his left, some forty yards away, the car barn dead ahead, the helipad a few yards farther on, to Bolan's right. The generator and communications hut were coming up on a collision course as the Executioner dropped the M-16 and scooped the 40 mm launcher from his dead companion's lap.

He veered a bit off course, allowing for his speed and forward motion as he aimed the piece one-handed. It wasn't the method taught in boot camp, but he had no time to stop and do it right.

The HE round went in on target, flattening the prefab bungalow and taking out the generator in a smoky thunderclap. The sudden darkness was illuminated only by the headlights of his jeep, and Bolan cursed his own forgetfulness as he reached down to switch them off.

Wild firing came from every side as sentries on the ground and in their lookout towers tried to score a hit with pure, dumb luck. It would be moments yet before their eyes adjusted to the sudden dark and they improved their aim. In that amount of time the Executioner could take advantage of his narrow lead and make it stick.

He braked outside the car barn, scrambling around behind the driver's seat and shoving his second dead passenger away from the Type 57 machine gun, a 7.62 mm weapon identical in all respects to the Soviet SGM. The weapon's heavy recoil thrummed along his

arms as Bolan held the trigger down and swept the
compound with a stream of automatic fire.

The helicopters would go first, though he could only
cover two from where he stood. No matter. He took
out those two with bursts that shattered windscreens,
turned the instruments to tangled wire and scrap, and
destroyed the engines. Sentries on the helipad went
down like headless chickens, flopping in a slick of
blood and fuel from ruptured tanks.

He swiveled toward the bungalows where he'd last
glimpsed Michael Lee, another long burst ripping
through the flimsy walls and windows, raising hell inside. The Executioner couldn't have said if he was
scoring any hits in there, but he'd at least keep their
heads down for a while.

The nearest tower guard was firing on him, the bullets marching past his jeep in spurts of dust and sand.
The man on top has an advantage in that kind of duel,
but Bolan had a death card up his sleeve.

Releasing the machine gun for a moment, he retrieved the M-40, fed it with a fresh grenade and used
the sights this time to spot his elevated target. Squeezing off in reference to the static muzzle-flash, he rode
the recoil out and watched the crow's nest of the tower
come apart, a fireball swallowing the lookout and his
weapon, hungry flames eclipsing any sound the gunner made.

The fuel pumps deserved his attention now. Returning to the mounted machine gun, he cranked the barrel hard around and sprayed the pumps. The smell of
gasoline and aircraft fuel was heavy in the night, more
piercing than the cordite reek of gun smoke on the
breeze. The pumps were flimsy, jerking underneath the

first few hits and finally disintegrating, jets of fuel erupting from their severed hoses.

Now!

He palmed a frag grenade, released the pin and lobbed the bomb overhand. The flash was all he needed to ignite the spreading lake of fuel, and any shrapnel generated by the blast was frosting on the cake.

Bolan was off the jeep and running as the tanks blew, carrying the M-16 and launcher with him as he sprinted for the compact quarters occupied by Sun Jiang Lao and Michael Lee. He might not be in time, but he'd give it everything he had.

Fire and thunder exploded into the night with a force that shook the earth beneath his feet.

THE GUARD on Ne Kyat's bungalow was crouching with his weapon raised when General Li arrived. His eyes were wide with fear, but he'd held his post as ordered, and the general complimented him on his efficiency.

Inside, the Burmese guide had wriggled off his cot and dragged himself halfway across the floor, in the direction of the exit. He was gasping from the pain, visibly exhausted by the effort, and his shoulders sagged at the sight of General Li.

"Your friend has joined us," the general said, startled to discover that he felt no irritation at the peasant's effort to escape. It was a futile bid in any case.

"Belasko?"

There was hope in Ne Kyat's voice. It almost made the general smile.

"We're going out to see him now," Li said. "You'll have a chance to say hello."

The guard was there beside him, helping General Li hoist Ne Kyat to his feet. The pain was staggering, their burden turning into deadweight instantly, but days on a starvation diet made him light enough to bear.

"Outside," Li snapped, the guard obeying instantly.

And it was hell out there, with weapons hammering on every side, no seeming rhyme or reason to it in the dark of night. Disabling the generator was a masterstroke, but one man couldn't hope to beat two hundred, even in the dark.

They crossed the threshold with their rag doll just in time to witness the explosion of the buried fuel tanks. Dirt and concrete levitated on a wall of flame, the heat intense enough to singe Li's eyebrows where he stood some eighty yards away. In that ghoulish light he saw flames spreading toward the helicopters, two of them already damaged, and he knew that he was on the verge of being trapped, cut off from contact with his reinforcements and the outside world.

"The pilots! Fetch them to the helicopters now!"

"But, sir—"

The soldier hesitated, holding up his own side of the man they carried until Li produced his pistol and leveled it at the private's face.

"Go now!"

The soldier went, and Li could only hope that he'd follow orders rather than escaping to some darkened corner of the camp where he could cringe and hide. The light of leaping flames revealed raw carnage in the compound, bodies scattered here and there, vehicles pocked by automatic fire, a number of the buildings with their windows smashed, facades defaced by bullets.

General Li Zhao Gan couldn't believe his eyes. Two hundred men at his command, and he was looking at disaster, one man running rings around his best and wreaking havoc in the compound. It would only take one shot to bring him down, and still two hundred guns weren't enough to do the job.

A new explosion, this time from the barracks where a crowd of soldiers milled around half-dressed, with weapons hanging idle in their hands. Confused, some of them half-asleep, they didn't understand what they were seeing. Even with the state of readiness they had maintained for several days, his soldiers were surprised by the ferocity of the attack.

The shock wave—a grenade, perhaps, or something larger—blew a portion of the barracks roof away and sent it sailing like a kite across the compound. Flames were leaping from inside, men screaming as they burned. Others ventured back to save their comrades, tossing guns aside as instinct made them play the hero. Few if any of them seemed intent on searching for their enemy inside the wire.

Li started dragging Ne Kyat toward the helicopters, knowing they would be his only chance to slip away. Retreat would once have been unthinkable, but he'd seen the enemy in action now, and a withdrawal from the danger zone was preferable to going down in flames.

If he couldn't negotiate with the American, at least Li could survive to organize a hunt that would inevitably bring his head back on a platter. It was little in the way of consolation for a man who saw his life and his career in flames, but Li was a survivor. He could turn the situation to his benefit, if he was only given time.

How long?

Ahead of him he saw the private who had guarded Ne Kyat coming back, a smudge of soot or mud across his face. He pulled up short in front of General Li and snapped off a salute.

"The pilots, sir! I found them!"

By the light of leaping flames, Li saw small figures milling near the helicopters, peering into cockpits.

"Help me!" he commanded, and the private took his place on Ne Kyat's other side, a burden shared.

A few more yards, and—

Using every ounce of strength he still had left, Ne Kyat shook off the private, turning like a wounded animal on General Li. His fingers scrabbled at the general's face and throat, as much to hold himself erect on shattered legs as for the damage they might cause. His screaming sounds were mingled agony and anger, ringing in the general's ears.

Before Li could respond effectively, the Burmese stiffened, jerking like a grounded fish. Li didn't see the knife until it came between them, slick with blood already, opening the wounded peasant's throat.

Blood spattered Li, his face and tunic, as he shoved the dying hostage to the ground. The private stood before him with the bloody knife in hand, uncertain whether he should cheer out loud or try a fresh salute.

"You idiot!"

Li's first shot struck the private in the chest, his second drilling through the dead man's upper lip to drop him where he stood. Ne Kyat was blowing crimson bubbles from the ruin of his throat. There was no hope of saving him with the facilities at hand, and Li took time to squeeze off one more shot before he turned and ran in the direction of the helicopter.

But wait. He hadn't lost his hole card yet.

He slipped the automatic in his belt and doubled back, grabbed Ne Kyat's lifeless body underneath the arms and started dragging him in the direction of the helipad.

"I HAVE BEEN saving these against our time of need."

As Sun Lao spoke, he drew an ornate Chinese trunk from underneath his simple bed and opened it. Inside, beneath some folded clothing, lay two Uzi submachine guns and at least a dozen extra magazines.

"But General Li—"

"Has other things to think about." Sun's tone allowed no argument from his subordinate, as he reached back and passed a weapon to the waiting hands of Michael Lee. "We must defend ourselves against our enemies."

The submachine gun's weight reminded Sun that he'd been a young man once. Such things were second nature to him then, and he'd never flinched from duty in the service of his clan. Outside his quarters younger men were writing history with blood and fire. He had to be a part of it, or he'd lose his self-respect.

They shared the extra magazines, Sun filling his pockets while his incense master tucked a few inside his belt. The sound of a tremendous blast ripped through the camp, and firelight blanched their faces in the room that had been nearly pitch-dark since the generator had blown short moments earlier.

"The fuel pumps," Lee suggested.

"It is time for us to go."

"Go where?"

"To meet our destinies, perhaps."

"Master—"

"Enough! A man must sometimes stand and fight, if he would call himself a man."

Embarrassment sometimes worked wonders in the face of fear.

They crossed Sun's smallish sitting room, where automatic fire had shattered windows, raked the flimsy walls and trashed the inexpensive furniture. Small loss, he thought, and made for the door.

"Master, let me."

Some courage remained in Michael Lee. The young man went out first, his silhouette described by firelight as he scanned the compound. Beyond Lee's shadow Sun could pick out bodies lying on the ground.

One man, he thought. Could it be possible?

He followed Lee outside and stood beside him, conscious of the Uzi in his hands, the magazines that weighed his pockets down. He was a warrior once again, regardless of his age.

A shadow raced toward them, backlit by the flames, and Sun Jiang Lao was conscious of a deadly difference. This man was taller than the average Chinese soldier, heavier, and he was carrying a weapon that wouldn't be regulation for the People's Revolutionary Army.

"There!"

Sun raised his weapon, firing even as he called out the warning to Michael Lee. The Uzi's recoil startled him, and his initial burst was wasted, raising puffs of dust a few feet to the running target's left. As Lee joined in the chorus, Sun had tightened his grip for more control, the runner firing back with what appeared to be an M-16.

The sound of bullets striking Michael Lee was nearly covered by the muzzle blast of Lee's own weapon, rising as he staggered backward, finally pointing toward the sky and spewing rounds as if he hoped to ventilate the stars before his magazine ran dry. Another quick burst from the runner dropped Lee on the porch, heels drumming in a last reflexive spasm as he died.

It was enough.

Sun Lao retreated, dodging bullets, and he lurched around the corner of the bungalow and out of sight. The American would be coming—there was no doubt in his mind, but this wasn't the place to lay an ambush. He could still attack from either side or circle wide around to find another angle. The Elder Brother of the Yi Kwah Tao could not watch every compass point at once.

He broke and ran in the direction of the gate, as if his very life depended on it, hating every step he took, disgusted with himself for trying to escape when braver men were standing fast and dying all around him.

Sun Jiang Lao discovered, with a blinding flash of insight, that he had no wish to join their company.

As if he had a choice.

The burst that cut his legs from under him had no sound of its own. He heard the impact, true enough, with flesh and bone emitting thick, wet sounds, his balance giving way to sudden, blinding pain.

Facedown, Sun realized that he had somehow kept his death grip on the Uzi. With a force of will that cost him everything he had, he pushed out with his free hand, straining, rolling over on his back. His legs were twisted, broken things that didn't follow suit.

He heard the American coming, tried to lift the Uzi, but the submachine gun weighed too much, as if a giant magnet somewhere underneath the surface of the earth had been switched on and held it fast. The effort brought more pain, and Sun Lao whimpered as he let the weapon go.

Above him, looming in the firelight, was a giant of a man, his face obscure.

"You're out of business," the assassin said to him in English.

"Others follow after me." It was the best Sun could do.

His executioner wasn't impressed.

"I'll see them later." And then his rising weapon blotted out the world.

THE SOUND of helicopter engines revving into lift-off startled Bolan, drawing him away from Sun Lao's prostrate form. One of the ships was lifting off behind a screen of fire, and Bolan didn't have to guess about the ranking passenger on board.

He fed the M-16 another magazine, reloading on the run. A Chinese soldier leaped out in front of him, then dropped as he took a short burst to the chest. The whirlybird was airborne, rising out of range.

He wasted half a dozen rounds, then gave it up. Two down, and there was no way he could chase the general from here unless he sprouted wings.

The camp was in chaos, soldiers running here and there without direction, some of them attempting to control the fires touched off by flaming gasoline and aircraft fuel. The car barn was in flames, the largest barracks likewise. Where the fuel pumps once had stood, a crater smoked and simmered like the gate to hell.

The Executioner took advantage of the general confusion, doubling back in the direction of the jeep that had delivered him to General Li and company. One of his silent passengers lay sprawled beside it on the ground; the other still slouched in the shotgun seat, held upright by the belt around his chest.

As Bolan neared the jeep, a Chinese soldier was approaching from the other side, apparently intent on moving it beyond the reach of spreading flames. The new arrival hesitated when he saw a dead man sitting in the jeep, edged closer for a better look, and finally leaned across the driver's seat to prod the corpse with trembling fingertips. The soldier glanced up just in time to see a shadow looming over him, and then the lights went out as Bolan raised his M-16 and clubbed him once across the face.

Escaping from the camp was an entirely different thing than crashing in. He lacked surprise, but rampant chaos was the next best thing. If he could keep his head down, make it to the gate without a major hit...

The engine gave him trouble, and he was afraid it might have been disabled by a lucky shot, but then it finally responded, grumbling into life. He shifted into gear and gunned it toward the open gate, two hundred yards away.

A gunner in the southeast lookout tower saw him coming, and let loose with an automatic weapon. The M-16 was chancy, and the warrior didn't want to stop and duel the tower guard with the machine gun mounted on the jeep.

Instead, he slowed enough to give himself stability and lifted the M-40, loaded with another high-explosive round. He left the jeep on automatic pilot long enough to aim and fire, approximating in the place of pinpoint accuracy.

Overhead a ball of fire erupted from the lookout tower, spewing wreckage to the ground. A flaming two-by-four bounced off the hood of Bolan's jeep as he accelerated toward the gate once more.

In front of him three Chinese soldiers scrambled for their lives. Two were quick enough to make it, but he clipped the third and sent him spinning into the shadows on the right, his scream a startled, birdlike sound.

And out.

He ran another fifty yards before he flicked on the headlights to keep from running off the one-lane mountain road. His rearview mirror showed reflected firelight for a while before the road began to curve and it was lost.

# CHAPTER TWENTY-FIVE

Bolan ditched the jeep two miles downrange, before it took him any closer to the army outpost at Simao. He had no way of knowing whether General Li had battery-operated radios in camp, but he could certainly communicate with reinforcements from the helicopter. They might be on their way already, racing north to find out what the hell was going on.

The last thing Bolan needed at the moment was to meet a flying column of the People's Revolutionary Army on a narrow mountain road when he was doing sixty miles an hour in a stolen jeep and carrying a dead man in the shotgun seat.

He parked across the road, as near a curve as possible, and shut off the engine. With any luck the point vehicle of a rescue column would collide with the obstruction and create a roadblock that would stop the reinforcements in their tracks.

The downside was a solid pointer to the spot where Bolan left the road on foot, but it couldn't be helped. He meant to have a decent lead before the hunters got this far. Li's backup from Simao would take at least two hours, maybe more, and that gave Bolan time to gain a two- or three-mile lead if he was quick enough.

Retreating into Burma wouldn't be an easy task, but Bolan had a plan. Instead of going back the way he'd come and risk ambush in the forest, he'd strike off toward the Mekong River, follow it due south until he hit

the Burmese border and begin to navigate from there.
Two hundred miles or better, but he might secure a
boat along the way somehow, and food would be more
plentiful along the river's edge.

As would the prospect of encountering patrols.

No matter.

He'd weighed the options, and the river was the way
to go.

The compass gave him his direction and he followed
it, aware of all the ways in which a skillful woods-
man's "better judgment" could defeat him in the dark,
much less on unfamiliar ground. The river lay southwest, some ten or fifteen miles if Bolan's survey maps
were accurate. He wouldn't get that far tonight, but he
was on his way.

As Bolan traveled, halting periodically to feel the
forest out and listen to its sounds, he let his mind review the mission and assess how much he had accomplished in the past three weeks, since leaving Stony
Man.

Australia was a toss-up. He'd called attention to the
Triad presence there, destroyed a major stock of heroin and Michael Lee was dead. But while the market
for illegal drugs remained, the dealers would continue
to supply their customers. The traffic might be slower
for a while, less organized, but it would soon be up to
speed unless municipal and federal police got on the
ball.

In Bangkok, casualties aside, he knew that he'd
barely made a dent. The Yi Kwah Tao was damaged,
but he hadn't touched the larger Triads—Chiu Chou,
or the 14K—and they'd quickly fill the gap in leadership occasioned by the death of Chou Sin Fong. If Thai
authorities had been unable or unwilling to confront

the Triads in the past, he had no reason to believe a two-day bloodbath would revise their attitudes. In short Bangkok would still remain the leading port of call for Western buyers seeking China white to breed new addicts back at home.

Rangoon was something else. Authorities were visibly preoccupied with the guerrilla menace from the north, but recent violence, culminating in the death of Chiang Fan Baht, might help them focus on the creeping rot within their capital. If not, at least he'd been able to disrupt the narco traffic for a time, perhaps increase the overhead for buyers on the other end.

And he'd left two outposts of the Yi Kwah Tao in chaos, touching off a scramble in Rangoon and Bangkok for the post of incense master that could easily produce a not-so-civil war among the rank and file. It would require a firm hand at the helm to steer the Triad through those troubled times...and that was where the Executioner had scored his greatest coup.

The death of Sun Jiang Lao would shake the Triad down to its foundations. At a time when local leadership was being swept away, the Elder Brother was himself deposed, and that in turn would agitate his brothers all the more. It wouldn't be enough to doom the clan, by any means, but with some fervent competition from the other families, it could be years before the Yi Kwah Tao regained its former strength... assuming that it ever did.

As for the Red Chinese connection, he'd missed the boat with General Li Zhao Gan. His mark was off and running, bound for parts unknown, and Bolan's consolation prize was the disruption—make that near-destruction—of the general's base camp in Yunnan. Embarrassment would follow, and he might unseat the general yet, if honest politicians in Beijing got wind of Li's involvement with the Yi Kwah Tao. But Bolan couldn't count on an official sanction from the top.

For all he knew, the Chinese government was perfectly aware of Li's participation in the smuggling of opium and heroin to Burma from Yunnan. Brognola's files contained no solid proof of any narco allies higher up the ladder, but a gap in information was anticipated when you tried to look behind the Bamboo Curtain, even in enlightened times.

Assuming Li explained himself to everybody's satisfaction in Beijing, perhaps indicting right-wing Burmese rebels for the raid, he could rebuild his camp and send new shipments south within a month or two, at the outside.

And if the Executioner had managed to remove Li permanently... then what? Who could say that his successor wouldn't find the fruits of crime as tasty and seductive as the loser he replaced? The Triads had been coexisting with a host of outwardly antagonistic governments for centuries, and they endured. Through bribery, intimidation, murder, subordination, they survived to deal again another day.

The warrior knew he'd be seeing them again, if he could only make it to the river, trail the Mekong south and find another contact who would help him make his way back home.

An hour passed, and Bolan estimated he'd put the best part of a mile behind him, traveling on foot. He thought he could do better if he tried.

And then he heard the helicopter somewhere at his back, a sound that he couldn't mistake or misinterpret in the circumstances, with the forest serving as an echo chamber for the engine sounds.

Pursuit!

He blanked his mind to everything except the raw mechanics of survival and began to run.

DISCOVERING THE JEEP was more a fluke than anything. They'd been following the road, due south in the direction of Simao, from which direction Li Zhao Gan had reinforcements on the way. He planned to meet them, set down in a clearing—maybe on the road itself—and lead the fighting column back to liberate his camp.

Assuming that the enemy hadn't been killed—or managed to escape—before they got there.

Carrying the bloody corpse of Ne Tin Kyat had been a whim, his hole card saved against a chance encounter with the American. No one in the helicopter dared to question General Li when he insisted that a dead man share the ride, and Ne Kyat had a window seat, strapped in beside the loading bay.

If nothing else, his corpse was solid evidence that Li's assailants hadn't come and gone unscathed. Such evidence might yet be needed when the word of the attack got out.

Li couldn't keep it from Beijing indefinitely, not with soldiers dead, expensive gear destroyed and waiting for replacements. He would need a cover story, witnesses to back him up for the inquiry, if it came to that.

Hill bandits.

Lacking an American to prove his story in the flesh, he would report a clash with outlaws. Captain Chou had been dispatched to seek out members of a local bandit tribe, and he had captured one, a renegade Burmese. The junior officer would bear Li's story out . . . provided he was still in camp, and still alive.

What else?

The bandits had retaliated, first by downing one of Li's scout helicopters, then by launching an assault upon his base camp. If they needed corpses other than Ne Kyat's, the general could send his men back to the village razed by Captain Chou, collect a number of the men and haul them back to set the stage. Advanced decomposition in the tropics was to be expected, and a medical examiner's report wouldn't be called for in the circumstances.

Feeling better, General Li was smiling to himself when the copilot hailed him, directing his attention to the jeep below. It had been parked across the narrow road at a diagonal and just beyond a curve, the lights switched off, as if it was intended for the purpose of a roadblock.

The American!

Who else would dump a vehicle in that position, blocking access to the camp?

"Go back!"

The pilot did as he was told, a wide loop that would place them back above the stranded jeep.

Which way would the American have gone? He might not have a decent map, but he would still know north from south and east from west. It made no sense for him to head for Laos, much less to strike off deeper into China.

Burma, then. But which way would be quickest, theoretically the safest for a runner on his own?

"The river," General Li decided, speaking even as the thought took shape. "Turn on the infrared device."

"Yes, sir."

"How much fuel do we have?"

"Two hours' worth," the copilot replied.

So they were limited in terms of hunting time. Li made a hasty calculation in his mind. Considering the time that they'd used to circle wide around the camp before they came back to the road, Belasko would have dropped the jeep sometime within the past half hour or forty minutes. It was twelve miles to the river by the shortest route available, but the American couldn't be sure of that. Allowing for mistakes, his path lay somewhere in a cone-shaped corridor between the highway and the Mekong, roughly west-southwest.

"This way!" Li pointed, spitting out rapid-fire commands. The pilots hastened to obey, their aircraft sweeping back and forth across the darkened jungle, covering the small end of the cone as they began their search.

Two hours. Less, if they allowed time for returning to the camp. Li checked his watch and scowled, aware that he could still be robbed of victory by circumstance.

With the American in hand, he had a vastly different tale to tell. Perhaps a CIA invasion of Yunnan—or, at the very least, some kind of devious conspiracy involving Westerners, the Thai and Burmese governments, perhaps the scheming Soviets. He could refine the details as he went along, play off his audience and tailor his remarks to their requirements as he went along.

Detente was dying in the Far East, as it was. Li's parting shot would merely be the coup de grace, where China and the U.S. were concerned.

And what of his escape plans, all his visions of a life beyond Yunnan?

Still possible, if he was cautious, spent some time rebuilding damaged bridges and allowed the heat to dissipate. There was no reason for Beijing to think that he was planning to defect or slip away to lead a life of Western decadence.

It would be General Li's surprise.

"A reading, General."

He started forward, glanced at the machine and realized that he could not interpret what he saw.

"What is it?"

"Man-size, from the indications, sir."

"Could this be a mistake?"

The pilot shrugged. "Unlikely, sir. We use this on the hill tribes, in Tibet."

Li knew about the long war in Tibet, suppressing rebels in the mountains where you had to track them by their body heat or not at all, because the peasant population wouldn't give them up at any price.

"We must be certain."

"I can try and take it down," the pilot said. Uncertainty was written on his face, along with something much like fear.

"Unnecessary," General Li decided. "Bring us back above the target. Hold position there. I have a plan."

He moved back toward the loading bay and Ne Kyat's body, slouching in its jump seat. Close beside the corpse, the private Li had dragged along was watching him, his automatic rifle braced between his knees.

"The door," Li snapped. "We need it open quickly."

Something close to panic was on the private's face, but he complied. It took him two attempts before he

got the safety line attached, then he had to struggle
with the door another moment, finally rolling it aside.

"Help me attach this rope," the general ordered,
lifting Ne Kyat's arms and waiting for the private to
complete a hasty noose. "Be sure the knots are firm."

"Yes, sir."

"Now, then, we're ready."

As he spoke, the general smiled and reached for Ne
Kyat's safety belt.

BENEATH THE ROTOR SOUNDS, and yet more sinister,
was a thrashing in the trees. He heard it coming down,
at first, a deadweight plummeting through fronds and
branches. It reminded him of the grenades that had
been dropped on him before, but the plunging object
sounded larger, vastly heavier.

Now came a different rushing, scraping sound, oc-
casional collisions with the bulk of tree trunks, as the
chopper started circling, the pilot working up to search
grids soon. Bolan hesitated, risking it to find out what
the hell was crash-bang-slamming after him among the
trees.

At first his mind refused to recognize the man-shape
skimming toward him, pointed toes a yard or so above
the ground. No sooner was the shape identified as human, when he recognized the blood-smeared, battered
face of Ne Tin Kyat.

Deadweight.

The warrior ducked aside and let his former guide
skim past, colliding with another tree and spinning like
a huge piñata, sweeping on for several yards before the
chopper turned and doubled back.

A little psywar from the general, right, but Bolan
wasn't having any at the moment. He drew his combat

knife and had it in hand before the swinging corpse came by a second time. He saw the rope was looped beneath the arms—the head would be too easily detached, on bailout—and he fixed his target as the taut line that protruded over Ne Kyat's head and disappeared among the treetops.

Now!

He swung the blade with everything he had, remembering to keep it on an angle for a better cut, the impact thrumming up his arm, across his shoulders, down his spine.

Almost.

The rope wasn't completely severed, but the cut was close enough. The next time Ne Kyat struck a tree, he hung there for a moment, snagged on smaller branches. Then the final strands let go with an explosive *twang*. The helicopter engines seemed to change their pitch, relieved of all resistance on the ground, and Bolan watched the rope whip freely back and forth until it disappeared among the trees.

The first grenade was off by thirty feet, but only due to Bolan's speed. Behind him trees absorbed the worst of the concussion and the shrapnel while he kept on running, bearing toward the river that would be his only highway home.

The hunters knew where he was going now, and there was nothing to be gained by any desperate ploy like doubling back in the direction of the road. His two advantages were ground mobility and the consumption rate of fuel for a chopper stalking mobile prey. An hour and a quarter, anyway, had elapsed since he'd seen the bird take off from Li's base camp. They wouldn't want to set down in the forest, even if they found a decent landing zone, and that meant that their hunting time was strictly limited.

Small consolation, that, if they got lucky with a frag grenade or burst of automatic fire.

The best and cleanest way would be to take them out, but that meant physical exposure to the enemy, a heightened risk. He had to find a clearing, preferably of decent size. Unless...

He chose a tree with good, stout limbs and started climbing, knowing that the infrared would pick him out, but hoping it would take a second pass, at least, to tell them he was stationary.

The warrior was twenty feet above the ground when the grenade fell past him, five or six feet to his left. He hugged the trunk, determined not to fall if he was hit by shrapnel. The grenade exploded four or five feet short of contact with the ground, a ring of lower branches screening Bolan from the worst of it. He felt a needle stab his flank, and fingers came back bloody when he checked himself.

Not bad. His leg still functioned on command, and he was ten feet higher when they dropped the second frag grenade a few feet to his right. He shifted slightly on his perch to put the trunk between him and the blast, already counting down to zero hour.

Six seconds, and they weren't adjusting fuses, which informed him that they didn't know their enemy was climbing. In his mind he pictured General Li, believing Bolan cornered, huddled underneath the tree. He might be hurt, or simply terrified, but they couldn't imagine him attacking from the forest floor.

Surprise.

Above him, hovering, the chopper's running lights produced a giant shadow, tadpole shaped. Leaves rippled from the rotorwash, and he could feel it on his face.

Climbing.

This time he could see the frag grenade before he heard it, plummeting directly toward his face. He jerked his head aside and took it on the shoulder, grunting as the lethal egg bounced free and fell away, exploding twenty feet below. He heard the shrapnel this time, but it didn't touch him.

How long would they wait in one position? Bolan grimaced, knowing he was running out of time.

He chose the squat M-40, loaded with a high-explosive round, and slipped it off its shoulder sling. Bolan threw one leg across a sturdy limb for some support and braced his elbows on the trunk, the wooden stock against his cheek.

It was a lot like firing from a prone position, if you didn't count the awkward pull of gravity. The range was thirty feet or less, and he corrected to avoid a couple of the larger branches as he aimed. He had one chance to do it right.

The Executioner stroked the trigger, counting down before the HE round struck home beneath the slim tail of the fuselage. Hot shrapnel rained down around him, smoke and flames, before the chopper veered away and disappeared from sight.

He heard the crash and marked its general direction, knowing he should have no trouble with the smoke and fire to guide him. Back on solid ground, he left the 40 mm launcher on its sling and flicked off the safety of his M-16.

A simple mop-up errand, more or less.

He found the chopper hung up in a tree, but the collision had expelled its occupants through doors and windows. Even belted in, the pilots had been pitched out through the windshield, landing in a broken heap below their aircraft. Bolan gave a mercy round to each, in case, and went in search of more.

A private lay on his back, eyes open, staring at the canopy of trees with a surprised expression. He was still alive, but fading fast. The HE round had taken one leg at the knee; the other had a corkscrew twist that months of orthopedic surgery could possibly correct, assuming that he lived that long.

No way.

The guy was losing blood like it was going out of style…which, in his case, it was. He tried to speak, and managed to produce a little wheezing sound that passed for words. His eyes swam in and out of focus, drifting toward the Executioner, and back in the direction of the helicopter, hanging nose down in the trees.

Another mercy round, between those eyes, and Bolan moved to stand beside the final body. General Li Zhao Gan had been ejected from the open loading bay, some forty feet in all, considering the angle of his drop. He lay facedown, unmoving, but the Executioner could see and hear him breathing. When he turned the general over, Bolan was prepared for anything. A hideout gun, a hand grenade…a warrior never knew.

The general's hands were empty, and he seemed to be unarmed. Not that a weapon would have served much purpose, with his broken neck. Just breathing was an effort, and if Bolan's estimate was accurate, Li wouldn't manage it for long.

Calling on what little strength he had, the general spoke.

"Belasko."

"Bolan."

If it registered at all, there was no hint of recognition in the general's eyes.

"Sun Lao?"

"He's dead."

It might have been a grimace, but on Li it looked more like a fleeting smile.

"You will be hunted to the corners of the earth."

"I wouldn't be surprised."

What else was new?

He put a mercy round between the general's glassy eyes and took himself away from there. He still had time before the sunrise helped his trackers navigate by means of smoke ascending from the burned-out chopper. It would be tomorrow before he reached the Mekong, but he had a hunch that he would get there all the same.

And anyone who chose to follow him could stand in line to take their shot.

He was a long way from home, but he was headed there.

For once the Executioner was coming out ahead.

## EPILOGUE

The half-ton truck trailed plumes of dust behind it on the long drive north from Tennant Creek. The vehicle didn't have air-conditioning, so Bolan kept the windows down and drove as close to seventy as he could manage, letting desert wind whip through the cab.

It was a long shot, granted, but Minmara's people had been sighted two days earlier, their approximate location reported by a flying doctor out of Alice Springs. Assuming they'd moved along by now, the chances were that they wouldn't have traveled far.

Two days.

In that amount of time, a man could find himself a river, steal a small canoe and paddle for his life until he felt as if his arms were made of lead, outdistancing his enemies. Connecting with a friendly face in Burma took more time, but in Rangoon the name of Ne Tin Kyat still opened certain doors.

The rest had been routine, preparing to evacuate and picking up reports of what had happened in his absence. The assassination of a cultural attaché from the U.S. Embassy was still an item of debate, with the majority opinion blaming the attack on Communists. The dead man's name was Jason Stark, but it meant nothing to the Executioner.

Before returning home, he had a job to do.

The truck was easy, purchased with a bag of liberated Triad dollars, when he got as far as Alice Springs.

He went shopping for supplies, leaning toward cans and dry goods, nothing that required refrigeration or immediate consumption on the trail. He had a choice of bags or bottles on the water, and he chose the bags because they'd be easier to carry.

Done.

The truck could carry more, but he was thinking of the people who would have to pack the burden on their backs. A gift they couldn't handle would be worse than useless, forcing them to linger in one place until they ate and drank enough to ease the load.

It didn't seem enough somehow, but Bolan knew that there was only so much he could do.

He found the tribe that afternoon, by the expedience of parking half a mile from where the doctor had reported seeing them. He built a fire, unmindful of the heat, and trusted in the smoke to pique their curiosity.

Minmara brought two hunters with him when he came, their unfamiliar faces marking them as refugees from slavery under Michael Lee. At the sight of Bolan, a delighted smile lighted Minmara's face.

"My friend."

"I heard that you were camped nearby. I have some food and water for your people in the truck."

Minmara's eyes reflected his gratitude, but then a new thought tugged down the corners of his mouth.

"What of the dragon?"

"Dead. He won't be coming back."

The smile returned full force.

"More reason we should celebrate," Minmara said. "You come with us to camp and join the feast?"

And home was what you made it, right?

The warrior smiled and said, "I thought you'd never ask."

**Dan Samson finds himself a deciding factor
in the Civil War in the third thrilling
episode of the action miniseries...**

# TIMERAIDER

## John Barnes

**Dan Samson, a hero for all time, is thrown into
the past to fight on the battlefields of history.**

**In Book 3: UNION FIRES, the scene has switched
to the Civil War, and Vietnam veteran Dan
Samson works to free a leading member of the
biggest resistance group in the South.**

Available in December at your favorite retail outlet.

# Take
# 4 explosive books
# plus a
# mystery bonus
# FREE

Raw determination
in a dark new age.

# JAMES AXLER

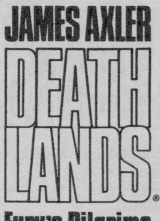

## DEATH LANDS®

## Fury's Pilgrims

A bad jump from a near-space Gateway leaves Ryan Cawdor and his band
of warrior survivalists in the devastated heart of the American Midwest.
In a small community that was once the sprawling metropolis of Chicago, Krysty is taken captive by a tribe of nocturnal female mutants. Ryan
fears for her life, especially since she is a woman.

In the Deathlands, life is a contest where the only victor is death.

Gold Eagle brings another fast-paced miniseries to the action adventure front!

## by PATRICK F. ROGERS

**Omega Force: the last—and deadliest—option**

With capabilities unmatched by any other paramilitary organization in the world, Omega Force is a special ready-reaction anti-terrorist strike force composed of the best commandos and equipment the military has to offer.

In Book 1: **WAR MACHINE,** two dozen SCUDs have been smuggled into Libya by a secret Iraqi extremist group whose plan is to exact ruthless retribution in the Middle East. The President has no choice but to call in Omega Force—a swift and lethal way to avert World War III.

---